Arron and Alem have been fri
both come from an ethnic g
persecuted by successive gove₁
only option for survival is to make the perilous passage
to Europe.

Arron has gone on ahead and is settled as a child refugee
in a small English city. Here he has to navigate his way
through the complex friendships and lifestyles of his
college classmates and well-wishers. Terribly homesick at
times, he worries about Alem as he too starts his journey
after meeting Emu, a young woman escaping an army
prison, also intent on finding a better life.

Aba Tso, Alem's grandfather is the guardian of a prophecy
which he shares with them. He helps them on their way
through a mixture of teaching, mysticism and magic.

We saw the fire that we have set, burning them alive in their own homes,

Some running away to the ocean,

Then we saw the beasts of the ocean swallowing their children.

We also saw the desert burying them alive and we could do nothing about it,

But how unbearable to see and yet not see as we witnessed them being slaughtered at the hands of our own people.

TO THE MEMORY OF THOSE ERITREAN AND ETHIOPIAN BOYS
SLAUGHTERED BY ISIS

Libya, March 2015

The
Seventh
NECK

Thomas Tegento

ISBN 978-1-913218-55-3

Printed in Great Britain by
Biddles Books Limited, King's Lynn, Norfolk

Chapter ONE

April 19, 2015: Enderbury, UK

Kids are screaming while burning walls and falling roofs are all around.

'Tsirrr...Tsirrrr...snap...

Dindinn... dindin... drop...

Whu huhu whiihu...pop'

On his bed, Arron looks like a rotten and scrambled tiny globe, curled like a new born baby in his mother's arm. He doesn't even look as if he's breathing. All he can hear is a mixed up symphony of haunting memories accompanied by his frightened heartbeat; pinching and scrambled thoughts dragging him into his darkest place. All he visualises fills him with terror. *What's going on? Is this real, real? How did I end up like this?* He is feeling very low and yet very high at the same time. Arron isn't even aware of Charlotte's text alert dropping and hooping every second. He's deafened by his day dreams. Even if he can hear the phone ringing, he thinks it's just part of the noise of his pounding heart.

'Bridiimtimmtiww...hoop...

Wvoooopwup... Brim whoop.'

Suddenly, the repeated text alerts wake him up from his daydreaming.

'Dinidinwhupdindijnn....'

He switches off his phone and tries to get back to the painful moments where he can see no difference after all these years. *What's the difference anyway? The world is still hell.* He looks forward to being cured from his past memories. He wants a conscious mind, so that he can realise how blessed he is just to be alive now with the hope that he will see when this world becomes like heaven. But now, he feels that he has no choice other than wishing, dreaming, hoping and not giving up... He is alone. He curls himself up like a baby again, covering his ears with the pillows this time. He misses all those close to him. He hasn't seen his girlfriend Charlotte for three days. He hasn't seen his best friend Alem for three years, and he hasn't seen his mother for thirteen years. Alone, all he can feel and visualise is Alem's death, all he can smell is the blood of his best friend's execution; all he sees is a bloody red ocean. He's almost out of his mind with loneliness and the tormenting images that won't leave his mind. That's his life now - Arron's life - in this small English city.

In his mind are vivid, terrifying scenes of:

Injured teens stretching up their hands for help, while bullets fly all around

Women running in between their men and their families, men lying with their heads detached from their bodies.

Smoke and fire producing a dark cloud.

After just a minute of chaos everything changes into cries and then nothingness, a majestic silence. It's a mighty silence that bears memories of a buried repeating history, like an apocalypse revealing that this is the end of the world.

And again... the next old city... and the new ones ... he remembers that everything that was there turned into ashes in the blink of an eye until he couldn't recognise the place he grew up in.

Thick, hot blood spreads on the ground,

Running and shooting, as if no one will live there again. Men finishing each other off for reasons no one can understand clearly.

Unlucky mothers are crying near the corpses of a family member – including his mother, even if he can't see her – she's always crying too.

Fathers are giving their lives for their families; even so, they can't save them.

He suddenly realises that he has been struggling and fighting with himself on his bed. He felt relief for a moment when he transferred his mental pain into physical. He realises that all his pillows have been thrown to the other side of the bedroom, painted with his blood. He covers his hands while blood is running from his incessant scratching. After taking care of that, he prays that he won't be mad with himself like this for the rest of his life. He prays that he can laugh again like he laughed the day before yesterday. Before that dark night took over his life, before he started to browse on YouTube to help his loneliness. But, he wasn't expecting such a vile video to pop up. Now, things are not the same as they were before last night. All he can see in his mind is a series of crime scenes. He saw them for real when he was a child and they become mixed with yesterday's happenings far away in the desert- in his dreams - again and again. Corpses of young boys wake up with him and follow him like shadows on his way to college.

And now, he has to wake up early and go to that same college with the same low feelings and same dreams. He can't even remember what time he has to get to his class. He walks quicker than ever as if someone behind is running after him, like a ghost following him. He was dream-walking and thinking about something fearful, that has power over him. It's still following him but he can't look back. He stares down at his feet where he imagines small spirits are walking next to his feet. Then he goes faster to get away from them, but they follow him all the same.

Even in class, he still sees dead bodies, smells hot flowing blood...

As he sits in college, his classmates are noisy as always. This unpleasant noise grates on him especially now. Terrified of death, he is screaming inside. He looks strong, but that's only because of his culture. He grew up in a society that thinks personal problems have to be kept inside and that dealing with them tests your strength and ability to solve your own problems. He hates it when his class mates bring their personal problems into college and change the mood of the classroom into a place of problems rather than knowledge. It only seems to make their emotional status worse than before. He thinks that this environment is too soft and does not encourage you to find strength within yourself.

Here there is free access to help and advice, too much support, making it is easier to rely on temporary help rather than struggling on your own. Or maybe he is wrong; today he is weaker than any of his classmates. He is changing into a monster. He cannot control his emotions.

He gets off his chair and rushes out without saying a word to any of his classmates, to the smoking area to be by himself. No one asked about him or followed him like they did in the days before yesterday. They all are too scared to ask what's wrong or to help him. He's never seemed to need help before. How quickly he's got used to being by himself. The smoking area is crowded with students and a couple of teachers in the corner. He lights a cigarette and takes three puffs at a time. He feels like crying and finally the smoke pinches his eyes helping him to drop a tear – it's a relief. He tries again but can't. The cold weather has also made him tired and dry. He hasn't slept for two days either. He coughs multiple times. From his sick and scared face while he inhales and exhales for a bit of relief one can notice that he's a new smoker. He's seen people smoking and having fun at the same time and wondered how. *Maybe they are not having fun. Or maybe they are trying to have fun. Maybe they are sad deep down as he is sad now.* But, they can pretend as if they are okay, so they can have fun for now. *Smoking is a stylish way of punishing yourself so badly,* he thinks.

The day is still as dark as the night itself; but it's not as dark as his heart. He is not himself anymore, since he saw those awful images on YouTube. He might be considered lucky to have unrestricted access to the internet, but in this instance it made him a witness to his friend's harrowing death. He puffs three times more at the same time, without coughing, tolerating the blaze from his lips, tongue, all the way through his throat and down into his stomach. He feels the flame inside and exhales a darker curled fume. Damaging himself inside couldn't help him forget everything, but he deceives himself into believing that by doing so, he would feel better for the moment. He needs a stronger cure. His head feels dizzy and he sits in a corner on a bench. Inhale; exhale. While his eyes follow the curling smoke, his memories take him back to the night before yesterday.

The night before, he had seen a film taken in Libya, and shown on YouTube. It was a close- up of Habesha blood pumping up into the Mediterranean Sea, spraying up to the sky from brown necks. 1st, 2nd, 3rd..

I cannot watch!

One of them could be him. He imagines himself among them. If he were there he would be struggling not to give his neck, at least he would not make it easy for these dark angels of death who call themselves ISIS. He would not be like the others. But he realises that these boys have been traumatised and show no defiance, walking like zombies. But he can't stop watching! It's terrifying! Now comes the bloodshed and slaughter, young souls fighting death, dead bodies lying on the ground baptised with each other's mingling blood... 3rd, 4th, 5th, 6th ....They say it's to scare the western world, but why do those boys have to be sacrificed, they who have done nothing wrong?

For God's sake! I cannot watch this! But...

Sick to the pit of his stomach he noticed that the 7th neck was not just a boy or simply a neck. It was a neck he had known for years. It's a neck he had kissed when he was a child. He recognises the cross tattoo displayed on this long neck. This boy had protected him from harm just as a father would. He used to call him 'my brother' even though he was not. This was his friend who was well-liked and popular in the village where Arron had started the journey of his refugee life, a nice chap who nobody could fail to love. He was not only his friend; he was more like his teacher.

A name sprung out from his heart with burning tears.

Alem!!

He throws his already finished cigarette down to his feet, just before it burns his fingertips. He crushes the cigarette under his feet and smiles, trying not to relive the sound of that terrifying voice. He repeatedly hears it. The same voice, his voice, calling his best friend 'Alem' that still keeps ringing in his ears. He remembers all the graphic pictures he saw that night, the images still follow him like spirits. They still whisper '*Whisssppshsh…*' back in the class, inside his mind again.

In class everyone is still noisy, even louder than the internal screams of dying people! Noisy with silly topics: teenage issues, dirty talk, new slang, banter. From the stinking farts and the disgusting breaking of wind, from the funny jokes to the bullying, floods of bloody 'F' words that he had never known before. Unfortunately for now, Arron is not familiar with swear words yet –or at least did not know such words in his own language – called Ge'ez - the first, God - given language of his homeland. He had no way to match their crudeness. He feels detached from them all. He is already in a different world. Now, he realises even more than usual just how much he's not part of where he is. He wants to sit alone.

'*Are you ok?*' He hates the question. To him that sounds like '*It's hopeless; the poor boy is going to die alone.*' He smiles back accordingly as if to say '*I'm not, but I'm going to say that I am okay because I'm living a life of pretence anyway, all the time,* he thinks.

Shush…

The teacher is begging the students to listen to her, as always. All of them mimic her and then burst into laughter when she can no longer stand their behaviour. He wakes up from his daydream only after she has walked out of the class. He used to enjoy his class even if it was hard to enjoy it. He didn't mind about any trouble he might face as long as he was alive. But nothing causes him more distress than the pain of others. They said bad things about her and he felt sorry for his teacher. He'd prefer it if they left her alone and bullied him instead. His culture taught him to be able to dance through hell. He had always enjoyed the ups and downs throughout his life.

He remembers how he had almost died last year in the refrigeration truck, from the four long hours he'd spent in the lorry. He did not know how it had happened but he'd started to enjoy his life again because of his friend Alem. But now he is gone – it doesn't seem possible. He was not only his friend, he had been his saviour.

Looking back, everything he sees, hears and thinks reminds him of his friend. How had they met?

He remembers. People called Arron 'Askar' (traitor)[1] and that is how he came to be bullied. He burned inside more than he used to when people called him 'Amche' in Asmara[2]. Even though these are only generic, political names that don't refer to an individual, still he could not bear it. He thought only of his misfortune and that he had no place in his home country. He remembers once when he was watching TV with a family where all the neighbours had gathered round to watch a serious drama. All eyes turned to him when the TV itself called his people that same name followed by the news of a terrorist attack in Kenya. He would have preferred hell to have swallowed him rather than feel those evil eyes staring at him. He went away and climbed up a tall tree. It wouldn't take him long to get to the top of the tree and throw himself down. He would have died quickly if the angel called Alem had not come to break his fall. Still unconscious, both of them were taken to the hospital where they were taken care of until they recovered. Through this incident their two souls had become one. One dies, the other dies. One lives, the other lives.

Alem is dead now, so Arron dies too inside. Half asleep, half awake; half alive, half dead. When everything stops, it's a sign of death. Now for him nothing is moving; and if nothing is moving, time is meaningless. It's just nothingness. *What will happen when the earth stops rotating or revolving?* he asks himself trying to find an explanation of the unexplained mystery of nature. *Yeah. Day and night will be the same. Time will stop. Clocks will be broken.* That's how Arron feels right now. The more he thinks like this, the more he misses his friend.

His mind drifts back to their childhood.

He remembers what Alem had said after the incident,

---

1 Ashkar is a word used to describe people employed by the Italians under colonialism. It's now a derogatory name meaning deserter.
2 Amche, again a derogatory word.

7

'If you try to do such a thing again, think about the sacrifices I made for you, and then our friendship will die.'

They had taken an oath of loyalty to each other and from that time those two young boys were symbols of love and friendship for everyone around. Their chemistry was perfect, the bond was strong, even death wouldn't break it, sadness wouldn't dim it, distance couldn't alienate them from each other. Even now, Arron doesn't believe his friend no longer exists.

Here in this new land, his Japanese friend Miyuki has told him that in her religion one can't just die and go, but people turn into some other being, returning in a different form. He wishes it were so. He wishes his friend would come in the form of a god, so as to keep him safe, or as a form of inspiration so that he would find a purpose and feel alive instead of empty and paralysed by grief.

While the teacher was asking the class if they could remember what she had just said moments ago, Arron can remember nothing except Alem. He remembers that two years ago, after his arrival in England and on leaving the hospital after his rescue by the police from the refrigeration truck, he was still unaware of his circumstances until in some mysterious way Alem had awoken him. Somehow he'd managed to send him, through a network of contacts, a bottle containing holy water and holy oil called Kibate-Meron[3].

In doing so he brought me back to life, back to consciousness of my new reality!

Since then, whenever Alem had needed his help, he had returned the favour by sending him some money, but ...

I couldn't save him from the butchers of ISIS.

Still he wants to do something for him, even if he is dead.

I will still make him feel alive as though he has an everlasting and true friend even after death.

---

3 A special medicine in Eritrea used in religious healing.

As the class finishes, the teacher calls for Arron before he rushes out.

"Are you ok today, Arron?"

"Yes, I'm fine," he replies while packing up his bag.

He made the promise there and then that he would be okay. He promised to himself that he would set his plan for some noble purpose.

I will make my friend immortal, I will remember his story.

From that moment Arron started reaching out for his purpose, even though he didn't know how and from where to start. Let's see what happens.

Chapter
TWO

September 2014, Entoto, Addis Ababa – The Call

'Dong …' The loud bell suddenly sounds! Alem jerks awake and then settles back to sleep for a little longer.

"*Oh…Bloody hell! It's time to wake up*", he says even though he isn't really asleep.

Time to wake up from a half sleep with half thoughts; half dead, half alive, half in reality and half in illusion, hallucination merged with reality, only feeling half human in general. Half in hope and half in dream; it's always time to wake up! Fully. Wholly. Totally. His mind as usual is wrestling with deep thoughts.

He has already finished his proper sleep and his mind just drifts in thoughts of his friends all over the world, including those who are prisoners, the thought that he too could be one of them at some point, unless a divine miracle happens to change this failing state.

'Dong….' He cries for them first and then wipes away his tears for his future; he replaces his hopeless thoughts, his worst expectations and terrible visions with thoughts of the night's spiritual festivities.

'Dong…'

Almighty bell, like a phone call from the heavens enabling you to speak directly to God through praise, prayer and festivals.

Praise that can make you feel that you are truly immortal and prayer enabling you to communicate throughout the universe.

The festivities that you will never think of living without, making you love being human.

He feels he's on the brink of losing all this as millions of others have done.

'Donggg......' He might be one of them not so long from now, trying to escape from this blessed night and the usual dark days ahead. He fears the days more than the nights. He fears human eyes more than the staring stars above in the dark sky, the millions that seem to be smiling down upon him.

'Donggg....' Alem curls up in his hammock again, thinking he can forget his worries for this evening at least and enjoy the night's singing and prayers for tomorrow with his grandfather and lifetime teacher Aba Tso.

The church bell still keeps on ringing as a reminder to wake everyone up for the night's praise and prayer.

'Riiiing riingggg riiiiiiing'. It's a phone call.

"Arron?"

"Alem?"

A call from Enderbury, UK to Entoto, Addis Ababa, Ethiopia.

'Dong ...ding .... dong...'. The mighty church bell still calls out to remind people it's time to gather together and sing for the night, for the delight of the Almighty and all creation; for the night when all creation is silent and God's ear is not disturbed by the loudness of creation, at night when only nature reigns.

"Melkam worha Tsgie. Happy Worha Tsgie!" Alem wishes Arron, taking care not to make him feel home sick because he cannot attend this holy event.

"Is that what I think I hear?" They remember. *Worha Tsgie* is a season of nearly two months' celebration in the Eritrean and Ethiopian Orthodox Church tradition that commemorates the refugee period of the child Jesus and Mother Mary in their flight from Jerusalem to Egypt, Nubia and Abyssinia and back to Jerusalem. *Worha Tsgie* is the most exciting season, especially for wonderful childhood memories. If Alem and Arron had been together at this time, they would have reminisced about the precious times of their childhood which would never be experienced

11

anywhere else. It's after the New Year, after Demera, before Christmas, before Baptism…

"Yep, it starts today. How are you doing?"

"I'm lonely."

He realises his situation. He can feel it even here; when you are lonely, you may even forget where you are. Loneliness is such an addictive thing that you can't stop thinking about things that are far away. Loneliness is weakness and strength. It makes you lazy but it makes you find time for yourself.

"I understand…" Alem sympathises with him.

He knows it isn't easy for Arron to approach people and make friends with anyone he likes in a foreign Western land. There are so many barriers levelled at him by class, race, and language that the unconditional love in human nature seems have been suppressed by the patriarchal system rooted deep down throughout dark centuries. Anyway he keeps encouraging him as usual.

Arron continues complaining, *"Feeling alone in a foreign land is no fun at all. People seem to hardly know their neighbours. There are people who forget the days and hunt for their life by night like wild beasts do. Feeling alone is when you know you can't achieve anything by yourself, but only with the help of something that can give you a spiritual confidence that makes you think that everything matters to you and you matter to everything. You could feel that there's nothing to live for because nothing has changed and you are still lonely and nothing matters at all."*

Alem keeps encouraging him. Arron cries when recalling everything he misses.

"How's your friend, Arron?" Alem asks him to change the topic.

"She's alright, but she still argues with her foster parents."

"Marry her and stop her complaining about anyone anymore."

"Are you joking? Be serious Alem."

"Just kidding. It is not that easy to marry a white girl is it?"

"Haha... I still have no idea. You could be right."

"They like trying everything before, don't they?"

"That isn't all bad though."

"And it's not granted that they will stick with you forever as African girls do."

"Fair enough."

"Fair enough."

Arron explains how women are treated here, that they have to fight the battle alone in the name of 'feminism' and sometimes get attacked by an unbreakable male dominance that was established long ago.

"They don't even believe that females are the source of life, the source of power, the sun and the moon, or as we believe, the nucleus of a family. They believe that women were created after men. For them it's impossible to think that the first human being could ever be Asian or African. Everyone looks anguished, detached and lonely. People don't get on very well together. I really don't think this is the world I became a refugee for. I want a world that doesn't marginalise anyone over anything, that accepts diversity".

Arron keeps on complaining and Alem keeps trying to bolster him up. Arron cries as he talks about missing everything back home but Alem says that what he's missing has changed now; most of what he remembers has been sucked away by western fashion and brainwashing. Five years have turned his homeland into a distorted state whose borders were changed by historical disputes between rival colonisers and resulted in ethnic groups becoming hostile to each other. Alem longs for the time that he too can escape somewhere safe and live without fear and danger. Together Arron and Alem look for a way to escape and pray for a solution. They both want a society based on harmony and togetherness.

"Everyone faces some kind of challenge" Alem says, followed by a deep breath.

"Sorry, I know I sound selfish. How are you anyway?"

"Still okay, but God knows about tomorrow."

"You are lucky, bro." Arron extends his wishes.

"Yes, I am."

"Hehe..." he starts to recite a poem they wrote together long ago. They play the old game of poetic slamming rather like rap but without all the swear words and bad language. It's almost a divine rap in their tradition. They retrieve the nostalgia of their old life as much as they can. They also remember heart-breaking songs.

"Ha....lieeee....lu....ya. Hallelujah...aah..aa...ha...aaa...lie...eee... lu..." Arron remembers the melody.

"You haven't forgotten it."

"I've forgotten a little."

"I'll help you hear it tonight, if you want to remember that."

"You are a legend."

"Goodbye for now." Alem knows this phone call is costing Arron a lot but ...

"I'll call you back later." He is half here, half there.

"You could watch it on YouTube, though." Alem knows the internet is cheaper than phone calls for Arron.

"No excuses accepted. Don't forget to let me hear it tonight."

"I promise. Chaw for now."

Another call...

'Drrrrappp...'

There is rapid knocking at Alem's door, five knocks at a time, rousing him from his sleep, part nightmare, partly thoughts of Arron and worries for his own future...

Brrdrdrrr... raabbbb... rab...

"Hold on a sec, will you?"

Dbdbdbdbdrrr…

"Heyy! Don't break down my door, for God's sake!"

He never trusts his dreams. He doesn't believe his dreams until he overhears his friends laughing at him. It's because his dreams, especially the bad dreams always seem to come true. He dreamed he was on fire with his dead father and his grandfather, trying to save the house of a beautiful neighbour who they loved dearly.

Oh… please, God let it be only a dream. He prayed softly. *Take my dream to deepest hell and to the bottomless sea.*

The previous week he had written a political article, uncovering what the government is doing, creating more war and exploitation to destabilise people from asking for their basic rights and to increase its power. He wrote of the governing TPLF party's plot to divide the country into more than fourteen states, so it will still have a territory to exploit even if it loses power over the country. It went viral because it described the reality hidden from the people but seen in practically every action of the ruling party. Some officials were furious and ground their teeth when his name was mentioned. They bought expensive jets and employed guards for their own safety while in fact there is no safety at all. The country has fallen into a paradoxical situation, where the oppressors have been granted more safety and the oppressed toil under still greater oppression. It's only a matter of hours before he will fall under their control. He thinks it would be better to cut his own hands instead. He knows what is happening to those activists and journalists who write against TPLF – truth has eaten her sons. They go to jail and undergo beatings until they die. The only escape is to lie – then they shut their mouths and submit in order to stay alive. Who cares even if you apologise? You become their prey. No one cares. Then you question why you wanted to be an activist in the first place. They even follow you to Kenya and Somalia to hunt you down wherever you go '*even to your mother's womb*' as the saying goes.

He is even more vulnerable and liable to be accused as he has the other problem of being related to the royal family. They give him the name 'Neftegna' which means a gunner because of his ethnic background. They all know that as a deacon under church rules he is not allowed to carry a gun, so he has never touched one. But they have waited for this moment to trap him. They accused him of being feudal. They accused him because he thinks differently, thinks that the Pan – African system was better than this one in so many ways. They accused him because he's different from them. They accused him because he disagreed with the reintroduction of slavery. He used to be a prince, but it's all over now since the downfall of Emperor Haile Selassie I (Ras Tafari), he who gave away a five thousand year old crown to a military junta. Alem has been keeping his royal blood hidden for his own sake and that of his family, constantly concerned for their safety. The world has become different for him since that event. Since the battle of Adwa, it has become a different state now. Now this new world means he's just a refugee in a world of ethnic divisions, ignorance, poverty, degradation of historic, traditional, religious traditions; the degradation of generations....

Now Alem is not only a prince of course, but also a poet, an activist and journalist which is a crime in the eyes of government officials. Whatever articles he writes get published, and have a wide readership, but he upsets the government. In fact, he's on a government blacklist mainly because of his background but also his profession. His grandfather Aba Tso had been arrested by the last Emperor for writing an allegorical play portraying a mighty country being ruled by animals. His father had been killed by the military government just for belonging to the royal family. Now, the same old card is being played by the new, so-called democratic government, so he's already aware that trouble will come someday. Where can he go? He is tired of the hide-and-seek game of political intrigue that his life has become. He prays for a better life but he fears that the worst is yet to come.

Brruurrraaadaradaratata...

He jumps down from his hammock.

He opens the door of his little hut exposing it to the bloody sunrise. His face is protected by the tall shadows of his friends' heads.

"Hello...."

"What?"

"Yenta⁴ summons you."

He has not heard *'Yenta summons you...'*, for a long time.

"Now?"

All of them nod their heads.

He hasn't been called for his poetic computation since last month. He's wanted to talk about his worries with him. In addition, he doesn't know if he has passed and qualified to be a teacher like his grandfather so that at least he could live farther from them. No one has told him and he wonders why. He doesn't waste a minute to hear from his aged teacher and grandfather Aba Tso, 'Yeneta Tso' as he addresses him. Despite their age difference, Alem and grandfather Tso have similar characters but they keep their secret to themselves; nobody knows they are related and nobody in this campus knows their background. Of course, everybody agrees that no one can replace them as the brave student and the respected teacher. But nobody knows what makes them such geniuses and adored at the same time. Aba Tso has been administering this traditional education centre for more than forty years, and he's never found such a brilliant student as Alem. He is the only boy Aba Tso proudly describes as being his match: *"you remind me of myself in my youth."* He's smiling as a father who sees himself in his own son. They are real poets as well. Every month it is their tradition to hold a poetic battle, but Alem and Aba Tso can never beat each other.

Alem doesn't waste a minute to go to Aba Tso.

Timtimtimm...taaa

He knocks on the door softly.

---

4 "Yenta" is a name for the highest teachers in Eritrean and Ethiopian Traditional school.

"*Who is it?*" A golden sound of voices rises inside the teacher's special hut.

"*It's I.*" His voice slurs, trying to slow down and be heard at the same time.

"*Who is I? Don't you have a name?*" replies Aba opening the door angrily.

"*Good morning, my lord.*"

"*Ah... Only God is Lord.*" Aba Tso smiles broadly at him and then his expression turns serious.

"*Is it better to live as everyone lives or is it better to fight back against what you cannot defeat and die, for what glory?*"

"*I don't understand.*" Softening his voice as if he's lost for an answer, he isn't really ready to take on his shoulders the curse of being born in this land, within this system and family. He's just unlucky, that's all.

"*Is it really so important for you to tell your history to all and sundry? Are you going to let your story be published, with you as the hero? Who do you think you are?*"

His heart hammers inside his shaking body.

"*What do you mean, Yenta?*" He knows what he means.

"*Only you and I are left from the house of Empress Hendeke[5] and the house of Solomon the wise. We need to take extra care just to live as normally as everyone does. Let me ask, what did you write? Tell me please. Did you call them 'hyenas?' did you expose what they are stealing from the people? Have you told them that one day all their bulging greedy stomachs are going to explode all over themselves? Have you told them that they will pay for all the damage they have caused throughout the land, huh? Tell me? I swear you have. It's all right, I know, for better or worse.*"

Agh..... Damn the curse! he said to himself. Their family have long been hiding their ancestry trying to conceal the family background. He'd grown up in an ancient forest leading a wandering life as his father and forefathers had struggled to conceal their true identity.

---

5 An ancient Abyssinian royal line

They both bend their heads as if they're tired of the curse and can't hold its weight anymore. They have been hiding in a forest in a remote part of the country just for this. Now, their country has neither forest to be hidden in, nor countryside free from conspirators and spies; there is no one with a sign of compassion, no one to plead with for life and protection. The officials don't have time for history; they have no respect for heroic deeds, no time for glory but only their own dirty politics and sleazy conspiracies. They're too busy fighting each other, killing the innocent, depriving people of freedom of speech and a free press, expanding war zones and turning the world into hell. Here being a poet is considered a job for cowards and there is no place for such kinds of cowards here.

"*I want to live.*"

"*Ohm… you need to move somewhere; rumours are spreading fast all over the place. Most of the political journalists released from the detention centres are starting to come and ask me more about you.*"

"*They still believe in the tale.*"

"*It's not a tale. It's a prophecy.*"

"*Ehm… Forofessy.*"

They know that almost everyone in the country believes that 'a young prince from the house of both Empress Hendeke/Saba and King Solomon the Wise will rise and his name will be 'Tewodros III'… He will overcome the dictators of the continent and replace them with the fathers of Africa and lead all the people in complete unity to give rise to a prosperous civilisation. That's as it was written in the sacred books of the Kingdom of Ancient Abyssinia. Not just a prophecy but also a hope of the nation that things can change. Officials are still scared of the name. That's why they detained Teddy Afro the musician.[6] See? Even the musicians are being hunted for singing about their own life and dreams?"

---

6 A famous singer

"I will go somewhere, but how about you?" "I am not a young prince, am I? I'm not a writer, am I?" Aba replied. *"Besides, I have learned the magic of how to escape from such evils. I have lived for a hundred and ten years with my curse without any trouble. But you need to go far away until I can teach you that magic, until you eat from the tree of life. Now go away! You won't be free here, until you have become immortal first. They will worship you then. They will think you were a man of God. But not now! From now on you have to become a refugee."*

"I am a free man; I am neither a prince nor a refugee."

"You might be a free man, but you are a prince and a refugee." A huge silence falls again.

He starts to think of the alternative. What if I were not a prince and I could be a free man? Why would I write and fight when I'm just an ordinary person, when I know there is no hope of a change, but only an endless fight. What if I had been born a farmer? I would have children by now... I wouldn't know anything about human rights, how time changes and how the world works; I'd just be caring for my family and myself just for today: that's all. Why wasn't I born in a remote part of the country, where the only safe way is to be free from worldly knowledge, to be illiterate, ignorant of all this... Sleeping until bad days pass like a dream, until dying in my sleep? How good it is to sleep anyway. How good is it not to feel pain, to shut my eyes from seeing my friends dying? To deafen my ears to hearing Parliament's insults and learning the numbers of people killed and drowned at sea... To ignore the fact that life is more than this. This is just a human nightmare.

He wants to escape from all this and be reborn as a farmer. He thinks it would be better. *'The common everyday life is a better way to live here,'* he thinks. He's going to lie to himself; he wants to get drunk and go crazy in order to find the courage to lie. Then he denies himself and pretends he is someone else for the moment; he imagines a miserable man in front of him, a poor farmer staring back at him and he starts to interrogate himself back and forth.

"Do you really want to be me? You are joking".

"What about your children's future."

'*God knows! But, I'll teach them to live like me as a father does.*'

"No no no..." He realises that he is talking to nobody but himself. He's even forgotten about Aba, who has also drifted away from his thoughts.

Alem wants to buy his life at the expense of his heritage. That's what almost everyone in his country is forced to do. To get a job they swear to be a loyal slave to the leaders; 'dogs of a single mad master' as he calls them. It's a system established by bloodshed between brothers. He felt like crying and he did, but inside, as he's done hundreds and thousands of times. Life taught him how to cry inside, he knows he's not alone though. Lots of people do the same.

He thinks,

Is there such a place where men can live without punishment because they hate holding guns and don't like fighting and war, because they prefer love, not because they are cowards but because they are capable of love and forgiveness, and do not fight back? A place where just being human is enough to live and enjoy life, where being a prince does not mean anything, a place where you can freely ask for a break when you are fatigued, or starving to death; where you can ask for a home, a mother, a father, a family?

Aba Tso knows what's on his mind. He is thinking the same thing too. *Yes, there is. If you can dream about it that means there is such a place. Only time will tell and you must wait for that time, when the truth will be revealed.*

'*Ohm...*' Aba Tso has already decided to send him away from this own country for his safety. Once the media have exposed him throughout the country, he will not have a single safe place to stay.

"But why?"

"I will not add anything. I don't want my church to become a political stage." He knows that apart from this church – Entoto Mariam Church - most churches around are already political stages. *"You may ask me, 'when have you ever seen religion without politics?'"* Alem agrees. Aba

continues explaining: *"I'm sorry, but the church cannot save her children anymore."*

He reminds him of what happened the last time when students went into the church of the patriarch seeking refuge from the beating by the government security guards. Even the patriarch hadn't shown pity on them as a normal human being would do, let alone act as a responsible religious father. A divine state is failing shamefully. A proud nation has raised its hands to beg. The lions are tired of the heat. The tiger is too old but it hasn't changed its colour, yet. There is still hope but you hope as when you have nothing left to hope for. You keep hoping because to still have hope is to live.

"It's the way it is."

Therefore, he decides that he must not waste time in seeking refuge somewhere safer, before he is caught, so he can live longer.

Chapter
THREE

Emu-Hiba Tsegay's life

Red

Black

Red blood... her brain has stopped identifying colours.

She has forgotten how to breathe normally. She's forgotten how to focus on one thing; her eyes have forgotten to tell her what they see. Her mind is wrestling with her soul. Her hands are out of her control, her legs can't walk straight. Her fingers are dripping with thick clotted red and black blood.

Emu's world is different from the world most of us know.

There's a bright yellow desert with more than three hundred islands scattered over the Red Sea, the green and beautiful shoreline. All of this seems dead to her now, the natural attractiveness is only what you see on the outside. The yellow city of Assab, Eritrea, with its abundance of seasonal yellow flowers and the green and red landscape of the highland breathing fresh perfume across the countless Red Sea islands, tells an ancient romantic story for those who like love stories:

> *Here, on this spot, seven and a half thousand years ago there was a creator (God of the sun) who was only a word, alone and bored. He lived in the region between the rivers of Gion, Tigris and Euphrates. He created a man in his own image, from a drop of water and clay. Then he created Eve, also in his image, a beautiful lady who was to live a loving life with her man and fill the world with peoples. That was the ultimate purpose. Princes*

and princesses tried to accomplish this ultimate purpose, till modern inventions come to end their stories. Their memorial lies at the grave of each prince and princess. Statues are timeless books to be read, still telling the legacies of dead romances. However, here in this present world, past and present are as far from each other as heaven and hell. One is not even close to the other. There is something which breaks the link between those times and now. It is called politics.

Now the camp which looks like a magnificent palace on the outside in fact holds a number of stinking cells for the detention of forcibly-trained young soldiers reluctant to fight, including Emu-Tsegay. It's as quiet as a graveyard, at least for the moment. It seems that it's prohibited even to make the sound of humming. Suddenly the silence is broken as one man roars as he fires his gun into the air, holding the gun in one hand and throwing a bottle of blood towards the crowd with the other.

"Our freedom is in our hands!" Bullets rocketed up to the sky with a sound like a disturbing drum roll.

Well, if firing a gun up to the free-flying birds is a declaration of freedom, it is like killing whoever protests just because you can. But you had better not misuse your power over innocent birds because that's the logic of hell. Satan can't change hell into heaven because his job is to make it worse – that's what is happening in this place – the Horn of Africa in general. Sadly, every group which comes to power pays with its own blood and continues to keep power by sucking the blood of its own people. No power is surrendered without further bloodshed. That's the logic of hell.

Emu is in hell now. She has killed her enemy who was employed to make citizens suffer. But she knows others will be sent to punish her. Even worse, she feels lifeless. She must find a way out of here to feel alive, if that's at all possible. *She knows she is still alive if she can remember; if she worries, if she breathes then she's alive.*

Welcome to Emu's world.

Here life stinks more than death itself. The ruined state of the city makes the feeling worse than tragic, imagining the city's plunge from heavenly grace to deepest Gahanna (hell). Once upon a time, this was a place full of life where rulers of great kingdoms celebrated holy days with Greek gods and held luxurious feasts; but now it is a place of death, all the deaths of the world and where human bodies stink like fish.

It's been hell for most of the young people of the city for a century. Seventeen – year – old Emu-Hiba, who used to look young and fresh, has spent almost her entire life here and now it has turned her into a miserable hag. She has been here together with her poor father since they killed him in the room next to hers and brought her here to prison. She still remembers her father's last breath – still fresh; she followed his heartbeat to the last. She grew up here filled with hatred, liking to be here just in order to wait to bring punishment and judgment to her father's killer who had never stopped watching her until his own death.

Red. Black. Thick. Blood.

Broken breath, nervous reflexes and harrowing thoughts are slowly killing her.

Now, her small room is filled with thick black blood flowing from a fat man's body. It's still and quiet. Head bowed and hands down, she seems to be giving thanks at the same time as asking for forgiveness, praying to her imperfect God, begging for help to escape after killing her enemy. This same man who had been watching her was only meant to keep her from escaping from the cell, but he had attacked her. He had even forgotten that he was the one who had killed her father. Well he was no different from the others, an evil man like all of his colleagues. It was one of the daily duties which he had to perform in order to stay close to his masters. After several attempts she won the fight. Although she had been forced to train for National Military Service, she had never fired at anybody before. She had preferred a quiet cell to the sound of gunfire until finally her compulsion for revenge had awakened. Now, was the time. She didn't feel fear at killing a man for the first time. She was proud of herself as her father would have been if he had seen her win the fight and kill one 'bastard' as he used to call them.

But, what next?

I don't care. It's called justice.

Though she's not sure about what she's doing, her instinct tells her to leave the silent camp in secret. She can't even remember the route they had brought her and her father twelve years before. After taking the narrow way out through the tunnel, she stops. She's been kept locked in the stinking cell for more than five years. It's even quieter here, only there is a soft wind, sun, nature all around. She's out in the wider world, leading her in uncountable directions and long routes that could lead her far away. The sun is beaming down on her. Protecting herself from being seen by anyone, she covers her miserable face. She follows the line of bushes, almost hiding herself from any exposure. She keeps on going to find a place where no man can even exist or see her, just walking to nowhere through the dark nights. Hiding by day because she doubts whether the sun can prevent exposing her to people she does not trust, she loves the moon and stars instead. At least they don't expose her bloody hands. She realises that the moon is both following her from the starting point but also leading her to the furthest point ahead. She feels that when she stops walking, the moon does too. Emu is feeling the company of other forces for the very first time. She wishes to chat with the moon, and in her imagination she does.

"*I am no longer alone, am I?*" Talking to herself, she imagines a reply from the moon:

'*No, you'll never be alone. You are joined with so many peoples in the world just as the stars are with me.*'

"*How do you know?*"

'*If you were up here with me, you could see them all. That's why I am up here, to see and give them company in need.*'

She asks the moon to tell her where she's going.

"*Advise me,* she says, *Tell me where I should go. I have no destination... but in a way I have.*"

'*Please, do tell.*'

"Anywhere where there is freedom to live."

'That's what we all want.' the comforting moon replies.

The lonely moon leads the way.

The biggest moon.

The brightest moon.

The full moon.

The moon.

Behind and in front of the moon there are huge clouds like fierce flying dragons following and hindering her journey. There is a brooding tension between them all, until the heavy cloud fades away by the breath of the sky and the moon shows her full and cheerful face. Emu wishes for cruelty to fade away from the sky of her country and make her own people smile with the joy of freedom, and then she could stay at home and enjoy the warmth and companionship of her family. As the moon gets older and bends her neck down to the horizon, the same young sun is born again on the other horizon. This is not by her choice; it's the nature of the universe. The cloud starts attacking the sun as well, covering her light and heat.

The sky, which is the backdrop for this scene, has started to cry and every living thing around has stopped and is bending over. Even though she feels as though the welcome rain is washing away her sin, she hates walking through the storm, through this desolate landscape.

Emu's world is about to change from the confines of a narrow cell to a wider storm. That's her life anyway and she doesn't complain. Even though she hates the days as she hates mankind, she tries to smile as she sees a loaded truck which has stopped to let the storm pass. Seizing her chance, she climbs unnoticed into the back of the truck, covering her bloody body by sinking down into the cargo. She doesn't even realise that she has buried herself in a truck which is full of raw salt until her wound gives her a painful jolt making her scream unexpectedly.

The female driver quickly stops and gets out of the car. She guesses that it's one of the unlucky girls who have somehow managed to escape from the prison. *They call it the door to hell.* It's because no one has ever came out free. Emu screams inside the salt truck again. The driver sees her groaning and then suddenly become silent. Realising that she has fainted, she takes her out of the salt-laden truck and she gives her first aid as best she can.

"Are you okay?"

"Yes, thank you."

"What happened to you?"

She doesn't know what or how to tell this woman, but she utters some words even if she's not sure about them.

"I killed him." She fears herself. *"It's because he tried to force me to… and he killed my father."*

"Oh, that's what is happening every day." The driver cries as if remembering the same happenings in her life. It's like an inside scar which can't be forgotten.

"And of course, I was waiting for revenge, and I did sin. I killed him." She gasps, *"I know they will find me. But I don't really care."* She was lost in thought for a while.

"Don't be afraid. I am Samrawit. What is your name?"

"I am Emu. Emu Tsegay." She felt proud to recall her dead father's name, making sure she would never forget him.

She reflects that he would have been proud of her now. She finds him inside herself. She sees him inside the driver's helping heart. She must live to make his soul happier. She wants to make him proud of her.

"I'll help you."

"Will you help me to get out of their sight, please?" She now smiles for the first time since her father died, realising that people *can* help each other. *"Please, get me out of their sight, please?"*

"I can take you as far as Sudan, at least."

"Wherever; take me out of the danger zone, and I'll pay you back for your good deeds."

They smile at each other. When two women smile together it's like a smile between the sun and the moon. From every direction there will be light and hope. This smile brings relief. It makes them forget about every wound they have ever experienced in their lives. It's like seeing a rose; you don't need a reason to feel excited, you just smile as you rest your eyes on the other, a natural smile like flowers that burst open to see the morning sun after waiting for the moment to spring out from their dark experience. It's like a rainbow appearing to smile through the dark clouds. It's an event only seen once in a yellow moon; two women understanding and opening to each other's hearts.

"Let's go."

Here is how Emu came to know the world that we all know – that of escape – that of a refugee.

Chapter FOUR

Enderbury - Charlotte, soul-mate

'Din din...

Trererereree...

Voooop, up!'

It's Charlotte's text again. She cannot stop herself from texting Arron even though it's not her character to persist. She's lost her decency because of his weirdness, she thinks. She wants to know what's changed him into being so selfish. She deserves to know. That's what lovers do, when they love their partner more than themselves. They don't care for their self-respect when their feelings take over.

Arron has realised he is weakened by thinking what he has lost in Alem. He was like his only brother with whom he has shared secrets, advice and got inspiration for his life. Now, it seems he's lost in life with nothing to share with anyone else. Charlotte also feels as though she is lost in a way. She doesn't want to lose him at all. She calls again.

'Trrrrrr...

Din din...

Whoop whoop...' the more he keeps ignoring her, the more she keeps texting.

She is typically English. Not only does she like knitting while having her tea but she is confident and seems posh. Arron had met her at a club where he had been playing the guitar. There they became friends and their friendship developed from that meeting. She had helped him so much and never regretted having done so.

His heart beats each time he receives a text alert from her.

"What do I mean to you?" she asked him.

Then he texted back, *"You are a perfect friend. You are more than a sister to me."*

"What a nice thing to say!"

She knows he will not appreciate it if she asks him to say it in words. She wants to know his feelings through more than words.

She knows him better than his social worker knows him, knows more about him than the government knows about him. He knows her more than her parents do. It's now been three years since they first met. She has been trying to help him trace his friends for about two years, but without success. Then they decided to be together.

Charlotte is in love with Arron, not because he writes her love poems every day, not because she loves his innocent silliness, but unconditionally – like his mother used to love him, so that her feeling for him remains unchanged. She has never viewed him as a foreigner. Here is one instance of his silliness.

"I am here for you, to free your feelings to let me through.

I'll do anything you desire,

Be it to swim under the fire,

Be it to fly up above the sky.

You are my queen forever.

That's what I feel, that's who I am."

"Thank you my Arial."

A year on..

Now she's reading it again and can't get the strength to throw away this treasure. She puts it back in the frame where it has been for ages. He's still in her heart – spiritually, but physically they are no longer together.

Now, Arron seems to be ignoring her for the first time. It's a shock for her. She doesn't know why, nor has he told her anything. She can't recall anything that could be forcing them apart. Nothing! She is the sun for him, the moon. Smiling is her signature. *"You know you are sweet,"* Arron used to tell her in response to every special smile she had for him. Next to guitar scales and chords, simple smiles and fun were their first language before his English got better. She didn't deserve a winter face, nor is she here to add beauty and brightness to his winter. Even the clouds here are beautiful as long as she is beside him. More importantly, she is his main girl. She is not as complicated as she looks. Her philosophy in life is easy to understand. Every day she dies and every day she is reborn and ready for 'Life'.

Here is her story ..

Her daily rebirth is when each morning is so much brighter than the one before – she would cry for it!

Her childhood? It was full of freedom. She could ask for anything she liked and it would be given to her. If not, who cared? Teenage years! She used to turn everything into whatever she wanted. She could make earth heaven. As an adult? Her dreams were real; she could talk to the future. Now, she is mature. Being mature is when you know you are a combination of heart and soul – the other elements are mere extensions. When you find no meaning and explanation you will stop asking. Life is money, money is work and work becomes slavery. If you have the same routine every day, you are just normal. She dreams of when she will be old, life will be 'was', a long way back. When you are old you will know the human race to be divided into only two types – dead and alive. If she is not alone, she will tell this to everybody. Heaven! It's never strange for her, heaven is love and love is her life with Arron. Death - is when life becomes a blank. She knows what darkness is anyway because she has seen it lots of times. But this one will be an absolute darkness for the flesh. Then you don't have any idea what will happen but you feel it's infinite and eternal. All you can do is wait patiently.

Now, that's what she is feeling, but she doesn't want to tell anybody, even him, as he is the cause of it. She can only guess he might be in a worse situation than her. The more she wants to forget about him, the more she realises how she loves him. He needs time to heal before he meets her. He has decided to wait for himself to settle his mind first. Therefore, she decides to wait for him. They decide to wait for each other in a better time.

In his class, students have seated themselves forming a cross without realising it. Arron and John are on the opposite side wings alone; the others are seated around the centre column. Arron wants to be alone, just for the moment hopefully, but John has always been excluded and forced to sit alone. His classmates say they don't get on with him. Arron still doesn't understand this culture of segregation, homophobia and how this can happen in modern societies. When will it stop? Arron has just started to understand why people in such countries easily get depressed, feel hopeless or even commit suicide. He too feels so lonely and less inspired. *When you cannot hide your problems anymore or when you let everyone know about it or when your appearance defines you entirely, life is different. It may not be only your problem, but it's your fight. It becomes too personal. Or you alienate yourself from the reality around you; you become known as weird,* he thinks. He remembers why he has never felt these kinds of feelings before. He then remembers Alem. He listens to Alem inside himself saying *'If only we realised that we are created for one another, the world could have been a better place.'* He realises now better what Alem meant by that. Arron finds himself within John, he finds John within himself. He wants to help John. He wants to help himself as well.

First he started sitting with him and then they became friends. He's known him for about a year, but they've only become friends recently. They remember a story John is famous for.

John's always been bullied by his high school mates, even now. Once when he was meeting his first girlfriend in the park, he suddenly saw the boys, those boys who had been dragging him down into the mud, bullying him for more than ten years. This time he promised himself that whatever happened he must act on it accordingly. They walked around him in his space.

"*Ay baldy!*" said one of them.

"*Oy, you too baldy.*"

"*Ay? Me too, what? You rat!*"

"*You're the rat.*"

They kicked his arse like a 12-year-old, leaving him at his girlfriend's feet. Diane got scared and ran away looking for help but, he couldn't bear the situation anymore. So, he turned himself from victim into aggressor. He remembered every kick he'd had before, but not as heavy as this one. He started to think the same way as them. He wanted to fight back, remembering each and every punch he'd had over the last years.

All the spitting

Every assault

Every evil stare

He wanted to pay back all of it. He wanted to do the same thing for the next decade. He stopped thinking about himself. Even though they beat him a lot, he stopped screaming the way he had done before. He stopped talking back. He stopped writing about it.

Over the next days, he started watching violent movies and studying the history of the most violent men in the world. He started to play all the violent video games that he could get hold of and he wanted to apply what he saw to every bastard.

His life was all about getting revenge.

Nothing to think, nothing to plan.

Nothing to feel, nothing to fear.

Just – Stab … Stab… Shoot, kill.

Remembering each and every evil action done throughout human history…

He said *'being human is too complicated.'* At least that was the system available to him at the time; a complicated system where humanity is distorted by so many contradictory demonic   -isms and systems. Bullying slogans like *'All we saw was a cloud of smoke.' 'They didn't stop pulling my hair; I didn't stop pulling the trigger.'* He had heard so many quotes from a number of social media sites. He wants more than these words. He wants innocent, pro-life and encouraging slogans. *'A good selfless heart is enough,'* he thinks. He doesn't have divine access to everyone's' hearts, though he wished there could be some divine force to stop the bullies. Religious leaders have become different forms of bullies and political leaders are developing their skills of insulting and pointing at each other. *Only consciousness or a divine self in every human heart can cure all this man made disease,* he suggests. It's not easy, he knows the brainwashing, and the language that has been used, deep rooted for hundreds of years of human experience. Thinking of this, he hated everyone except his mother. Feeding him every day, she gave him the body to re-enforce his revenge or to enjoy his fate, like today.

"*A mother is a mother, after all,*" Arron says supportively.

John smiles.

Who knows what it means to grow up motherless more than this boy who has known hunger? No one knows what water means more than the camels that live in the desert, Arron thinks.

"*Yeah, I come to realise that now.*" They smile together.

"*Do you remember last year?*"

Again… they remember… On the way to his college, John was riding his bicycle under the bridge through the tunnel, along the side of the river. As soon as he was in the middle, the boys rode faster towards him and pushed him till he bounced back and was dragged into the river with his bicycle. He could think of nothing other than paying them back. He was not sure how he could do it though.

People saw him struggling to get out of the river; being dragged down into the river again and again, being punched simultaneously.

He was spitting blood into the river from his mouth and nostrils.

People stood around watching him struggling as if they were watching nothing but a boxing match.

They didn't call the police or do anything to help him. Arron was the only one who came to get him out of the river. That's how they first met. He jumped into the crowd and shouted at the boys who were all over John. They left immediately, realising that he was not alone.

"Why did you help me?"

"In my culture, I cannot see someone like that, struggling, and just pass by ..."

"I was enjoying it," said John as if proudly.

"What do you mean?"

"Welcome to my life! That is what I'm used to."

"Really?"

"Do you know the risk of what getting involved in this shit with me would be?"

"I can guess. I know you from college. I'll watch out for you."

Remembering it now, they smile again.

"You helped your classmate, unexpectedly."

"That was meant to be."

The fight wasn't only for the victim; the fight was for all mankind. Everyone has the right to be free from bullying they think.

Chapter
FIVE

Farewell to Addis Ababa, Adu Genet ... 2014

Alem's singing as usual.

He's sitting in the same spot where Emperor Minilik II used to sit to watch over the city a hundred years before, probably thinking how he could lead his nation to a new civilisation without leaving the old and divine civilisations of Africa behind. But, Alem is neither a king nor a soldier. What can he do, what benefits him standing at the same place of HIM Minilik II? What can he even free himself from? He is probably just thinking that this place is historical, a blessed mountain, and a strategic spot on the top of the mountain, where you can see the darkness of the city clearly.

'Whistlewhiswhisssll...

> *Arë beleŵ arē beleŵ..*
> *Enatiem lij yelat, esum wondm yelew,*
> *Areee bellleeewwww...'*

He keeps singing....   *Meaning*

> *Hark! Hark! Hark!*
> *My Mama doesn't have a son,*
> *And her son has no brother.*

He does it whenever he feels very lonely. The melody of angels he calls it. Alem knows the first ancient notation system. The story goes like this:

> *'About one and a half thousand years ago the inventor of Abyssinian traditional music that has lasted centuries – the scales, conducting methods, notations, compositions- Liku*

Yaredm, was a simple and lonely child who wasn't very good at learning. His teacher tired of him and sent him away. On his way, he rested under a tree and he saw a spider trying to climb up the tree, but each time it fell down. On the seventh attempt it finally climbed the tree, and Liku Yared learned from this and returned to his teacher. As he walked back to his teacher, three birds from heaven came and accompanied him with heavenly melodies. Ge'ez, Ezl, Araray. From those he invented notations and formed scales. Requesting one more chance, his teacher accepted him and was surprised by his gifts of wisdom, art, knowledge and spiritual strength. He appointed him as a 'Lik'[7] and he used to sing to King Gebre-Meskel. Then he immediately became a scholar. Since then these melodies have been become an indispensable therapy for any illness. They linked so many generations together, closer than through knowledge, wisdom and arts. They even served during the Great Black African victory – Adwa!'

Remembering this history makes him have hope that one day generations will learn good from history.

Entoto Mountain is high up from the city of Addis Ababa. Here you can see all the heaven and hell of the city. A hundred years ago there was a wise queen – *Etegie Taytu* who established the city and called it Addis Ababa – New Flower. Alem misses it most when he remembers it full of flowers. It's still an impressive and progressive city. He has no idea why he has had to leave. The only thing he knows is he's always been chased away, from his childhood even until now. He has been forced to leave many beautiful cities. From his birth place *Gonder* – The Home of Palaces, *Bahrdar* - the symbol of heaven on earth, *Lalibela* – the second Jerusalem, *Afar* - the home of the first human being, *Wollo, Nazret, Harer* – the home of beauties... He has been called 'Capitalist' 'Neftegna / Gunner' because of his forefather's unfortunate deeds.

---

7 'Lik' a traditional scholar title as Laureate, given to exceptional scholars and inventors in Eritrean and Ethiopian traditional school.

Now, he's singing an operatic melody, high pitched, emotionally dynamic...

This may be the last time he'll say goodbye. He has no idea. The only thing he knows is he's being chased because of his forefather's deed over which he had no control. Even in church services, he has been excluded, rejected, insulted just because he was born in one particular ethnicity and as a prince, though still he loves to be here. He loves everything here: his country, his friends and his family, some of the girls who could have been his future wife. Love is a problem sometimes, love is embarrassing sometimes. The more he stands on the side of love, the more he feels deep down that he is powerless to change anything. Now freedom is what he needs more than love, so he is at the point of having no choice but to stop being strong and instead to walk away until one day he can fly freely.

Across the sky a large full moon lays bare the city so that he can see it clearly and bid it goodbye. Across the city: Shromeda, Sdst Killo, Amst killo, Arat killo[8]....the palace lies deep inside the forest. Since most of the forests across the country have been cut down, the only area of tall trees left is around the palace. He wonders what is happening out there. He feels that he has to get there but doesn't know how he can pass the brutal gate keepers who have no mercy even on flies. They are the so-called federal police. People call them "fedish, faddish, fetish, fiendish, ..." stuff like that. Everybody hates them and looks on them as worse than donkeys, not because they look ugly. In fact they are strong and really fit, but fit like wild animals, worse than brutal animals. They've been trained in how to kill their own relatives, friends; they've learned how to kill each other to keep their oath to protect their master, the so- called prime minister. He remembers the incident that happened last week, when a Jamaican Rasta kissing the ground to honour Ras Tafari I near the old palace got a beating from a federal policeman. What a disgrace and what a shame. Hospitality used to be the greatest characteristic of the people, but the government always acts against the traditional values of the society. Traditionally, if somebody is inside a church and needing

---

8 Name of the places in Addis Ababa city centre.

mercy, they would be safe, but that day students were killed inside St. Mary's Church. Hundreds of other students were taken prisoner and no one has heard of them since. It's a common occurrence nowadays.

Remembering all this, he starts to fear, to be selfish. He wants to stay longer, to see what the future will bring. Remembering all this makes his soul tired, he really needs some way to find relief. He doesn't know what the future holds for him. For better for worse, he's going to follow where his legs take him; it's his destiny.

Would you follow me? he asks the pitying moon.

Would you follow me? it asks him back.

Of course, that's my destiny.

Mine too.

Yours?

Yes, mine. Have you ever seen me stop in one place?

No, but why is that? he wonders to himself. *It's the law of nature! What other reason could it be?*

Not only that, of course, the reason is, I couldn't find what I wanted and even knowing I will not find it, I will still not stop looking for it.

What is it that you are looking for?

My love

Who is your love? He feels shy even with himself.

Freedom

It's the same for me.

We are on the same road then, right! Join me! Hurry up!!

The moon leads the way.

The biggest moon.

The brightest moon.

The full moon.

The moon.

Selena – Eritrea

'Kakakakaka...

Diwww, diww...diiwww.' Bullets are flying all around the poor truck transporting Emu. They wish they could fly, they wish anything could save them from the combat vehicle called '*Oral*'. After smiling, the angels of death are quickly upon them.

Nearby in the town of Selena, two military cars are racing towards the poor salt-loaded Isuzu truck. They rush at the truck and sandwich it from back and front. A mushroom of dust falls over the road. They shoot at the driver four rounds at a time. She slumps on the driving wheel. Emu fights back helplessly but she cannot resist them and she's taken by force all the way back to her cell.

Even though she thinks she will spend the rest of her life there, in fact it is only for one night. It was at this point, Emus' story took a mysterious turn, when instead of being a victim like the poor driver who had tried to save her, she felt herself being caught up in something bigger, some greater purpose. She felt it was not her fate to die in some remote place, lost and forgotten, but she was being led for some greater purpose. It started mysteriously in the night, someone came to release her, but she didn't know how or why it happened.

The night after being returned to her cell, from midnight until the morning, the weather turned the prison in to a battlefield; storms and lightning wrecking everything around. The windows and the gates of the tunnels were unable to resist the elements and stay strong and unbroken. Water flooded in to every cell. Everybody became breathless and faint including Emu until she felt that she had come back to life, drawing a long breath as someone lifted her up from the water. She'd nearly died in the flooded cell but she saw the top half of a man, naked and red, like a fire. She noticed that the water was swallowing them up to the chest. He grabbed her and placed her in his arms. She felt as though she had been placed safely in a strong, secure cave, comfortable and warm, at least for the moment. He reminded her of her father. He smiled, but not the smile of a father, more a seductive smile as she fell asleep in his arms until they met the sun.

"Good morning."

He said these words for the first time in his life. Zen had never greeted anybody before he met Emu. He has been involved in many dark practices, but he has never been involved in such a miracle as he feels this girl is working in him. He realised the effect of her charm while fighting with his nature to accept her beauty. He realised it even more when she opened her eyes to uncover the light of her pupils. They have a special light that invites even the devil to kneel down at the vision of her beauty. Still in his arms, running fast through half storm and half sun, now walking fast, they were miles away from the tempestuous prison village. She was not looking back. She was looking into his eyes, wondering who he might be, wondering whose prince he might be.

"Why did you save me?" she asked him, calculating how she could repay him. His face closed in on hers as if they were about to exchange a kiss. He asked himself, '*Why is this even a question?*'

"Because I have to ask."

She noticed he took in her breath and returned his while speaking ever closer. It was a bachelor's breath that smelt fresh and hot like a spring steam. They looked at each other before she rejected him, avoiding his advances as he tried to kiss her. He can tell she has never been kissed before.

"Not now." She'd rather kiss his right ear. Zen was still happy, perhaps for the first time in his life.

He looked around and at himself and it was real. He was standing in the shadow of a beautiful girl and he felt love for the first time. He had never felt like this since he turned into a Real Devil. 'Real Devil' is a nick-name he'd had since his childhood. It's because he used to do tricks and magic to fool people.

Her soft and strong arms were around his neck. He placed her in a comfortable rock-hewn bed. He was surprised and felt glad to have received such a romantic mission from those anonymous bosses. Even if it only lasted a short time, he could still enjoy her until he had to destroy her. He wanted to start new life, even if he knew it would end in horror. As part of a suicide group he would be forced ultimately to poison himself. Participating in a terrorist attack he'd nearly died along with 200 children, yet he survived them all. He is a loyal servant of the devil and he is proud of it. That's why he came to this world. But he didn't want to remember his past life at that moment. Even if he wanted to he wouldn't have a clue about it. Money, mission and the eternal darkness were the key words of his life. He has been given multiple devilish gifts to perform his duties without any humanity or compassion.

He was born in 1966, though he looked to be in his thirties. He has taken the lives of many people: children, pregnant women, poor villagers, freedom fighters, charity workers, refugees, subjects and subordinates. Honest activists, responsible leaders, brilliant scientists, humanitarians and talented artists have all fallen into his death trap. He hated such kinds of people. He called them "perfect obstacles for life in the imperfect world." He especially hated poor people who couldn't kneel down for money and power; activists and freedom fighters who did not keep quiet after they gained power, people who felt sorry after they had killed someone. That's her – Emu, but he liked her. Before he considered killing her, he thought about her; it may have been the first time he'd ever considered another person's feelings. This girl fitted into most of the above categories, and yet he adored her. She was telling him her story, even though he knew it already. He loved listening as she told of her past life, enjoying as he listened to what she had been through. He was happy to learn that even she had killed at least one man.

"You are a criminal just as the bloody bible says." he remarked, making her feel the same way he felt about himself, an accomplice. He added, *"Revenge is a cure."* He now showed a different face, not romantic as

before. *"I hate human beings to the point where I feel I do not belong among these miserable creatures."* She didn't like his view, but she respected it. Besides, she had nothing and no one but him in this strange, lifeless place, four miles away from the prison, four miles away from the storm. They were on a rocky mountain, the sun beating down on them.

The burning sun was staring at them.

The angry sun.

The sun.

Falling in love with the devil

Burning sun

Blazing air

But safe from her enemies for now, at least.

He's a fire, a wicked fire that could turn all the colourful flowers in the world into grey ash; that's what he was born for and that's what he was born from – grey ash. He hated his nature, he was his own prisoner. His devilish nature was beyond evil itself – pure evil.

But now, he found that he was changing. He started to like himself. He was appreciating his fieriness. He didn't care for anything so long as he was always at her side. At least for a while he felt a sense of liberation. Love can be a relief.

And sex as well, Zen assured himself.

Even with a devil, he confesses to himself.

When he had sex with girls it was not natural; it was a bloody hellish ritual performed only behind the stage. He was very violent. He had killed lots of girls on his beds. Only God knows what he'd done. Emu didn't know about it, she didn't really know him at all.

They had been kissing and pressing each other for long, tedious hours; she couldn't allow him to have sex with her because she was feeling too much pain, more than she had ever known before.

"Keep it down! I have never had sex before."

He pretended as if he hadn't heard.

Suddenly she pushed him away as she witnessed strange pictures appearing all over his body- like magic tattoos.

He received a message. The code read 'Travel across the Atlantic.' She'd never seen it before.

"Is it ..."

"A tattoo."

"I haven't seen it before."

"I made it moments ago." He lied to her, at least for the moment. He knew he wasn't allowed to tell her anything. If he'd told her that he was a messenger from the devil, his mission would be too difficult. She might have even thought that he was not a man; rather he was a living robot, wired to fall in love with her. He had never seen himself as more than that of course, though these kinds of feelings had to be kept inside. He knew that after some days she would not consider him to be a normal man anyway. But what choice had she other than to be with him? He was planning to change her into being like him. He'd promised himself that he was going to make her feel like a queen of the world before he was ordered to destroy her. He was going to show her how he was the richest man in the world, how famous he was throughout the world, how many admirers he had. That was his mission now, to distract her completely.

Chapter
SIX

Arron- there is always someone for you

'Knock

Knock knock

Knock knock knock...'

'If you want to help yourself, nature is on your side most of the time. All you need is to focus and take time to see, listen and realise. If you want to get out of your trouble, truth is there for you nearby. All you need to do is remember. You could feel tired of playing hide and seek with it, you might feel sick. But, the truth is there and the ability to heal is within each one of us, stronger than the sicknesses this world causes. One day all the madness of mankind will explode and be gone as at the end of the world. It's the beginning of heaven or God's kingdom to come - whatever you call it.' He starts thinking about something positive as he used to.

'Knock knock knock...'

He wasn't listening to the door even though someone keeps knocking repeatedly; it's as if he was listening to himself deep down within. Yes, he's thinking about living for others, those he can find himself within, those he can find as friends. Alem is within him. Intuitively, he started to find Alem within everyone he met. Then he starts to think about someone else he should have been thinking of all the time – Charlotte. He feels lighter as if he is dreaming of flying. Flying away from the Earth's sorrow and touching the divine sky.

'Knock knock knock...'

He leaps up from his alarming but hopeless wishes and visions.

'Knock knock knock!' He still wasn't sure that he had heard someone knocking outside. He worries that sometimes he cannot identify what's in his dreams and what's really going on around. He's chosen to be alone for some time, but he is realising that he can't be like this for that long or else he will die of loneliness. His ignored college assignments need to be done and submitted, Charlotte needs his attention. John needs his company and so on. *And so on. And so on.* He keeps sinking deeper into his thoughts.

There is always someone desperate to have you, wanting your company. There is always a lonely soul, waiting for you. The most frightening thing is not being alone but missing that twin soul who has been waiting for you for ages. He has been locked inside himself, inside his room for several days. No college, no calls, nothing. He couldn't even answer his social worker's call. He's just lying as if dead. He doesn't notice that the bell is ringing. All of his house mates are out. There's only him in the huge silent building. The door is already open. Again he doesn't notice that someone has been knocking on his door for a while when Charlotte enters. She'd been ringing the front bell and then knocking on his bedroom door for ages. He didn't expect to see her at all, especially at this sort of time, but she can't just let him shut himself off without any reason, a time when he's down, messy and dirty like this. He's never been so low before. She has never seen him like this. She only knows him when he's being optimistic, saying *'you can do it.'* She knows him by his unconquerable confidence, his smile and courage. She knows him when he's calm and graceful, looking as when he's walking with her down the streets of Enderbury, proud like a lion. Now, he is like a dot on his bed. *'So what's broken him like this?'* she wonders.

"*What are you doing?*" she whispers to soften her question.

"*What am I doing?*" looking for an answer from his confusion.

"*Repeating my question. You don't have to tell me if it hurts, but you know I am always here for you.*" Silence. He likes the silence. It gives him a power he can't explain. Sharing silence with someone else is even more profound. He is happy that there is somebody who cares for him. But he is also sad that he can't have that same sense of humour that he had a couple of days before nor have the guts to explain what has happened to make him change. He's been lonely for a week. Well that's what he wanted to be. More silence. Finally she breaks the silence as she tidies up his room. He thinks she is too good for him. *She is a bright star in my life*, he says. He remembers a meeting with her, not long after their first meeting. It was in the youth club where he was playing the guitar. Playing the guitar makes him feel grounded, stable and able to forget the terrifying life he spent before. It makes him feel comfortable and connected to lots of happy souls instead.

His house is better now, it smells better too. *Now, it's weird to sit and stare at each other like this,* he thinks. He's still silent. She sits on the corner of the bed. He's curled back, securing his personal space and she stares at him quizzically. She does it when she misses him.

They remember the good times.

She used to meet him every day after she finished work to make sure he was okay. There was not a single second that she was not thinking about him. It was as if everything she saw, everything she did, everyone she met reminded her only of him. She was blind, but she could see everything in the universe in him. She changed him a lot. She made him forget his loneliness as he did for her; she made him feel he was at home. She was his therapy. On his bad days she used to tell him, *"everyone has days, when the sky and earth smash you in between, towers fall on you, when you are frozen in a massive ice cube then poured in the lava of an active volcano, when life is frightening – full of fears. But don't worry; you will survive – to your surprise – to face the next episode."* For him she is like the girls he knew back home. Like his mother. Like his guitar.

"Did you have a mother?" she asked him once as they were staring at each other. He thought, *as if anybody has ever come into this world without a mother or without somebody who wants to replace a mother.*

"Yes I did." He replied staring ahead as if he could see his mother in front of him. He had lost his mother when he was young during a youth demonstration. He remembers it like a distant but unforgotten dream. A federal policeman shot at her. He still remembers every detail about her.

It seemed as if he had seen her yesterday, today in the morning, now, even tomorrow waiting in his dream. Charlotte has a similar character to his mother, they are both caring. They both have large eyes and long brown hair.

In a timeless silence, staring at each other's souls, they remember the sweet times; their first date, a long time ago.

8:00pm Friday

He often recalled the first time they'd met, after he had finished practising his guitar solo and everybody was clapping. He remembered there was one bold clap which lasted longer. He saw her for the first time. She was at the door and he felt as if she was waiting for him. It was like a call to let him in. *What's this smile for?* He asked himself. *Typically British.* He answered his question himself. She smiled again and again until he felt dizzy, until he felt numb.

"Hi, do I know you?" he said.

"Na... aha."

" Really? Do you have a name?"

"Nobody is without a name."

"For example me, you can give me a name if you like."

"That's nonsense."

"Thank you, that's nice name for me. I'm Arron."

"I know."

"Is your name 'I know'?"

"Charlotte, or call me Charlie." It felt as if he had known her for ages; she felt the same. She washed her face with milk, and her hair was as bright as if it washed it by the moon. He was as brown as burning gold, she was as bright as a diamond, and the chemistry was good between them. They'd walked back home together as they lived in the same direction. They talked a lot as they walked side by side, talking about nothing but

common subjects. They were finding out about each other, exploring each other's' views – it was rather like reading each other. It was as if one spoke what the other was thinking. Time passed. They started to touch each other as if they had known each other for decades. She invited him to her house on the pretext of "a cup of tea." He hadn't regretted it. He was rather happy.

…. back in his house

Papers everywhere; leftover food, unwashed dishes. Typical. Pieces of paper everywhere. She'd picked one up and read it aloud. *'Life is smoking to its end. It really stinks like a cigar, with an odour of a ladies' perfume attracting you to let you stick with it. Life does smell like this. …'* He'd always covered his feelings by smoking, at least for then. In fact he'd neither been able to control his anger with it nor had he ever really enjoyed smoking. The more he'd smoked the emptier he'd become …. empty… feeling finished, vanished, dead, lighter… very high as if near to the highest sky, all so that he would have the courage to face the ghost of a friend he loved most, before he became one of them. *"I saw…I think I've missed …"* he omitted the last word. *'Alem.'*

Another Friday

She'd taken him to her house again.

"Are you a writer?"

"I am a student." She'd been working on her dissertation.

"Well I can't blame you, because I don't know how tough university is, I haven't been through it." He'd helped her to tidy up. Rather than making him a coffee, she'd invited him to look at her laptop and shown him all the pictures of her family. Her grandfather was French, her mother English; another grandfather was German.

"So you are like the EU," he'd said trying to make her smile, but she was too sensitive to want to laugh. She'd given him an amorous smile while

leaning towards him, forcing him to swallow her between his arms, their eyes never losing each other.

"I wanted somebody who knows my weakness."

He'd kissed her saying *"I know your weakness,"* whispering while kissing her right ear lobe.

"Tell me my weakness..." she wanted to let him die between her legs. She'd felt the pain of happiness. She'd added, *"We are rushing."*

"Yeah." He'd stopped.

"But it feels alright."

"It feels awesome."

She'd let him die in her again and deep down this time. He'd liked the idea even if it was his first time to do so. He'd thought, *most of the time people die of the thing he or she loves the most, if they are lucky.* It'd continued the same for the whole of the next four weeks.

"I have never felt the same feeling like this before. I feel happy only with you." That's what she'd told him. They hadn't found any reason why they shouldn't stick together.

"I feel you look like my mother."

"You fancy me, don't you?"

"I am shy to tell the truth."

"I've been fond of you from the first time I saw you with your guitar, to be honest."

"Which one do you like most, me or my guitar?"

"I like your hair most." She felt shy about exposing her feelings too much but she couldn't control herself. *"Oh my God, your eyes are ... excuse me."* He hugged her tight till she found out his hugs were the most powerful thing he had, and she felt his breath till she lost control, till she placed her mouth on his and discovered his kisses hot and passionate.

"I have never felt as good as I am feeling right now. I have never felt as happy with anyone as I do now." She agreed again.

They had been together since then. Only this week has he ignored her, and she doesn't have any idea why. But she guesses something must be wrong back home. She also knows when he needs her help.

Now...

She rests her back on his legs across the corner of his bed. He pulls his legs and curls himself away from her presence again. She wants to curl up with him, inside his dangerous arms. And she couldn't stop herself trying.

"Get off me!" He violates the silence.

She leaps up from his bed in terror.

"Would you like a cup of coffee?" she asks. He smiles with a feeling of pity for both of them. *"I take that as yes."* They smile at each other. She hugs him, more tightly than ever. She reminds him that once she told him he was a number one hugger and he had laughed at her. A long hug, embraced in a sweet daydream. She wishes she could be hugging him like this for ever. He finds that there is no more comfortable place to be than in her presence.

"You are trying to make me forget everything."

*"I am trying to make you live for **me**, baby."*

"I can only live for myself."

"There is no better way to live for me than to live for you."

"I mean, perhaps I am very selfish."

"Yes you are." She kisses him hard.

Then she promises that she will be by his side no matter what. He begs her to give him time instead. They agree to see how it goes.

Chapter
SEVEN

Emu - A trip from one hell to another

"ABeGeDe...Zibadaa..."

Dadada...papaqaga...

Tsetsitsestsestee...'

Zen held her hand and talked to himself in gibberish.

"Tête-à-tête... Totototo..."

Then they took off on a mysterious journey, speeding away. She noticed that they were flying very fast, faster than any technological invention would ever allow. As far as she knew, she couldn't fly but here she was, one foot above the ground. She only knew this kind of miracle from legends told in the Jewish Christian community. Three thousand years before, King Minilik I (the son of King Solomon the wise and Queen Saba) with the priests of Zion, brought the Arc of the covenant to the land of Abyssinia. They travelled as fast as the wind, hovering above the ground. According to legend, it took them only forty days to travel the distance from Israel to Abyssinia. She didn't believe it anyhow. She didn't believe in her religion either. Her mother was Christian but her father with whom she spent much of her childhood was a kind and wise Muslim father who she is proud of. He is a martyr to her. She didn't believe, but somehow this was happening to her.

It felt as if they were flying under the clouds.

Bright cities, teaming jungles, burning deserts, bombed battle fields.... The world looked vast but no more than a miserable planet. Now, she could see the world as a diminutive star, as a small ball with which people like Zen play. This ball is not safe for everyone to play with, it's a fire ball. People can only play with it if they know how to play with fire. Other people have different roles in the tournaments. Some coach, some commentate, most don't care about it, and most, like Emu, have no idea about it.

The more new things he offered her, the more she lost interest in him and he became strange to her. She was growing bored. He was figuring out how to make her stay with him by creating a seductive mood.

"I will make you play volleyball with any planet you like; I'll show you how to play Frisbee with the sun or the moon if you like. I'll make you play tennis with all the stars if you want. I'll ride with you over the orbit of Jupiter if you like. I'll even take you to a universe where no one has ever been. I'll show you how to lead the moon in any direction you want, I will make you the queen of time, so that you can stop and unstop time. I'll make you immortal."

They arrived on an island in the middle of the ocean. She knew only the name of this mysterious place. She didn't have any real idea about it. He introduced her to lots of things to make her feel like a queen and to want to stay with him.

Then, just as Zen had appeared in her life back in the prison, so another character appeared in this remote place; one of the inhabitants was creeping up to her without letting Zen notice it, an old man. She recognised him.

"Don't do this, my dear. Don't let him use you!"

"What?"

"Get away from him as soon as you can."

"But he has been good to me, and this place looks nice. He wants me to stay here. Can I?"

"This place is a prison, a life time's prison. Nobody gets in and nobody gets out, except by the help of those messengers of the devil."

"The devil?"

"Yes my dear. You are falling in love with the Devil".

"How did you get here?" He explained that he used to support the freedom fighters in East Africa and the Middle East in order to re-establish peace and order. And he had a plan to establish a satellite centre in East Africa, which was NASA's nightmare.

"My dream was to see peace in all Africa and the Middle East, just like everyone in the world."

"And?"

"And my idea was insane for those groups who don't want that."

"I don't understand. They said you are dead."

"Yeah, that was better. You know almost all these people you see here have similar circumstances. You could find well-known engineers like Mendel and Montoya…"

"I used to work for NASA, I was a satellite systems engineer."

"You were a top man."

"My name is Kitaw."

"Engineer Kitaw Ejigu? I know about you. I am from Eritrea."

"I know. Emu-Hiba zeAseb – Azieb."

"How do you know me?" He had developed a system to help him see what was going on around the Globe. He told her that his traditional school teacher Aba Tso had taught him all this a long time ago.

"He is more than a hundred years old, this man, but he is stronger than any young man, my child."

Doctor Kitaw was happy for her when he heard the news of her escape.

"Congratulations!" He put his hand on hers. *"At least you have escaped from that secret international prison from where people hardly ever return. At least you are out of this eternal prison."*

"But am I going to another prison?" she enquired.

"It could be, or it might not be."

"Why should I be in prison all my life, is that my destiny?" She hadn't considered it to be her inevitable destiny; she'd always wanted to live in hope of her freedom.

"One day you will be on your own."

As soon as he noticed the old man advising her, Zen took her back to the flammable part of ERTALE, the hottest and deepest place in the world. There, water and fire live together. There, you can see what is going on at the heart of our planet. There, fire is king. It breathes an acidic steam. It produces acidic flowers to be seen but not to be touched. It has poisoned water, a smoking dry wind and burning bright flowers throughout its a massive stony territory. There, you might think the world is built of rock and fire but nothing else.

For Emu, her whole life has been strange to her anyway, so she couldn't find anything to be impressed by.

Their journey back was fast, faster than the speed of light. They arrived in Dallol, among the hottest places in the world with temperatures over 100 degrees centigrade - the centre is volcanic, encircled by lava, acidic landscapes, burning ponds, barren land. She knew the place from when she was doing her compulsory training. But the training centre was farther away from the volcano, so it was only forty degrees centigrade. But now, here, it is as hot as hell, burning underfoot.

"Why are we back in Ertale?"

"Because it's our home." She's been confused all the time. *"I want you to live with me here."*

"No, I can't. It's too hot here; you don't want me to be burn here, do you? Besides, I'll be exposed to my enemies."

Suddenly a voice was heard coming from behind a giant, lonely, leafless tree. It sounded like the voice of God saying, *"You have no enemy greater than this devil next to you"*. Zen - the real devil was shocked by the magical appearance of this old wizard at such a critical moment. Aba Tso came out from behind the tree.

"Don't get involved with my mission here." the Real Devil shouted.

"What if I have a more important mission, then?"

"It's an order!"

"What kind of order, a 'new world order' an order of destruction, an order of uncertainty, an order of demobilisation and disunity...to kill the first born? Genocide? Tell me, what kind of order?"

"It's none of your business!" Zen howls.

"What are you talking about?" Emu feels rather queer.

"He's an agent sent from the devil to kill you or your first son as he does everywhere – clearing humanity from the world."

"Why are you doing this?"

"Your son will be..." Aba paused in order not to confuse her more about what was really happening there.

"A game changer'...., anyone can be... I'm that myself... " Zen picks up from Aba Tao's words.

"Oh... a prophesy." She remembers and then rejects the idea. She doesn't have a clue how this legendary story could be related to her life. Maybe that's the reason why she'd had such a sad life. *It's better not have anything to do with this curse,* she reflected.

The prophesy stated, *'There will be a great leader and thinker by the name of Theodor the Third who will bring eternal peace to the entire world. He will learn wisdom from the immortal king of peace – who had taught leadership to Moses the Liberator and King Solomon the Wise, words to Martin Luther King, resistance to Gandhi, Mandela even Jesus Christ. He is known by different names in different incarnations. Some of his names are Melketsediek, King of Salem – peace, Yotor among others. He has been eternally fighting the dark forces and helping people to resist dark temptations.'*

"It's not only a tale, it's a real prophecy" Aba proclaims.

"How did you find me?" Zen asks regretfully.

"Because, I am as strong as the green and fast as the light."

"You are dead!"

"Yes, but still alive in a different form, so I am not going to scare anyone because they think I am dead anyway." He laughed aloud.

Zen grabbed Emu and put a knife across her neck. She applied her training for the second time. First, she escaped from his reach, taking his pistol from out of his armpit as she did so. Before she could take aim at him, he threw a knife straight to the back of her shoulder. She didn't feel anything for the moment; rather it helped her to make a quick decision on what to do next.

She shot all the bullets in the pistol straight to his heart before he could throw another knife at Aba. He felt pain for the first time. She felt his pain for a moment, but then he came forward towards her, smashing her across the face. She rebounded and blacked out. It happened so quickly. Then Aba flew at him, grabbed his legs and threw him back into the acidic lake, where he burned until he was no further trouble. His bones together with his pistol sank into the fiery hole and deep down to the earth's core, where he melted away, consumed by the flames of the magma which swallowed his soul.

"Why did you throw away the gun?"

"I hate guns." Aba replied.

"You are ..."

"And... I have a phobia of guns and all kinds of weapons."

"As I expected." She remembered what the old man told her in that place.

She also remembered what her father told her when she was very little, about Melke-tsedeq. She is starting to believe. Aba knows what's going on in this young lady's mind. They are hopeful about her faith.

"You okay?"

"Do I have to be okay?" Aba understands her situation completely. It's easy to guess what life means to her, she who has spent more than half of

her life in a stinking prison cell. She needs help to heal sooner. Aba tries to explain her situation bit by bit. He tells her briefly what will happen to her in the future.

"Some are born this way, some the other way, some people learn this way some the other way. It starts with a destiny, a prerequisite for the start of your life. It's given not by choice or free will but by chance concerning where you are born. The older you become, the wider your world becomes. The wider the earth, the sky, the universe, the cosmos becomes. Then you would say that you're alone."

"What are you saying?"

"Does it make sense? Mysteries are hard to take it in."

"I can only follow at the level of my understanding."

"Well done."

His encouragement reminds her of her father. She's beginning a new journey with an old man, who talks like her father, who believes and tries to make her believe that his myths and tales are true, like her father used to believe.

"So, are you my next prison?"

"No, you are free."

"That's what people say when they first meet you, then they end up being enslaved by you."

"Not this time. You can go wherever you want."

"I want to go anywhere away from this place."

"Do it then."

They travelled a long way together, but now with her leading, Aba following. The sun and the moon followed them as their natural course. A long way they walked. Accompanied by Aba Tso, she walked away from this barren land to another equally desolate place until she felt totally lost.

Chapter
EIGHT

Alem - good day and goodbye mother...

'Tiptiptip

Tepteptep

Taptaptap...'

He knocked slowly on the wooden gate of the poor hut, as if not to damage further its fragile structure. Alem had no bright memories of being here in his birth place, at least for now. He hated everything out here. He had only come to see his mother, just for a quick chat. She had been unlucky her entire life just because she'd loved a prince and given birth to the same cursed prince's child. She raised her son while hiding in a forest. She told everybody the lie that she was barren, and preferred to be known officially as a 'barren woman' rather than exposing her child to an executioner. When she'd felt him moving in her stomach, she'd prayed for him to be a woman so that he would not face his father's fate. Now, no more a child, he is old enough to be easily trapped by his hunters. His mother was curious at the unexpected visit and happy to see him after such a long time - happy at least for the moment.

"I came because, I have to say goodbye to you."

His speech was precise and bitter, as he cried inside. That was what her husband had said to her before he left her for imprisonment. But he made her promise to keep their son as safe as she could. She looked up into his eyes. He had his father's eyes. She still sees her husband in his eyes: bold, honest, wise but fragile.

"I thought you came because you missed me."

"Of course I miss you a lot, and I'll miss you always."

"I thought you had come to live with me", murmuring to herself, lost in her thoughts. She's emotional whenever she sees him not only because he is her son, but there is another emotional attachment because of his father in him, too difficult to put into words. She rushed to the bed and brought something to him. She gave him an old picture of his mother and father together. She realised that she had met his father at exactly the same age her son is now.

"You two look like twins, don't you?" she forced herself to say with a wistful smile – still fresh. He replied hopefully to her smile. He took his parents' picture and placed it near to his chest, in his pocket. She hugged him tight. Knowing she could no longer protect him, her heart fell into a well of sorrow. Losing hope of seeing him again made her eyes fill with tears. At least she would not see him being killed in front of her eyes like she had seen his father killed. Twenty years before but feeling like yesterday, at the market place, she saw her husband – rounds of bullets fired into his body, people staring at her while she was painted with his blood. She had been crying ever since. Until now, nothing had changed. The power is always with the dictators.

And there she was, washing her tears away with the back of his jacket before he would see her eyes flooding. He noticed it anyway; he was doing the same thing behind her back.

"What can I say?"

"As tradition dictates, give me your blessing, mother. I am not going to die, I am only moving away." He bent down at her feet; she held his head up between her arms and her breasts. Giving him a last warming maternal embrace, she started giving him the power of her blessing.

"May St. Michael - foremost angel of all the angels guard you wherever you go. May my forefathers' arch of St. George direct your path and follow your steps, Let the God of Abraham and Ysaq be your umbrella from the burning sun and your sandals from the desert thorns. May my God.... May St Mary.... All the saints... God of Abyssinia...... Emanuel...." her blessing faded from her voice into a silent prayer or sob.

She wrapped up as much food as would help to sustain him until he arrived somewhere he could provide for himself. She gave him all the money she had saved for him for such a time as he would need it. He told her he didn't need her money as he had been given lots of money by his grandfather Aba and his best friend Arron. She still insisted that she had saved it only for him as she had promised her husband.

"I will be sad for the rest of my life, if you let me down. Your father will be sorry looking down on us."

She wanted to follow him to the end, but she was too old for that. She was tired. She would rather give up on life, become a nun and pray for him for the rest of her life. She wished to follow him but how could she bear to watch his sufferings? She wouldn't be any help to him at all. She wanted to follow him but her legs are too old… What good could she do following him? When staying back and saying goodbye is more helpful than keeping an eye on your only son, you can understand this. He is too big for her to hide him under her scarfs anymore. So, the safest way was just to say goodbye and let him go until a better time comes. She followed him until he disappeared, her eyes still staring at the point where she last saw him. Until he returns she will always wait for him in the same spot - until he can come back to her again. She started praying.

'Kiryalaysoo, kiryalayson… kirialay…son.'

And he's gone.

He didn't even look back at her as he thought only of the trouble facing him in this new life – the life of a refugee. He knew there was no going back from somewhere he didn't yet know. He felt that his mother was following him, but he was sure that she wouldn't keep up. He felt that she could see him through the moon and could tell how he was doing. He knows her as if she is with him, as if talking through the moon.

The full moon

The bright moon,

The full bright moon,

The moon.

"Mother, stop worrying."

"Okay, son." (He wishes she would reply).

"Just pray for me."

'What else can I do?'

"Then, I'll never be alone."

"I'll be always with you." (He imagines his mother promising him through the moon).

"I'll always be with you too."

"Ehm... Endashah! (As you wish) *Then what does it mean, when you say 'I'll always be with you?' when I'm moving further away from you? Ehm..."* They both know what it means now.

He had stepped out on his way towards the dark unknown searching for a light – if he could find one - a journey without any destination, without any company – countless steps, limitless roads, climbing up and down, in a vast death trap just searching for life. Everything around him was so quiet. No governments, no humans, just silent nature, a terrifying peace. The sky and the earth came together and he was in between them. Downwards, Lake Tana no longer seemed beautiful. If it had, it might have felt like a deep but beautiful hell. Upwards, the cloud was almost over his head resembling a dragon vomiting chilly foam. He wished the lightning would make him go down to hell. He wished he had never been born. Of course he knew that no one has the choice not to be born into this miserable world. Who had ever said I want to be born anyway? Who knows what will happen to each of us on earth? He accused his mother's womb, his father's wish. He accused his luck. He accused Aba, finally he accused himself.

Hoping there was still hope was the only thing he had to hold on to.

There is always a way even in a darkened prison, a dream, faith, and determination; keeping on going until the sun sets. Keeping looking forward until you see a sign of light, keeping going until the sun sets and rises again and again - keeping searching for yourself until you are completely lost. Keeping working until you die, hoping even though there is no hope at all, and being strong until you have lost all your power. Breathing till your last breath - that's what we all do whether we like it or not, anyway. It's the law of nature.

The mountain in front of him was massive. It's the mountain of all mountains. He wished that he had even a small amount of faith, just enough to order it to move away from his path, but he hadn't. This mountain is not ordinary. It's a historical place; he understood its significance even if nobody else did. This mountain is a patriot. It served as a bodyguard for his ancestors. It kept them from attacks from foreign invaders. This mountain is a place of black lions. It sheltered them for centuries. This mountain is the sacred place - Ararat, where Moses heard the voice of his and his people's God, took orders for their liberation from his God. This place has been a place of protesters, freedom fighters, promised leaders up until now. This place was the home of the immortal scholar, priest, and king, Melkezedek, Yotor – the father of Sipara, who taught Moses how to protest peacefully against the dictatorship of the Egyptian Pharaoh. Here he was taught leadership and the true law for his people. From the top of this mountain you can see half the world. In one direction you see Shewa, the place where Nelson Mandela was trained. There, the greatest king of all, Alexander the Great was captured by the Abyssinian queen Nikawla Hindekie, disguising himself to spy on her kingdom before he attacked, though he was captured instead. Teaching him a lesson and protecting him from the fierce guards of the palace, she led him to escape to safety. Alem had studied all those historical events.

"If you want to win, don't come with war, just come with peace and love."

That was what the queen had said to Alexander the Great. He had not only admired her, he had immediately fallen in love with her even while he was in danger of his own life. But now, all this is only history, mostly unknown. Even if known, it's now assumed to be only a legend. The government has changed the reality of the area in order to destroy people's patriotism and dehumanise them so that they become ignorant of the principles of freedom, equality and are more easily exploited.

That's why the greatest scholars of history have become the targets of politicians and been forced to find work in other countries.

Alem managed to climb up to the top of this mountain in order to look over the landscape and decide where to go although he couldn't see beyond his village. He reflected that the entire world was covered, separated and bordered by distances, so that it wouldn't be easy to set his destination. He would never know where he would end up the next day. He had been here when he was a child and been afraid of the forest, but it no longer scared him.

Over the top of the mountain giant trees created a large shadow in the unearthly moonlight. He knew each tree individually. Some of them had been cut down by charcoal labourers to prepare the daily meal but some of them still stood firm and strong so that nobody would even attempt to cut them down. Instead of fearing them he befriended and communed with them about ancient proverbs, riddles and historical facts. Trees were not just life in fact. Thousands of years ago they were considered as gods by some peoples. There was a time when no one was allowed to cut down a tree, unless it had dried up and became lifeless, so that they could grow tall and wide before dying. So they could protect the place and the people around with their graceful spirits.

When he was a child, Alem used to fear them as he would fear a graveyard. In day time he used to enjoy climbing on them, but at night they were different. Every night, as he went to his church class and had to pass through these giant trees and the huge old graveyards, he panicked. But now, he has no fear of them, now he fears people more than anything else. He remembered Yeneta saying:-

"The thing that made you fear yesterday makes you laugh today, a thing that seems tough today will be simple tomorrow."

Now, he was not afraid of those elegant gods, rather he wanted to have a last word with them all.

"Can we have a chat?"

Reclining at the top of a tree had always been his practice when he was here.

Not only did he not trust the ground, he loved climbing anything but not only for fun now. It's just part of his life; climbing up or down had saved his life from several near-death incidents. He knew the same thing could happen at any time. Fortunately, he was well-experienced in finding a comfortable bed high up in a tree. That night he wanted to have his last nap in his own special place but as soon as he fell asleep he dreamed of falling from a cliff; the nightmare woke him up. He decided to keep going. He saw all the trees one by one. Some of them had names carved in them, names of people who had died; he shuddered as he noticed that one of the trees that had featured in his nightmare had his name carved on it.

"Would you give me your blessing?"

His request blew with the whistle of the winds, and made all the trees laugh out loud until their breath dropped their fruits from their branches. He picked some up and ate them. He had never tasted them before, never tasted them throughout the long years.

"You are tasty and sweet!" They laughed out loud once again and dropped all the fruit they bore until he had collected enough. *"... I am going to miss you, because I am going far, to the end of the world where you are not able to protect me any anymore."*

He knew they had sheltered him years and years ago when they were thick enough. But since then they had been attacked by the people sponsored by the uncaring government officials. He blamed himself that he couldn't do anything to repay their favour. All he could do for his friends was just bid them goodbye.

"Farewell, I am going far beyond here to where the earth and the sky kiss. There is a large curtain called distance, and neither I nor you can hear or see what will happen to us."

Poor old trees, half alive half already dead. They couldn't even give him shelter from the pouring rain. They got wet themselves as if they were sweating or crying for him. Kneeling to the wet cold, bowing to the aggressively beating wind each time as it came towards them. Waving and whistling a goodbye to him until the moon exposed their emptiness, it made them look naked all over again. He realises that he won't have them as friends anymore, because they won't accompany him nor follow him even an inch. He looks for a friend, some company that could at least move. He keeps walking until he finds it; something going in the same direction as him. He sees a graceful river falling over the cliffs, tearing at every slope while looking forward to its destination – The Mediterranean Sea. It's the Nile, more than a human being, it's a river. *Rivers are sources of life*, he thinks. Rivers live longer than humans. Rivers can flow faster, rivers never get tired. They're made up of millions of drops of water. Each tributary contains innumerable drops mixing with each other without segregation and flowing together to reach the ocean. He has heard the history of its formation from Aba Tso: that its direction was altered by ancient African civilisation to reveal the potential of African togetherness for the rest of the universe.

Arron's first vacation …

'Siii…tstsss…shihuu…'

The speed is intimidating together with the sound of grating metal, the sound of the London Underground. It helps to distract Arron from the nightmares he's had for a whole week.

There's an awkward silence within the train.

Passengers are facing each other, pretending that they are not aware of each other. They all look to be day dreaming or lost in their thoughts, trusting that the train is going to get them to their destination safer and faster. They seem to be reading papers to distract themselves from this squeaking tunnel or the eye contact of strangers. They look even more miserable than him. *What has happened to them that is worse than what has happened to me?* He wonders.

After they learned what had happened to Arron, his friends John and Charlotte took him to different parts of the country on trips, and now to London.

He fears the piercing eyes of staring people who seem to be reading the pages of the life of the person they staring at. He's overcome this intimidating situation of people staring at him; it was strange and uncomfortable at first. In fact he's happy that he agreed to travel to London with John and Charlotte. Each time the train stops, it fills up with more and more people.

As they get off the train, Arron sees London as if for the first time. He has been coming and going every week for work but he's never discovered the whole city. London: building over building, people over people; it's such a diverse place with so much to see and so much to ask about. He remembers Alem saying '*England and Abyssinia are the same in one regard: they are places where you can find the universe within a museum; a world new and classic at the same time.*' Yet, London is a spectacular museum where in actions and reactions, all kinds of people live not quite together but side by side in a lonely life style of individualism and respect.

Yet, Abyssinia is more like a hidden mysterious museum; nothing is direct, open and easily seen; it's difficult to understand. There you can find the first humans buried under ground, the first human language forgotten and buried in thousands of temples, the first state rotten or perished underneath. It's a mysterious museum that doesn't looks as if it belongs to anyone; where no one in the world is just a visitor but part of it instead. *The time of recognition hasn't yet come for Abyssinia – sister of London, Mother of cities and stream of civilisation.* He misses Eritrea, he misses Ethiopia, and he even misses Khartoum where he began his refugee life.

They arrive at the British Museum.

While inside the British Museum, they see items more ancient than the country itself, borrowed mummies from Egypt, ancient foreign statues and artefacts; all the spirits of the world in one place. The history of the whole world is there, all together. Anyone like him who comes from anywhere in the world and is missing his home should visit this Museum he thought. They see the Abyssinian Prince Alemayehu's and his father's belongings. He tells John and Charlotte the whole story of Emperor Theodor of Abyssinia and his beloved son Prince Alemayehu as he heard it from his friend Alem. He could tell it better than any tour guide could tell.

"*I'm proud of you.*" Charlotte leans her head over his neck and he side kisses her over the top of her blond hair.

"*Where did you get all this knowledge and confidence from, college friend?*" John is proud to have him as a friend.

"*From my mother's womb, the first land I kissed and the air that I breathe.*"

"*Eritrea?*" John enquires.

"*Yes, Eritrea – Abyssinia – Kush – Meroe – DMT – Punt – Axum – Ethiopia – Sudan...*"

"*Or is it one of the stories that your brother told you?*"

He suddenly becomes silent, staring at the name "HIH Prince Alemayehu Tewodros (23 April 1861 – 14 November 1879)", over it is a note saying, "*I was a stranger and ye took me in.*" Not only does the similarity of the name affect him but the whole atmosphere reminds him of himself and his friend again – his friend Alem and the Abyssinian Prince Alemayehu, whose name means '**I see the world and I see happiness.**' He saw history repeating itself in different variations. *We are all variations of that ultimate being – humanity – in different times, in different places and within different bodies,* he pondered.

Westminster is much more majestic than when he saw it on TV or in films. He realises why the area is so famous.

London is like a different world, from the underground to the museum and also the skyscrapers. It's commercial with everyone trying to make money through dealing, gambling and merchandising, each bringing artificial gratification. He loves the bridges crossing the River Thames. The big London Eye standing on the bank lets you watch a different rollercoaster world - there's Shakespeare's Globe staring across at the cathedral, quoting Shakespeare's, "*All the world's a stage, and all the men and women merely players*". If the world is a stage then London is near to the centre stage entrance, the focus of the world where everyone is in a rush.

Arron sees people as the modern day players, making a life out of busking or selling on the streets; some feeling marginalised, some feeling lost like Arron himself. He likes the fact that he's distracted for a while. He's found the pleasure of travelling as if for the first time. He sees lovers and families taking pictures trying to make every experience they can get last forever. Charlotte is taking a selfie. John talks about London nonstop, even when he knows no one is listening to him. He's rather boring compared to the spectacles around: strangers zigzagging, trying to find a way out of a sudden crowd. Across the bridge, through the London Eye, he sees a tall building pointing up to the cloudy sky. Across the sky…, Arron thinks Alem might be right there. His attention flies through the many layers of grey cloud until he can see the rays of the sun with its true power, so bright and clear. A heaven, vertical to London, beyond the dark sky and the bright sun, there he pictures Alem flying over and waving down smiling to him. For a moment it seems real until stranger steps on his foot, bumping into his face. He responds, *"Sorry, thank you"* and comes back to the here and now. Arron doesn't respond, but he misses a time and a place where strangers would say to strangers *"How are you?"*, *"It's a very hot day"* or talk about things that could remain in the mind as a good experience and distract him from thinking about home so badly.

They took him to watch a ballet. It was his first time and it was miraculous. It had the power to take him anywhere, but not from thinking about Alem. He saw him among the performers, the main character as they jumped, ran down, up, forward… looking for his beloved friend dancing or singing. It was a great performance in which he could lose himself, and as he did so he found himself crying freely. But he couldn't cry enough; he would have to wait to come back to Enderbury for that.

*The next day…*They wandered through Kent on the way back to Enderbury, thinking it could help. They took him to the historical and recreational places in Kent. He'd been feeling bad for several months, and alone. Now things were turning green; green is magic for him. He wished Alem could have made it here with him. He knew it had been his dream. Green had become his dream too. As John was driving and Charlotte reading a book, Arron was daydreaming, observing the green Kentish countryside through the car window. To him Kent is a wide, green romantic and mysterious county where you could find a castle in the middle of nowhere. He thinks of scenes he's seen from Bond movies. No amount of time would be enough to finish reading all the mystery that Kent presents. It's the stepping stone for foreign travellers to enter the country. The Roman Empire had entered here for the first time. It also happens to be warmer than other counties of the UK. He tries to find something interesting to take his mind off things. He rests his eyes upon those colourful flowers and poor trees. Grey trees that are bare in the freezing winter but are dressed in beauty when it's dry summer. The grey sky is mostly hidden by darkly overlapping clouds, the cheeky sun looking down across with her cold, steamy and blinding rays. What if England could buy or colonise the sun, he wonders. Pale faces smile even if facing the biting wind that pinches the heart. For him everything is trying to survive the weather here and he's trying to survive his sadness and wandering thoughts too. He wants to be happy again. *Everything is going to be alright. It's just nature, with its abundant gifts and misery.* He tries clearing his mind.

Back to Enderbury

Enderbury seemed smaller than it actually is in the winter, but safer than London for him where he can live inside of himself, curled in his bed looking like a basketball. It's warmer here for him too. It's a place he calls home, at least for now. Nothing can take this away from him for the time being. Enderbury is like a mini-London, yet London though busy, noisy, crazy and messy is still the heart of the world. He used to like going to London every week for work, but now he'd prefer to die in his bed. It seems to him that he's found no meaning after all his toiling. All the people he saw dying on YouTube are still disturbing and traumatising him badly. He needs more time to heal, to focus on himself, to collect himself and become his real self again.

They thought that taking him away would make him forget about things, but it made him think even more about Alem. The more he tried to forget about him, the more he hated himself, feeling useless and impotent. He couldn't tell what he was feeling. The only way he could feel happy was just by keeping quiet, dreaming and wishing to see his friend somewhere in a better place. He dreamt of Alem being a king in a heavenly kingdom. He wanted to know what was happening to Alem after his death, trying to imagine his situation. He hoped and prayed that he was in heaven. He felt that there might be a great kingdom where those innocent people could enjoy the life they had missed on earth. He imagines that there is a world where mankind lives with its own true and divine essence with no patriarchal madness that has turned this beautiful world into such a mess; a life where no one would be punished for historical mistakes made by his predecessors, a hopeful future. He imagines a free and innocent world where being different is being precious, being strange is still okay and just being human is enough. Heaven. He imagined how it would be. Water is milk, there's no bloodshed and everybody is equal to a king. That's how it looks in the world of heaven he was told when he was a child. He didn't want to think there was no heaven or life after death. This doesn't make him feel better. *Half a life isn't enough, and how about justice,* he thinks. It was too unbearable to think that his friend had just vanished, robbed of his life. He thought, *of course there is life after death, it starts in the very heart of existence, but it has to be told or imitated to make it real, seen and revealed in the 'actual' world where we are now.* For Alem's sake, he wishes to collaborate with all mankind and build Alem's heaven for the love of humanity. He wants to build his real world in this fake world, a world built by the will of friends and new generations for the memorial of their beloved ones and the betterment of humanity. He wants to tell people about his world, but he knows it's was only a wild dream. He feels impotent, unable to find his way for the present.

Giving up on things, he's becoming hostile to his friends. However, he has their love, Charlotte and John's. Charlotte invited him to her house again. He used to like being with her family. He used to have a lot of fun, but now he is downcast. All he can see is blackness and by day he dreams of what lies beyond that blackness.

"You came back quite soon, Charlie." At Charlotte's house it's lunch time. Her mother Mrs Dickinson enquires if everything is alright with both of them. She's addressing Arron and her husband to initiate a healthy conversation. Arron replies with a subtle gesture, bending his head to one side, silent. Silence has become his story. All his answers are with this silence. Charlotte explains their visit to London and the reason why

they came back earlier than she planned adding that Arron has missed Enderbury. There's another awkward silence.

"Arron has got a point". Her father called his name for the first time, but Arron doesn't respond. He has nothing to say. Her mother asks him again that if he is okay. He doesn't know how to answer, so he keeps silent. None of the people around him make him feel alive and comfortable. All they asked was,

"Are you alright?" He doesn't know how to respond to that right now.

"Arron has got a point." Mr Dickinson continues his conversation without worrying that no one is bothering to listen. *"Even if we pay half of our wages in taxes, the other half for bills and insurance, the rest to charities and on the top of that... and so on; it's worth paying to live here anyway, worth paying for the ringing bells of the cathedral at night saying 'its bye-byes, beddy byes. More tomorrow, now it's time for bed, safe to sleep.' And in the morning, 'Good morning, it's time to face the day.' Yeah... it's worth paying for the future possibilities that lay in the dreams of generations to come".* Enderbury has a mystery that's worth paying for. Enderbury is eternal. With the variety of its residents we call her *'our little London'.* They all laugh and for a reason Arron can't understand as he wasn't listening, he couldn't resist smiling softly and precisely. They keep forcing the laughter and good cheer for him until he gets confused and they all stare at him strangely.

Could he tell them that they were all boring him, that they were not alive to him, that they were nothing to him? Could he express the banality of all that was around him? He feels selfish and he feels vulnerable. He used to fight to hide his feelings as a boy, but it's not easy. So he wants to be alone. He misses his bedroom. He wants to escape within himself and himself alone. He tries to speak the truth but Mrs Dickinson asks a question first.

"When will you go back to your country to visit... or in case you can find peace... I mean your family... you can introduce them to us... I mean...eh?"

"I told you about his family, mom!"

"She's asking him, why he doesn't answer for himself. Eh?" Mr Dickinson tries to chastise him.

As all eyes are on him, he feels so much pressure that he cannot bear it anymore. He pushes his plate away slowly and quietly. He doesn't understand why these people consider his life as an adventure or a holiday where he can do whatever he wants or had planned, that he's lucky at having the privilege of living as a refugee. He is not expecting them to understand but at least they should not question him every time they have conversations with him about things they don't understand. All his life he has never had accepted failure, dependency, inferiority, oppression and involuntary manipulation. That was one of the reasons he left his country. He's never understood why people have decided that this is a life he wishes to live or used to dream about. He wanted to tell them that he misses his childhood homeland, where he can eat his natural food, where the hours and the calendar seem to fit perfectly. He wants to have a spring New Year and a summer Christmas as he used to have before. He misses watching stars on Christmas Day rather than freezing snowflakes. He has all that he has never had before – freedom, yet he used to have all that he doesn't have today – happiness. He's just not used to all this yet; he's mentally a prisoner now. He wants to tell Mrs Dickinson that 'he will go back soon' in search of mental therapy. But, he has a very little hope for this to happen, unless he wants to die like his friends. So, he is out of an answer again. Silence is his only story. All his stories are within his silence. He bends his head down again.

All the family asked him in unison the same question and he hated it more than he hated himself.

"Are you okay?"

"Would you just leave me alone?" He ran away from them, so that they would not talk about him at least in front of him. Charlotte went numb.

"Now we know his true face," commented her mother.

"Do you think you have enough cause to blacken him?"

All was quiet and she didn't follow him, because she realised that her presence didn't help him. She gave up on him for the first time. But she couldn't stop her feelings. The more unpleasant he was to her the more she loved him, for no reason. Sometimes, you love when you get only hate in return. Sometimes, love is visible when it's covered with hate, as when sometimes you see more when it's dark or close your eyes; you sometimes feel happier in life when something hits you and you say *'It's okay. It'll be alright!'* You know everything at a time when you can't do anything, and you say *'life is good'*. When it's time to die, you say *"I want to die"* as if it's a way of saying I am on or ready for the next level, going forward where it takes you. That's what life is anyway! That was her emotion, and anybody could easily tell it from the expression on her face. She went to her bed for no reason. After contemplating a while, she picks up her phone and calls Arron.

'The number you're dialling is out of the service area.' She will keep trying until.. she has no idea what to do next, to keep calling again after a while ...

He has switched off his phone and wanders looking for natural healing. He wishes he could go into a forest or into a jungle. On his way back home, he found himself walking slowly to a park near his house, where a group of teenagers and street boys and girls spend their time. He says *hi* to a group of friends sitting on a bench, who he knows from when they were bullying his friend John. He realises that they are smoking weed as usual. He has no idea how they could manage to do that every day, since it's illegal. He's scared and feeling intimidated by their practice, but he knows how to hide his fear. At a bench nearby he sees John with one of the boys who used to bully him. He realises something odd is going on and tries to find out what. John and Lucas are eating together, now. It surprises Arron. Eating together has definitely a broader meaning to him. It seems for them too, now - friendship. They remind him of himself and Alem a long time ago. He smiles. The moment they see him they smile back.

"*You guys are ok?*" he asks, pretending to be serious.

"*Oi, take it easy lad, we are fine. And you?*" Lucas burst into laughter, remembering the last time he saw Arron at that fight where he had got involved to save John from them all.

"*Here is my friend.*" John gestures his new friend to Arron.

"*Hi, Since when you have you two become friends?*"

"*Just very recently really,*" Lucas replies happily.

"*Of course he used to bully me.*"

"*Now, it's his turn that he can bully me for the rest of my life, man*" they laugh.

"*No more bullying, mate,*" he says, joining in the laughter.

"*You seem to be on good terms.*"

"*Yeah, and he got me a job, man… and bought me lunch, your friend. Trust me; he has saved my life now. He has taught me that people can actually help each other.*"

"*Yes indeed.*" But, helping your enemy to make him a better person shows a great personality, Arron thinks. Being bullied is the worst feeling but can be cured with forgiveness. But who can forgive? How does it feel to forgive? Who can feel it more than John does? Alem. He pictures what Alem might have said when he was being slaughtered by his enemies – the enemy of the world – ISIS. Did he say '*God. They don't know what they are doing, please forgive them.*' What else he could say? "*You got him a job too?*"

"*My step father is tired of taking my shit anymore. He beats my mother because of me being with them. He said I'm old enough to be on my own, man…. so I had to push myself to live on the street… to save my mom's marriage, man. It's just been three weeks… the cold, the hunger ah…*"

*man, but I get used to it man… but your friend… well, my friend now…
saved me, man."*

"*Well done, bro."*

*"Yeah. I learned forgiveness from the stories of your friends you told me,
bro. I just helped, 'cus that's what friends do, right."*

"*Thank you, man."* Lucas smiles.

"A friendship built on forgiveness."

"And brotherhood, man." They smile and want to celebrate this union
of friendship. Arron takes them all to his house after buying snacks
and drinks for them. They keep laughing at recalling their childhood
memories. Arron is contaminated by their laughter too. He starts
smiling, but now without pretending. He feels that he's getting his smile
back, the one that every one of his friends has missed. One of John's
friends joins their company later.

"Sorry, what did I miss?" He was in the barbershop to get his haircut.
Everyone was surprised at his unusual haircut.

"Hey, mate. What happened to your head?" John said boldly.

"You guys are scared of me because I've suddenly gone bald?"

"Not at all."

"You like it?" He puts his head down.

"*Huh?"*

"You cannot tell if it's a head or…"

"'Half a bum' you were going to say, Arron?" They all laugh at themselves.

"*Huh?"*

*"What happened man? Your long hair was the only good thing you had
man. I wouldn't expect you to get rid of it all and come here as bald as one
could be… haha."*

*"It's all about my one of my closest friends and I have to tell this to let
everybody know about it."*

"What is it we have to know?"

"You should know about my friend; his girlfriend died of cancer! And he followed her straight after."

"Maaan."

"Yeah."

"Oh... sorry."

She had said goodbye to all her friends and family the day before, but she didn't let them know why. Only he knew, she was gonna die. He promised her that he would spend every second with her. They had been to every party, club and sunny beach in order not to sleep and just wait for her death. He made her live a hundred years within a single week. He even took her to Ibiza for the last four days of her life. The doctor had said she was slowly dying. He'd been right. Nowadays doctors possess the spirit of prophets.

"You need to be strong and think that I am always with you. Yes, right here, at the centre of my heart."

"I don't want to die," she'd said it with all the breath she had, the final words of her life, but no one had heard it. Her boyfriend? He had silently gone before she'd died. She could no longer remember that he'd told her *"wherever you go I will follow you as I have already fixed my heartbeat with yours".*

He touches his bald head. They all sympathise with him, bending their heads down in unison.

"Oh... the sacrifice he made is beyond everything."

"Unbelievable."

"True"

Arron was touched, but the story suddenly made him love life again; love anything, even himself. He thought about his relationship with Charlotte. To be fair, she had meant a lot to him. She deserved a return for her love. When she was with him, she was always tripping over everything, but it was only because she wanted him to be strong and she never regretted her feelings as a free-spirited young woman. She had sacrificed her desire; she has been sharing his sadness. She is trying to help him out no matter how. Like her own self, she'd loved him unconditionally. She'd known what she was doing, every detail, and he knew all about her strength. She was his engine – he couldn't achieve anything without her beside him. He wants to call her back, but he still doesn't have anything to say. So, he decides that he needs more time to heal. More time with his new friends, more laughter that can help him refresh his troubled mind.

They went to the pub nearby, and then they headed off to the *Cuban Club* after.

Chapter TEN

Following the Nile...

Alem is not feeling alone yet.

He feels part of nature now, surrounded by all this silent beauty.

Right: cliff.

Left: river.

Daf... daf...fuua...da...

Looking up he sees soft white cloud with a clear blue sky as a backdrop; he imagines divine figures within the clouds. Across each of the river's obstructions, little fountains dance in the sunlight. Sometimes within the fountains and under the clouds he sees a tiny rainbow. Within a rainbow he sees a flag and within the flag, his mother. He sees them together, himself, his mother and father, and Aba Tso. They're within him. The colours are mainly green, blue, yellow and red, the colours of the Ethiopian flag, the Eritrean flag - African flags. He looks up to the sky and they remind him of that promise, the divine oath God gave to Noah , an oath that if we can learn from our past mistakes, we can find our blessings and grace from it – in between the sky, the fountains and the mountains. Meanwhile down on the narrow road he keeps on going thinking of all this. Aligned with his new companion, the Nile, he increased his pace walking in strangeness, in desperation but also in hope.

It had been four days since he'd eaten the last piece of his mother's pancake and finished all the fruits he'd brought with him. It'd been fourteen days since he started walking barefoot. Even if the going was getting tough he still kept going.

It's all for you, he said to himself. He missed somebody else's company so he made himself his own company.

It's all for you, my love. Freedom. Even if I've never known you.

Freedom – he'd grown apart from it since his childhood. He'd suffered to meet it. As soon he realised he was talking only to himself, he felt lonely and weak. He felt he couldn't go any further on his own. He was thirsty and hungry. He dived into a small pond and felt strong again when he saw the dark muddy river flowing rapidly and aggressively in front of him, long and straight, down to the earth's crust, then springing up onto rocks in the turbulent swell. He knew about it. It was one of the tributaries of the River Nile. In his loneliness he pondered on the history of this region. It's the lifeblood and sustenance of Egypt and the Sudan. The Nile is a symbol of all human life; old, young, wise and strong people migrated from the east of Africa to the rest of the world, populating the whole earth. Theoretically, everybody apart from those living in East Africa were refugees at some time he thought, and this consoled him as he wandered the same path. Born in East Africa, they travelled across deserts to the Mediterranean Sea and never came back; the whole mass of humanity, over the centuries, until they found their own place to call home. However, it seemed as though Abyssinian people, like the Nile River still haven't found their resting places. This migration has existed from the time of the creation, continuing until now.

He befriended the Nile – it became his best friend, at least for then, far away from their homeland by now. He looked back as far as he could to the distant horizon, the sun beating down on the sand. He recited a sad lament for his motherland as was his custom. Back home, back in time, it was deep in his culture, a poetic culture, to express ideas on love – country – freedom - in poetry.

'Greetings'

'Ethiopia tabetsih edewiha : havèEgziabhier. Ethiopia stretches her hand: to God.

Greetings, greetings, greetings for the sweetness of your name, received from your beloved wise King Etyopis,

All human nature, even man himself, is made from your rich soil and water mixed with the precious spirit of life. That blessed ash[9] and holy water is your priceless blood and flesh -Abyssinia. You even gave humanity to the world, a brain to an empty planet. Wherever human beings touch, you are there,

You are the heart of civilisation, yet now you are the poorest.

You are the source of the Nile that allows Egyptians eat, drink and sustains their life

Your remnant pyramids have endured for thousands of years, yet some are still not discovered.

You are the birth place and home of gods, their leaders far above all other creators.

You always tell your history as a simple fantasy, to become the content of legends.

Jah Ras Tefery, the earliest prophet and king of kings and god for the Ras Teferians

Without you there would be no Moses, as your king Melkezedek trained him well and made him the hero of Israel.

Without you there would be no answer to the origin of mankind, as you are the womb of the first man and woman who filled the earth and the entire universe as was promised. You are everywhere, even beyond human sensation.

You are the home of freedom, but not now; even though you challenged colonialism and helped to bring an end to it, you are not free now.

From your heavenly northern mountains 'Semien terara' to your devilish gate of hell - 'ertale' - smoking mountain, you are

9 The ash remaining from the burning of incense.

ironically blessed, yet cursed. Paradoxically heaven, mysterious
paradise on earth – utopia – Ethiopia, Eritrea - Abyssinia.'

He realised it sounded nonsensical, but it is his custom and reality to keep singing his personal lamentation.

> *'Hark! Hark! Hark!*
> *Netsanet sisheshegn, ene siketelew,*
> *Selam sisheshegn, ene siketelew,*
> *Enjera sisheshegn ene sketeleww*
> *Tinsh snzr keregn alemn lizoreww.'*

Meaning:

> *'Walking in search of freedom, peace and life,*
> *I'll circle the entire world from and to where I was born.'*

His lamentations are not just lamentations but also a sign of his courage and self-knowledge. His intense patriotism seemed strange even to himself. Everything seemed strange. But, he had a belief that he was not alone in this. He always said, *whoever I see, I feel an affinity with, all different people. I can see myself in those people; I only see one thing, one figure in them, our common HUMANITY! Humans in different person-ifications, the same beings each with a unique distinguishable beauty!* Through others' eyes he could see himself, and in that self were his mother, his father, sister, brother, friends and all the people he missed so dearly. Then it was easy for him to fall in love with whoever he saw, because he had already fallen in love with humanity. His pure and open nature had made him a victim to this divine law, and that law is nothing but LOVE!   Of course there were some people who had made his life difficult – clowns! false jokers! masqueraders! Covered with opaque veils, their true characters were far from what was seen on their faces. Staring into their eyes, looking at their humanity beyond the evil veil you can see other beings who you have never seen before. Strangers! That's what most corrupt political and religious leaders look like: strangers.

The river beats

'Riv... riv... rrivera... amon!

Doff...daff... buff...'

Alem sings

> *Abayyy... mola Alu (2x)*
> *Zares yalamelu...*

Singing together, they keep going – side by side, talking in a language no one can understand easily. He addressed the river, his strange friend who couldn't stop flowing forward and singing its own refugee lament. He asked questions as if he would get the answer from this river.

"Where are you running to, anyway?"

"Better if you first ask me why"

"Okay, why?"

"I go wherever it takes me to be with my love."

Crazy river. Can a river know love? Maybe. If it can run and can sing and have a life, then why not love? Well everything has something to hate and love he mused.

"Who is your love?"

"Freedom."

"Uuwaa!!! You have been running throughout those millions of years since you were born, and have you ever met your 'Love'?"

"Nay! ... I'm still searching."

"When will you give up trying?"

"Never."

They walked along with each other. A walk in company is far easier and safer than walking alone. They talked a lot and so he did not realise the fact that he was tired. The river had never tired in its entire history but humans tire more easily than any other creature. The more tired he felt, the more he felt the distance he had travelled. Trying not to be hard on himself, he still kept going before the flame burnt him, before someone delayed his journey to freedom. Though they had travelled for many miles, Alem was feeling stronger with the help of his friend. The river had become his best companion now, next to the moon. He smiled as he thought to himself that he really had these great and mighty friends who made him forget his troubles for a while.

He gave thanks as his forefathers did, but more poetically than ceremonially. He sang the river's song – a country song with the sound of the river as a backdrop.

> *Abay, bimola*
> *Chewatachn liela.'*

"Thank you, you are soothing me well."

"Hey, don't worry. That's what friends are for."

They smiled at each other and kept on going faster than before.

Until the next night and the night after, they kept smiling and going on.

Even if it was silent in the night time, it was incredibly beautiful. In the night beauty is naked, maybe because his friend the moon was free from any staring eyes that could make her shy and half cover her face. She is full today. He still kept on going because his friends the moon and river were still going, travelling together as he went, not leaving him to feel alone. But, he was afraid, because it was night and night time is the time when our fathers were afraid of the dark and called it night! Were they right to be afraid of the darkness? Who knows? He had become more afraid of people and the darkness protected him from them. He considered that human life is generally connected more to the sun than the moon and the stars; days are more frenetic than the calm nights, governed more by manmade rules than the law of nature in order to conquer nature. Imagine if our ancestors had taught us the reverse, that the night was the time to be awake and work; then we wouldn't miss all the beauty the clear sky provides and be denied all the miracles of the night. Of course, we would definitely miss the mother of all energy – the sun! But, at least we could teach ourselves when to work and we would sleep whenever we needed and wake up without being disturbed by an alarm. Life would be as it is! Keep walking till you want to sleep and you can't walk any further. Who knows where you will find yourself? His thoughts rambled on becoming increasingly nonsensical as fatigue took over.

When the going gets tough the Nile keeps on going.

The river, still flowing and smiling.

Alem, whistling.

'Wisslllll....'

'Dadadaaadaa...

Dufdufgda...

Dadadadaa..

Da..'

Singing together and flowing along together, going down to the unknown until another night and morning passes and then on again and again. He felt tired.

It's morning again. Alem realised that the further from home he travelled, the faster he went - to nowhere, but searching for a destination. He couldn't deny the aching inside. After passing numerous hills and valleys he was now walking on a path along long, flat barren land that stretched far ahead of him. It was boring but he just kept on walking.

"I can't go any faster"

"It doesn't matter as long as you keep walking."

"How do you manage to handle it?"

"I just keep flowing, as I said. Keep going, you will find yourself somewhere you can't even imagine."

"Yeah, I'll keep going. Have I any choice?" He said it as if no one could stop him anymore. He is on his own for sure. Nothing is easier than to be on one's own.

"I'll keep going as long as I possibly can". He encouraged himself.

But he knew it was not possible for him to flow like the river because he had legs, legs that tire. He could only walk. He wished he could flow or even fly. He wanted to be a river or a bird which of course was impossible. He began to feel really tired and his thoughts grew ever more fanciful. The dying sun was giving way to the new, bright, full moon. The cycle of life: day in, day out, the sun gives way to his friend the moon. He had a deep sense of joy; in his solitude he wondered at the fidelity of the moon, constant as time itself - a joy without human intervention.

Unable to continue further, Alem sat down between his two friends. The moon is his queen and the magnificent waters of the river reflect her beauty. Within a deep blue frame against the background of the dark sky, the darkness magnified her beauty. The moon and the river: he wondered how those two natures support each other continuously without a single day of fighting. Peace had come to him and he started to be lulled by the marvellous natural symphony of the river which led him to a deep, deathlike sleep. Such beauty it seems was the meaning of his life, nature in all its hues of green and yellow. At every page of his life he had admired nature, imagining himself in an enormous green room, the nuptial room. He dreamed of a green horse – a unicorn with a green horn with its mane blown by the green wind – green blood that runs with green life and green music performing in his green adventure. His soul was soothed and strengthened by the green. When he thought of green he thought of a world without war, no anger, no poverty or thirst. He thought only of festivities in a green field. In a garden with a free -spirited dove, he can only sense – green.

He slept and had a dream in green. He saw green people, desert, children playing with green and yellow toys, a green fairy beside him, and he himself, green. The overwhelming tiredness and hunger had led him to a strange place indeed.

He sees beyond his imagination as if a movie were projected on the sky, lying down on his back staring at the sky. He sees a world beyond that which anyone has ever seen, a world beyond all this trouble, where no one can be stopped from loving, living life as God has intended it to be

- a happy life with families around, a life where no one has control over his life but God himself.

Chapter
● ● ● ● ● ● ELEVEN

Arron's Recovery…

'Kuakuakuaa…

Kua kuaa…

Trrrrr…'

He feels as bright as he did before. He pretends that he can forget all he has been through, at least for today. He's decided to celebrate his mortal but saintly friend with his new friends. He wants to turn over a new leaf. He feels that he's healing.

Arron is having a party at his house.

Everybody was surprised he had called it, and he himself hadn't been looking forward to it. But it's a birthday party and nobody wants to miss a birthday party. He'd invited everybody - friends who had felt ignored for a long time were invited to recall good times. Charlotte was keeping her distance to give him some personal space; he felt alone but relished the solitude. He didn't want to involve her in his sadness. He hated being a negative vibe. He'd introduced himself to drugs finding they helped him when he felt his loneliness badly. He knew what to do. He went deep into his inner self, breathing in freedom to travel boldly across any border of the world, together with his best friend Alem. Today it's them together, yesterday them, tomorrow them, all of his life it's been *them*. He felt completely different each time. Then he saw that he was the result of all those shared experiences and he would say *I am not alone!* Besides, he's part of all of them. How could he be alone? But how is he to carry on? He wanted to become everybody's friend. He wanted to say to

90

everybody *"you are not alone."* He said to himself, *I love you Charlotte, (but I loved you first Alem).*

His whole life seemed to have a purpose now. He could work a miracle, or at least he could be part of that miraculous story of his martyred friend, conquering death on a quest for immortality. For him those thirty one young boys had never died. They are bolder than ever, they are more alive than ever, they are more known to the world than before; martyrs united the world at 9/11, at the Paris attacks and all other such bloody situations.

'Tirrrr...'

Arron is busy answering the door to his friends. Everyone is bringing a lot to eat and drink. He starts to recall the good times, to start towards his life again.

A year ago on 20th March, Arron remembered that he had rung Alem to wish him Happy Birthday. He could hear the melody of the church through the phone.

"It's beautiful!!"

"Can you hear it?"

"Yes, are you at a service?"

"Yes, today is the eve of St. Mary's Day!"

"Waw! Joyful boy. And it's your birthday as well. Melkam Lidet."

"Ameseginalehu!"

"I've sent you some money to celebrate."

"Thank you. I'll give some of it to St. Mary's Church. I'll give it to the chief priest, so that he will pray for you to protect your life."

The same time, the same day. Now, he has no Alem to call; the prayers didn't work at all, but he reminds himself that he has all the people he needs around him. His friends still keep coming, singing popular birthday songs. His room has filled with his friends and classmates who have come to the birthday party - except only he knows that it is not really his birthday. It is someone else's 22nd birthday, the one who'd died several months before. It is Alem's birthday.

Chapter
TWELVE

The first day of his rebirth…

Alem wasn't aware of sleep walking until he fell to the ground on hearing his name called by *a spirit*, or so he thought.

"*… Alem!*" called Aba Tso again.

He realised that someone real was calling him, probably Aba Tso. He responded at the third call when he could see it really was Aba Tso and he could not believe his eyes. He couldn't believe what he was actually seeing, Aba Tso together with a beautiful girl – Emu-Hiba. He didn't expect them to be in the middle of this barren land. But he remembered that he had heard that Aba Tso was a holy man, even capable of performing miraculous acts. It was said that he was able to make himself invisible and to ride on the wind but still he couldn't believe that he had come across Aba, there in front of him in the middle of nowhere. He was sure that Aba Tso was here to give him guidance and support but he wondered what kind of support he'd have now.

"*Why are you here?*"

"*I want you to take Emu-Hiba with you.*"

"*Emu…*" Aba didn't seem to hear him. Emu knew that Aba couldn't really know her name but she didn't really care how he knew; all she cared about was her own safety.

"*Why?*" replied Alem in confusion.

"*She needs help, and you need help as well, don't you?*"

"*I suppose I do.*"

"She is a hundred times stronger than you."

He wondered how a skinny woman like her could be stronger than him unless she was a witch. But she was too beautiful to be a witch and too wise, but who could tell from just seeing her for a couple of minutes?

Pause

For the first time they started a conversation, a silent conversation with no words, a muted conversation.

"Happy birthday, anyway." It was like his mother's voice. He wanted to hear more of it.

"Pardon?" he wondered.

"It's your birthday, isn't it?"

"Yes, how do you know?"

"I'll be twenty in August. You?"

"I am twenty one." Aba knew what was going on between these young ones. To break the silence between the two, Aba started a conversation.

"I dreamed of you two together giving birth to a son." Their laughter broke the silence.

"Are you joking?" Emu smiled. Alem heard her speaking for the first time: *my first impression of her is she's perfect,* he thinks.

"Exactly," he agreed with her.

"No, I am not joking. Disbelief is not a choice this time, but it's better to believe and see what is going to happen".

"Oh, what else have you dreamed of?"

"Just this," he said, speaking as he raised his eyes up to the middle of the sky, looking at a dark cloud coming with flashes of a storm.

Alem knew what Aba was thinking. Aba didn't tell the entirety of his miserable nightmare. It looked as if there would be trouble; there always is some kind of trouble.

"Why don't you go with us, then?"

"It's not possible for me son." He paused. *"Besides, I am a soldier…"*

"I have never seen a ninety-four-year-old soldier in my life."

"Have you ever seen a nineteen-year-old woman soldier in your life then?"

"Nay."

"Now, in front you, you see soldiers of both ages."

"Are you *a soldier then?"* Taking time to admire her, he interrogated her.

"I was." Emu assured him. He heard her speaking for the second time and she was impressive. *"It's not my plan."*

He stared at her. The longer he stared the more he felt he knew her. They'd started a conversation already, but continued with no words for the second time but as fresh as before.

"You must be more mysterious than anybody thinks you."

"I will follow you to the end of the world. Anywhere you go."

"You are from heaven, not from an earthly womb."

"Believe me, your mother's womb is a source of such flowers."

"I will be by your side till the end of my world."

"I will marry you."

"You will always be my king."

"I will make you my queen before anyone comes between us."

"I am not afraid anything as long as I am with you."

"And I will not mind about any trouble as long as you are with me."

He was absolutely sure that she was thinking the same thing. They were already able to read each other's feelings without any verbal communication. They have created their own language already, a silent and divine language; a peaceful language of love with stability – calming and encouraging. Her eyes darted magically, sometimes stopping to stare penetratingly into his, examining his forehead. Aba seemed comfortable about them, even if the human part of him was rather jealous that his grandson already seemed closer to her than to him. Aba seemed satisfied with both and wanted to give them time to see their limits.

"Now I'm leaving you, though I will always be with you in spirit."

"Pray for us, Aba."

"I will, always."

"See you later"

"Farewell."

After exposing the reality that they already belonged to each other, they became confused as to what to do together. Every circumstance they faced now was new to them. They were new to each other but they were together. They didn't have to be together. They could even leave each other at this stage. They had a choice to leave each other alone. But, that was not what they wanted. Love was what they wanted; standing by each other was what they needed. Eager to discover, they simply started walking along the long road that was taking them away from their homeland. They continued their silent conversation.

"Now it's only me and you. This is it," both of them were thinking.

"We've only just met," she thought strangely.

"Yeah, we've only just met."

"How we can believe in each other?"

"Because we have no other choice."

"And there is no one else for us."

"Just us."

"It's not hard."

"And it even feels exciting."

"That's true."

Of course there was no reason they had to be together; they had countless choices. They could have walked away in opposite directions, but they couldn't do it. They felt they were not able to push each other away; it was as if opposite charges pulled them together. She was a soldier and he was a priest. Well, they were not necessarily the same kind of birds having the same feathers to fly together, but they had to fly together, they had to pull towards each other, because there was nobody else for either of them. They felt that their being together was a law of natural forces, drawing them together, forever – they wished.

However, they needed more time to know each other; they felt they had to grow up together. But it was also too soon to be sure. They walked along without saying a word but she missed his voice that she had been getting to know, his tone of speech.

"Do you know where we are going?" It was the first time she had talked to him alone.

"No"

"A runner doesn't start on his course before he knows his destination."

"That's different, we are running for our lives, not for medals."

"Fair enough, only God knows our destination then."

He knew that she knew he had no idea where they were walking to, but he's better off walking away with someone in the same situation as he's in. She knew he was confused too. They didn't even know what difference they could make to each other yet. So, they kept walking side by side. That's the only choice they had and they were contented in each other's company.

Thirty miles they walked that day.

She was tired. He felt her tiredness more.

She wanted to know why she didn't die from walking such a long way for the first time. She knew why. He knew it too. He had been her unconditional strength and she had been his, even though they hadn't told each other that they had a special feeling for each other. They feared it. They wanted this new feeling to continue like this, a silent telepathy.

"I think I am falling."

"I am submitting to you."

"You are already compelled to be with me."

"No, you have conquered me."

Now, at last, it seemed that her miserable nineteen years of life had been refreshed by this twelve- hour walking day. She started to calculate her life. Nineteen years of three hundred and sixty five days in hell equals no life at all. Twelve hours of love is equal to a variety of feelings she is not sure how to calculate, but a lot. He also wished for more future hours of love, caresses and intimate happiness (he felt shy even to think of this himself with *Emu* - he stressed her name.) He wished to build his home right here in the middle of nowhere, but based on the love developing between them.

"Let's just stop and live here, Alemye – my world." She was thinking the same.

He talked openly to her again for the second time.

"I'll call you Tsion[10] from this time. Tsion - a promise of love, reunion, a spiritual bond, the land of the covenant..."

"But my name is..."

"Emu seems not a good enough name for you, besides it's my mother's name."

"Oh... I see, as long as you don't see me as your mother, I'll not mind about it."

"Thank you Emu."

"Tsion."

---

10 Tsion is a pretty, fairy-like name given to a girl in Ethiopian culture.

"*Sorry, Tsion,*" he said, pretending to approach her while she was pulling herself away from him. They started to speak in short phrases. While walking he came closer to her again without realising but he retreated again as he realised he was too close. She did the same again and again. Sometimes their shoulders and hands touched accidentally. Sometimes she wished that she could be as close to his chest and heart as she could be.

"*Too soon*" she thought, "*it's too soon.*"

They were not interested in having physical contact, not so quickly. They knew already that there was a strange force between them. They were still new to each other, and besides they had never before done the things which would lead them to explore each other's bodies. But despite the feeling of shyness, their bodies started to pull and push and pull each other. They still sensed the residual presence of Aba Tso, as if the thought of his sudden appearance was protecting them from going too fast, too soon.

"*Ehm...*" It was not just a sensation. Aba Tso had returned!

"*You've come back.*"

"*Yes, but not to interrupt you, Sorry. I hope I'm not disturbing you, coming at the wrong time.*"

"*There is no wrong time at all, Aba.*"

"*So fast?*" They became shy. "*There's no need to be shy; I am pleased for you.*" Aba kissed both of their cheeks.

"*Are you coming with us?*" asked Alem, full of happiness and smiles.

"*I am glad you decided to ...*" she opened her mouth, lips trembling.

"*No, I am not coming with you, but I have a plan to show you a secret that has been kept from generations, before you leave this land behind.*"

"*What do you mean?*"

"*You must visit my monastery before you leave; the secret ancient and traditional academy. It's like a university, where you can study and learn*" *from the books of our ancient civilisations and the original mystical books like the book of the underworld, the book of Enoch and so on."* Alem knows what the old man is talking about.

"Don't worry Aba, we won't forget our culture if you are worried about that."

"Monasteries?" Emu eagerly enquires.

"It's not an ordinary monastery. It's located underground through foxhole like tunnels"

"And there are the vestal virgin pyramids that no western archaeologist has ever reached and violated yet." Alem remembers being told about this story when he was a kid.

"The pyramids." Emu becomes fascinated; she doesn't mind where she's going as long as she's with Aba and especially with this young man.

"Another Pharaonic temple." Alem disclaims.

"It's not just a temple; it's a secret way into another world that no one has entered."

"But pyramids are the temples of kings."

"Yes, and they are symbolic of the knowledge to revive the sunken city of Noah, one day, if and when mankind come to its senses. It's not ordinary knowledge, but you are sharing this knowledge that I'm going to show you." Aba Tso walks faster and they keep pace with him.

"Why is it secret?"

"It's because our fathers managed to keep it safe and hidden from the eyes of thieves and warriors through all the dark history of mankind. It's like that unimaginable and wonderful civilisation that was buried under the sphinx, yet to be discovered until the time comes. It's the secret of our being, the wholeness and togetherness of Mother Africa and beyond. It represents the origin of the future, the hidden might of all human species; the undead past, the everlasting present and the exciting future all together."

Alem is slowly surrendering to Aba Tso's enchanted speech. He then dives deep into it and begins to dream about it as usual.

"Take us into that place"

"Do not be afraid. It's not as you imagine an underground monastery to be; it's a beautiful hidden village that was built before the time of Noah and the bloody destruction of Sodom and Gomorra. It's hidden because of the greedy nature of corrupted man-made religious and political institutions; the great flood and its consequences. It has many secret entrances including the great pyramids of Egypt and other ancient sites in different places throughout the world. All are locked forever with the death of their gate keepers. But my ancestors were strong unto death and managed to hand down the password of this one gate to successive generations. We have the passwords. This mountain defies time, and has stood high throughout history. At each gate there are small pyramids indicating their location, but only one gate is always opened and that one is at the highest peak of the great mountain." Aba points at one of the triple mountains ahead, covered over with giant trees.

"There. A pyramid gate at the top of the mountain! Incredible; no one would think of that!"

"You can see nothing from here!"

"That's the reason why it's been kept safe for millennia. Remember how our forefathers kept The Arc of the Covenant? Hiding it with numberless other covenants, as the safest place to hide a precious tree is a jungle. Just like that. It was also nearby the Garden of Eden that lies under the Great Desert and between the longest rivers. Let's go on." They steadily climbed up as he walked on singing an ancient chant. Alem knew this melody; he'd studied it as a hymn. He followed Aba and Emu.

Visiting the ancient underground monastery...

They arrived at the oldest monastery in East Africa, where giant trees and streams running off proudly posing mountains together with spectacular cliffs dominate the landscape. Raising his head up to reach the cliff ahead, Alem saw a complex structure of accommodation with decorated hut doors half way to the top.

"Do people live here?"

"Yes, monks and nuns obviously. Chosen ones."

"Chosen by whom?"

"By nature." Aba explains. *"Here, you can find people from all the tribes of mankind: the Jews and gentiles, the 'Gedions', the first Christian families, Buddhist monks, Muslim Imams. They lived here together; they lived here for one another. This is the only place you can find mankind in all its variety and dignity."*

"Where are they now?"

"You wouldn't be able to see them now, but be careful; it doesn't mean they can't see you. Walk slowly and quietly, instead."

They saw two persons running over the cliff.

"Can we speak to one of them?"

"They are messengers. They are watching over without us noticing. They don't talk as this season is a season of silence," Aba informed them by placing his pointing finger adjacent to his lips. A flock of singing doves flew over their heads and crying eagles flew around them. *"Well, not for birds obviously,"* Aba shared a smile.

"Ajahib!" They were astonished.

The mountain had covered its head with light cloud and it looked like an image of an aged local priest, wrapped around in a white garment. It looked as if it belonged in a fictional tale or legend, but Aba was telling them that all this was real.

Alem had studied many fantastical stories, mysterious and miraculous; old Abyssinian manuscripts most of them, but he was not sure that they could be true. He had never believed the fact that there may be old ruined towns and cities remaining buried underground, and that they would be so near to his home. He eagerly followed Aba to see miracles that he had heard about, dreamed of and known for ages through the oral traditions of his people. He couldn't wait to get to where he could see and believe in those legends that he had never seen with his own eyes or believed before.

"I was thinking they were all legends."

"You are not the only one to think like that. Even though I have lived there, I couldn't believe they were real sometimes."

"It's because it seems beyond all human understanding."

"Alem," Aba takes a long breath first to enable him to speak the truth about Alem's vague reply.

"I tell you frankly that human beings are way beyond what you have known before. Once upon a time, man was master of the entire universe, the master of Angels, the master of Devils, the friend of God; God himself, who used to live with humanity, compromising his super power – divinity - (I mean his natural gifts). He nurtured and cultivated most of the animals, plants, and the entire earth in fact. He gave them names, shelter and made them familiar with one another. It all happened a very long time ago. Humanity is greater than we think, but the greatest time is yet to come. Human beings are the masters who gave names to each and everything in the cosmos."

"When I was a child, I heard the story of Adam giving names to each animal that visited him. A child's brain is blessed; I used to believe all of it till I was old enough to disbelieve it."

Aba was happy. More than anything he realised he had found his successor to be appointed as a gate keeper for the next century. They were one soul with two bodies now, with the same title, purpose and understanding. Aba takes a deep breath, thinking of the future ahead –

it's going to be long and hard but it will always be worth it. He's thinking of seeing himself through his grandsons, through his great grandsons yet to come. He feels a sense of family after such a long and hard time. He kisses them both.

"I am not alone. Do you know the story of the priest and king of Salem, who lives forever, and keeps his people forever?"

"He's an East African legendary character called, Melke-tsedeq, as you yourself taught me." Alem remembers everything Aba Tso told him when he was little. Emu has heard this story too, from her father when she was little.

"Melke-tsedeq means 'a face of a saint'. He was the leader of the first human species. He was a peasant and a king." Alem remembers most of the stories. He also knows Melke-tsedeq has died as everyone does, but his name lives on. As a result, it's traditional to think that he's still alive and is immortal.

"You are now a part of that role." It was a call to awaken them.

"I don't understand."

"Soon, you will." There was silence and confusion. Emu asked for an explanation of this story as she was interested in it.

"I might not be a part of it, but I know this story as well. He's mentioned in the holy books several times, for blessing Abraham and teaching Moses. He is the one who guides people through the ages of history."

"You are to be part of it, that's why you are here."

She became confused and demanded further explanation.

"You mean…"

"He or she is the king or queen descended from that ancient and pure civilisation, until the Real Devil turned everything upside down."

"He or she? Ancient, pure civilisation?"

Chapter Twelve

"It's a spirit; it can be in a man or woman's body, but still it's the keeper of the secret and the keeper of humanity. All he has is the key - peace. The only one he fights is the Devil."

"Devil?"

"Melke-tsedeq and Noah fought him to save humanity. It's your destiny to fight along with humanity from here on."

She wanted to ask more questions, but couldn't figure out what to ask.

"I am excited." She tries not to show her feelings as her transformation from prisoner to an adventurer seems only a dream. *'Even if it's a dream it doesn't mean it's not true,'* she thinks.

Aba entered through the tunnel, leading the young couple. Emu followed, Alem followed.

It was just like a rabbit hole; it seemed no more important than a shelter for a fox or the den of some wild beast. The deeper they went into the dark tunnel the less they could see each other until when, in complete darkness, Aba Tso commanded the light.

Even the sun is not as bright as these ancient walls and brilliant man-made household items. They were not made of gold or diamonds but made of an untouchable material which generated its own light from within.

"Waaw! It's unreal!" Emu exclaimed. The tunnel seemed filled with a thousand suns, moons and stars; as wide as the limitless sky.

"You may sit. We are waiting in the reception room until we get the sign that lets us in."

Decorated with exotic classic pictures, the reception room made them feel as if they were part of the spectacle, sitting not on chairs, but on a comfortable floating sofa, like a duvet made up of colourful flowers on a soft green cloud.

While they were all taking a rest, Aba exchanged a pass code that enabled him to communicate with the gate keeper of the monastery. Alem and Emu felt ignored. They were forced to conduct their own

105

love rituals then. This real girl made him feel more relaxed the more he became acquainted with her; the real beauty to make him forget whatever troubles or joys he was about to face. She felt genuinely safe and happy in his presence. She forgot that she was hungry; she even forgot that she was thirsty. She forgot the fact that she was in the middle of a troubled but mysterious nowhere. It was as if she was opening the entrance to his personal heaven. She wanted to hug him tighter than ever before and he wanted to dive between the roundness of her breasts. Here, the ritual began not with sacrifice but with love. The colder the tunnel got, the more they clung to each other and the more they wanted to fight against each other to become a single entity. It was so cold. They might live or die, but at that moment they didn't mind about anything, as long as they were together. They were- for the moment- only fondling each other and didn't know what would follow.

"Well, we have passed the deadly cold tunnel, now." The waiting room was not only a waiting room but a multipurpose machine. *"It served as a lift to the city built across the dead."* Emu wishes it to be true. Her eyes open and close as she thinks that maybe it's all a dream. *Isn't life a dream anyway?* she reflects.

"It was called the death tunnel because it was a place of the dead. They kept the treasures with their deadly power, and cold, hallowing games. Only one spell could stop them from attacking." Alem is trying to filter what's real and what's not, wondering in between at what he is seeing and hearing. He wishes he had a spell that could make the whole world a peaceful place.

"Here we are."

Sandwiched in between two gigantic trees Emu by the left and Alem by the right side of Aba Tso, they enter the gate of the monastery garden. The trees with their branches are another world in themselves. Commanding a large space, covered in colourful dead flowers, dressed in green leaves from their roots to their stems, crowned with young flowers on the top, they give the place a divine grace. The stems are carved with names and prayers by people who had made pilgrimages here.

"Each part of the trees has a name written on it." Aba remarked.

Whatever this old man is talking about, Emu is full of happiness but she also feels hungry: hungry for their fruits, hungry for more discoveries, hungry for love while it's right in front of her eyes. She instantly picks and eats a fruit from the tree. Encouraged by her, Alem wants to taste as well.

"Can I?" Aba Tso picked one and ate it without replying to him.

"How would I know how you are feeling? Make yourself responsible for whatever you do, Alem. What do you feel?"

"Hungry." Aba picks from the left side of the tree and gives it to him. The taste reminds him of everything fresh. He bites more and becomes attached to the tree. He realises that it's been a while since he's eaten anything, but with just a couple of bites, he felt full.

"Now you have both eaten from the tree of knowledge. Once you come back here, you can eat from the other tree of life." Then, passing by a green park and water fountains he says, *"Drink here, you shall never thirst again."* As they walk through, they see a variety of trees that give the place unimaginable spiritual fragrance, almost as if you can smell heaven itself.

Aba ducks under a statue of a boy over a tiny grave. Shutting his eyes while taking a long breath, he opens his mouth at the same time.

"You see? We grow over each other. Previous generations, we on the top and the next one will be built over us. We have made a skyscraper with our bodies, not to die, but to grow wider. The branches are wide, spread out from one another but from one trunk, one life and one tree: you may say this is an African dream. The tree is our home, our family, the place of our elders. We are like the trees, calm, peaceful, the source of life yet dependent on nature."

Various people from the monastery appeared singing and dancing. It looked like a museum of people where you could see everyone you would want to see in the real world.

"We call this the city of Noah. All the people here are equal. It's the ideal of the world above, but here it's not only an idea, it's real. Here elephants fly, rats can pull a massive chariot, and unicorns are real..." Aba smiles thinking that Alem and Emu-Hiba might already think that he is talking nonsense. For Alem and Emu-Hiba, it's not so easy to get their heads around. What could help these two different generations communicate easily? There's the one who believes unicorns might be real, the others who think these are just fairy tales. What kind of communication can be more effective than just a smile, hoping that one day they will understand what all this means; a simple smile with the hope from a loving heart? She could have asked hundreds of questions, but she just smiles back instead. Alem replies with a smile too. They smiled back at each other. There they understand that if there is to be an answer for everything, then smiling is the divine answer.

After an adventurous visit around this sacred place, they called it a day. There were limits to what they could understand but they had awareness. Alem felt that he he'd understood some of what Aba had shown them, but he felt exhausted by it.

They rested at Aba's hut listening to ancient divine chanting that was slowly turning them into new people. It had nurtured and restored inside them an everlasting happiness, a hope and a compassionate love of humanity.

Alem saw Emu smile and laugh continuously. The more she kept smiling, the more she became new and attractive to him. She smiled again and again. It was deep, and genuine. He wished to see her like this after every trouble had passed, after they had settled down in a better place to live, the place they were searching for.

"Can't we just stay and live here?" she smiled, even though she knew they couldn't live there as easily as that. Not only would they have to commit to being a monk/nun before they could join the community, but also they needed to have worldwide experience, they needed to feel every pain the world has got to get into this paradise, and they needed to learn the joy of embarrassment that the world gives. Feeling that she was

made to belong to this place, she was still smiling, hoping one day she would be a part of it.

He wished she could always smile the same smile. It was as if she gave him a million years of life in a minute. He thanked God for these smiles.

"*I'll love you, no matter what happens.*"

"*What do you mean, no matter what happens?*"

Her question was more like words of comfort or encouragement; it was as if she was happy to express the first phrase "*I love you too.*"

"*I love you, more.*"

"*Thank God!*"

"*And, there won't be any problems as long as you are with me.*"

"*I want you to keep your smile.*"

"*Nothing will take my smile away other than losing you.*"

"*Even if I become a sad monster?*"

"*What do you mean, cheeky?*"

Aba wanted them to be like this forever, it seemed it was going on according to his wish. What is sweeter than looking at an adoring couple enjoying each other? It was like a mother breastfeeding her child in her arms, the two of them feeding love to each other – the first love – the first air that they could breathe freely, a curiosity about each other, leading to new discoveries - the future.

"*Only prayer could help this!*"

Here they made their vows to each other and promised to marry as soon as they settled somewhere they could lead a normal life. They pray for all of that.

"*I've blessed your engagement.*" Aba knew what was happening between them and what was going to happen to them. '*There couldn't be a better place than this holy town to feel the power of a new life. Unlike the rest the world, this place has been established with love and holy marriage, not with machine guns and blood.'* Aba proposed that they marry soon and not hesitate. Who could resist the power of love? Who could guess the journey of partners? Alem imagined what life living with her would be like, making a family built on love, peace and freedom. *Nothing would be a better life than this.*

Silence

Her smiling silence is becoming a safe place for him he thinks as he strokes his right earring while replying to her smile. She is already the soul of my soul.

"You are the heart of my heart," she reached out to his heart through hers.

"I am going to be your husband for all the years to come" he said in response, putting his arms around her neck gently, her long tiny neck covered with dark wavy hair.

"Yeah, I will, and I mean it," he says gazing at his eyes reflected in hers.

"You will marry me?"

"With pleasure!"

"Will you be my wife?" He kissed her cheek for the first time.

"With endless love," she replies kissing his throat. They took an oath, not just out of the responsibility caused by social pressure, caused by trouble, caused by having no choice, needing someone's support, or because of an accidental pregnancy. The only reason for this marriage is love. Temptation would not be their weakness when love was their strength to seek life in this lifeless world, hope on the hopeless journey, and faith in a faithless and unstable world.

Becoming betrothed...

In unison, they sang a song, a love song: love that will never end, love that will always stay fresh and never surrender. Their love would have no pretence; it would be a real love.

'Our love has no boundaries as the more we grow together, the closer we get. The older we grow the wiser we become. The more we consume each other, the more we are united.'

They slept together during the night, in one bed, side by side, but as a brother and sister. In between they created a burning magnetism, sweating with love and fearing that each would be melted by the love they felt for each other. Not even a kiss could give them relief but they were bound by culture and principle. One must not have sex before marriage and this was still only the period of engagement – it was a time to stay with each other, love each other till they burned enough for the next level.

It was time for the temptation. He thanked God for letting him live to see this miracle and he felt as if he had lived there forever. Then he said, *Now I feel old and happy, I can say 'I have seen your miracle, I will not be afraid of death hereafter!'*

The question was not to do with age; if it was about age then it shouldn't be measured by the numbers of days, months and years. It should be measured by the places you've visited, the things you have done, the dreams you have dreamt, the feelings of every fraction of infinite seconds. Life is infinite and everywhere, especially now that they understood their feelings were real and forever.

In the morning, earlier than the birds and the bright sun awoke to replace fading moon of the African night, Aba led them out of the monastery.

"Now you are ready to leave." They wished that they didn't have to go. They wished that they could live here as man and woman.

"You must leave; you have a long way to go." They felt vulnerable but at least being together made them determined. They walked in silence, a very long silence and in tranquillity.

Aba Tso bade them farewell outside the tunnel.

They were on their way again, together, to nowhere. They began their long trek together, with a new strength, energy and as refugees.

Chapter
THIRTEEN

The beginning of their future – border town, Galabat, Sudan

To make sure he's safe in case any TPLF or PFDJ spy catches them, she searches his bag and finds lots of needless papers, especially the political commentaries he wrote. They could expose him if any East African spies caught him with them.

"*All this must go,*" she says throwing away papers, feeding them to the fire as she's cooking their dinner.

He's still writing about almost everything. She takes the time to read most of it. He's watching her lying under a lonely tree, where they decided to take a break from the tiring journey.

"*This isn't good in our situation. We can't eat it nor can it protect us,*" she groans. He realises what she is doing, so he lets her do what she needs to do to protect both of them. They've made friends with a group of refugees they met on their way. They have all decided to stick together as an old African saying dictates: '*If you want to go fast, you go alone; but if you want to go far, you go together.*' They all understand that their journey is going to be long and they needed to be together.

She told everybody that she was his sister, to save him from danger. He told everybody that he was her husband to give her protection even to the point of risking his life. Just like Abraham and Sarah from the story of the sacred books, they knew how to keep right next to each other. She burned everything he wrote about her and about the journey they had made together. She said that she was keeping an invisible record in her head and that she would never forget each moment that she spent with her love.

"You can write it all as soon as we are at a safe place. I'll remind you of everything you tell me now, trust me." She promises that she will remind him of every bit of it once their time as refugees has passed. She thinks they won't need papers or pictures to remind them later. For her, their memories are more vivid than colour and words on paper. There was one diary which she started reading before she threw it into the fire.

'Suddenly, I got up in the middle of a deep sleep, and you were beside me – my star with the stars above. When I see stars I see you differently, I see myself differently. Without you I am half a person; you are the queen of the stars, and the full moon is our witness. We are twin souls like the two faces of the moon. Time is our road, endless but divine. As we travel, our hopes die each passing day but are reborn every night; for our love springs each new day from the sheer happiness of our own creation.'

She cried at his words and burned the diary after studying it word for word. Crying was madness, sadness was hell, and she hoped beyond hope that trouble wouldn't take her sweet love away.

Meeting the band of travellers

One thing that tells how our fathers expressed love and unity among our people is by eating together from one dish and feeding with our hands. They are all eating together as usual – agape – they call it. Especially, in the Sudan, it's the custom for people to eat outside so they can call guests passing by. Haven't we read the story of Abraham and Sara building a tent near the road, so they could devote their life to hospitality? It's a common custom throughout East Africa, a sign of unity that no one can take away from them.

"I'm full, praise to God." Alem took his hands away, just because he wanted the others to eat more.

"God will laugh at you."

"Why?" He smiles at her.

"You just said you are full although you have eaten hardly anything."

"You made me full with one Gursha."

It's all quiet and everything seems okay. In fact, it's better than the city of Addis Ababa for him to be on the road where he met his likeness, where she keeps feeding him and where he keeps pushing her hand away to feed herself.

There are a lot of desperate people like them passing by. The agent who had taken all their money had left them scattered in a land they had no idea about. Hence, instead of the false promises of smugglers, Alem preferred his squad with whom to continue his journey without anyone cheating and trading on them. It's safer than to travel alone too. They made a simple rule. Almost everyone here must help, support and take care of the others. Meeting other travellers, Alem and Emu felt much better; they were becoming like a family to him and especially, Emu. They'd joined a group of travellers all searching for freedom, feeling that there was more safety in travelling together. In just a few days, they had already adopted each other, looking after each other with no less concern than a family would. They had characters bolder than their names.

"Mewoled kuankua new" declares Alem, as if saying, *'Sibling is just a word; you can be a family as long as you have that commitment of caring for each other as a family. It was as if to say, you don't have to be born a family to be a family.'*

"Yeah, what are you saying young bro?" Paulos Amon reaffirms Alem's point, even if he doesn't understand Amharic. They have already started referring to each other as 'young brother, older brother and sisters...'

He loves it here just because of them.

There's Paulos who usually pays for everything he uses twice over because he has a body twice as big as two large men. Alem loves being with them, he likes listening to Moussa's news updates every hour. Moussa had introduced himself as a young Somalian boy. He's a good friend to Alem and even though his name is Moussa, people call him *BBC* because he always has heart-breaking news to tell.

He likes being a travel companion with Mohamed too. Mohamed is always on the radio, his ears are twice as large as normal ears – '*his face looks like a car with its two front doors open*,' is Moussa's description of him. Moussa loves teasing him to make him smile a bit.

Alem likes this squad so much, they've given him courage and hope in himself to take responsibility; one based on love and caring. Everyone seems to know their duties and responsibility to ease the burden of their refugee lives.

Paulos is with Rahel in the group; this couple are another strong symbol of love. Although, Rahel looks as if she has never eaten in her entire life, she's proud of her beauty and dreams that she will be a top model one day. She's had a crush on Paulos for long time. Her phone is full of his images.

"*How long are you going to keep being sweet on him?*" people ask her all the time.

"*Forever, as long as we live.*" She answers all the time.

"*We are already married, well not officially. But we will, once we've settled somewhere. Then your feelings may change*," he pulled her leg. When she's angry at him, she just calls him '*mushroom face pumpkin*', that's all.

"*What's the problem with having a crush on my husband?*" She gets hotter now.

"*Nothing*" he says, supporting her.

"*Do you trust me?*"

"*Do I need to? As long as I love you.*" They hug.

"*Nope.*" They kiss.

She always talked about him and her friends teased her as she was totally infatuated by him. She'd followed him on his long journey and risked her life multiple times. She dearly loved him and he felt the same towards her. *'She is my special world; she brings me to a different world every time. The worlds in her mind are uncountable. She can make me surrender with only a blink of her eyes.'* Alem remembered what Paulos Amon has told him and he starts picturing it all.

'Imagine that you were meant for each other even before you were born, because your father and her father have promised to keep their two families tighter than before, through the bond of marriage vows. They have made plans for your life already. You are a bridge of love between two different families, a hope for the bonding of generations. You are the new born tree; a hybrid. Together, you grew up learning how to take care of each other. However, as soon as it's the time that you were meant to marry and test the happiness of your own little family that you have been waiting for, your world is turned upside down for some unknown reason. In the blink of an eye, war has replaced peace. You have no clue what's going on because you have seen nothing like this before. It suddenly becomes a miracle to still be alive. But when the war keeps wiping out those still remaining, you must depart from your home, from your city, your ancestors' graveyard, from each other, from your memories. You must say goodbye, even if you have never said it before. No one told you that this could happen, because there was no one who could tell about what to expect.'

Alem realised that they were meant to be together for as long as possible, until one of them passes away. That was the paradigm they inherited from their ancestors; unconditional love and care that never fades. He keeps imagining how it went for both of them as he remembered.

'Imagine that you have shared everything your city offered the both of you: the smell of each flower that every season brings; the odour of your mother's spices, the flavour of your father's herbs; the memories of the names of each of your cattle. You remember how every fruit tasted different in its own season. You have never thought about the world beyond the clouds and the sky of your town. You never think of a world beyond, where the earth and the sky kiss at every sunset and sunrise: everlasting and divine; nature in its glory. It's the image of divine love reflected down over a clean mirror-like lake, the sky and the lake mirroring each other's dimensional

beauty. It's the image that you are familiar with. It's not war, not massive fires, not a corpse-ridden land which is now totally turned into killing fields with the smell of death lingering around. It's a landscape that burns with unstoppable fire on and off, unexpectedly. This comes from beyond, from the unknown. You never thought this would be true in your homeland; you never made yourself ready for this harrowing experience. You have just had occasional nightmares between the sunset and sunrise, but nothing like this. You were never allowed to find out or go beyond your own place anyway, because that's where you were told people go and never came back from. That's where you used to think people go to when they die. Now, the sky seems turned upside down and fallen over you. Your town is never the same anymore; that seems a world too small now. You see beyond it, but there is nobody left to ask, to guide both of you. You are outnumbered and unable to fight back. You know one thing- that it's time to escape if possible leaving everything behind. You don't even have the time or courage to say goodbye properly. You have never said it before. You just stare at each other for a moment and cry: it is final. There is no time to waste when every minute is a matter of life and death. You fight to die or depart in search of a life'.

Only Rahel and Paulos can make it, he assures himself. They are role models for all the squad. As the Abyssinian elders say, '*Spiders in unity can tie up a lion.*' They can be the strength of the squad so that together they can survive. They have made it this far together, preaching about love, about peace up until now.

He likes Moussa most, with his annoying pranks.

In the middle of the night when everybody was outside their handmade shelter, relaxing in the moonlight and Alem and Emu were lying alone, suddenly Moussa rushed up to them in a hurry.

"*Oioioo,*"

"*What's wrong Moussa?*"

"*Police.*"

"*Eh? Which ones?*" He knew that whether it was the Eritrean, Ethiopian or the Sudanese police, there would be no difference. They were all enemies now. Their job was to make sure there was no man living who didn't worship their dictatorial government and obey their unfair laws. The word 'police' became synonymous with the words beatings, killings and if they showed a degree of mercy they would throw you in a stinking cell from where you had to buy your freedom by any means possible. Either you died there or escaped if you could find a way. They cannot run away from here as there is not enough shelter to hide all of them, in this flat, barren land. Alem was very disturbed until Moussa laughed at him in his high pitched voice.

"*Damn you and your sick jokes!*" They all laughed.

"*Not today. They are busy today, man.*" He hands them a newspaper that has tragic news on the front page.

"*Who? Why?*"

"*Why do you always bring sad news, BBC?*" he asks, looking across at it involuntarily.

"*I don't make it up; I deliver it, that's all. Sudan is in an incredible mess. Look.*" He handed Alem another newspaper. "*Very sad news, another national shame.*"

'*Ethiopian woman sentenced to death.*' A woman's husband had revealed that he saw her secretly praying to Jesus as she was Christian before her marriage to him, a Muslim, arranged by their families. According to their version of sharia law, she would have to pay for her *sin* with her death.'

"*I don't understand.*" Moussa gets confused.

"*Me neither*" Mohamed was confused too.

"*But in our country...*"

"*It's because, in our country, sharia law comes under the state law.*" Gech explained.

"The true law of Allah states that one is never allowed to take anyone's life, to take life is only up to Allah. It was a wrong and fanatical interpretation of the holy manuscripts of the Qur-An; Islam is a peace- loving religion." Mohamed confirmed.

"Oh... God! It's worse to be here, then." Emu-Hiba murmurs to herself, ducking her head down behind Alem's back.

They had grown up in a society where differences in religion, colour and ethnicity were nothing but beautiful and unique elements of their constructed society. Differences were never seen as a curse but more as a blessing. Muslims celebrate Christian holidays, and Christians celebrate Muslim holidays all together. They help each other to build their churches and mosques. That's what it means to be Eritrean or Ethiopian. That is the history of East Africa which he knew had developed before the storm of European colonialism came, Arab inventions began dividing the continent and now it's the same; Africa has become a proper Christmas dinner fought over between China and America. This wasn't East Africa before the old king Emperor Haile Selassie I got killed, smothered with a pillow by the Soviet-centric socialist president; before the American gamblers from one ethnic group of Northern Abyssinia took over the power for themselves to gamble in turn on their poor people and country. It was another national shame. He is realising how the world has become polluted and disregards the real sense of humanity. *The world needs to come to its senses,* he thinks.

"Mate, our differences are uncountable, but that was our beauty until partition came, until greed took over our religious and political leaders. Look at us now" Moussa says.

They all pray that they will live in a world where everybody is treated fairly regardless of their belief. *Besides religion is not based on fear of punishment, it's rather enlightenment, formed of messages from those who can see the unseen, the future. It's supposed to mean love, peace and co-existence,* Alem thinks. He remembers the sheiks and Imams of Abyssinia building churches for their Christian brothers. He missed the times when he used to attend *Ed al fetr* with his Muslim brothers.

He also anticipates the time when he will officially be with his future Muslim wife: Emu-Hiba.

"People should give up picking on each other and concentrate on supporting and loving each other," he preaches.

"It was only a difference of religion, not something to be punished for." Emu felt sorry for the woman. She would prefer her cell where she grew up in darkness to witnessing this public shame. She missed her people. *'Eritrea is a blessed nation but has a bloody messy government,'* she thinks. *'There, religious difference didn't stop you from loving and getting married to someone different, someone you love, but here it could sentence you to death.'*

"So, Sudan will have no place for me and Emu to live, then." Alem seeks their opinion on what choice they'll have next; what'll be their destination.

"The group has already decided to leave Sudan and go to Libya."

"We will follow the herd; what choice do we have anyway?" says Paulos Amon fiddling with Rahel's fingers.

"I will follow you wherever you think that we will have a better place." Emu put her palms on Alem's chin and he did the same to her.

"I can go to the ends of the Earth to find a better place for you and me."

He put his lips against her lower lip, softly. She responded and he felt relieved. He started hoping for a life beyond this chaos, across the biggest desert: somewhere where they can forget about it all. They wish each day to be new and fresh. Trying to forget all that was troubling his mind, Alem began to enjoy watching Paulos and Moussa having a laugh playing the games they like.

He taught them how to play a game of riddles.

"Riddle, riddle"

"What it would be. Give it to me, then," Paulos replies.

"It has travelled through all the ages far and wide; it has neither tired nor retired."

"The wind."

"Silly"

"God"

"No!"

"A traveller?"

"Be specific"

"The Devil"

"God and the Devil don't need to travel, stupid!"

"I've never played this game before."

"Guess!"

"Ay!"

"No! Give me a country."

"I give you, Libya."

"After I get to Libya, I will be a king there and you will be my servant. I shall eat at a banquet and you will eat my scraps. My road is a gold carpet and your road is full of thorns…"

"Oh… here you go. I give in; tell me the answer."

"The answer is river, stupid." They laughed at their silliness. They knew that was how difficult times passed more quickly. They can do it all day long, while walking, while eating, while lying down.

Alem likes hearing the battle field stories of General Gech.

Even though each one of them has had their ups and downs, Gech's life has been a painful rollercoaster his entire life as a soldier, nothing but this. Now he's a refugee, freeing himself from his former life at great expense. Not so long ago he'd had a life full of power and respect, but the system he was in was so dirty. He wasn't able to stand on his principles;

he was supposed to be saving his people from all that oppression. He thought he was helping his people by being a soldier; he didn't know his leaders' motives to begin with and he served them well at the beginning, thinking that he was serving his people and his country by getting rid of the previous militant government of Ethiopia. That's what every single soldier thought.

"*Call me G4*," said General Gech Gibril the Gondor, trying to forget his full name and where he came from. His family had been proud of him because he was amongst the brave young soldiers who overthrew the military government and handed the power to others empowered and assigned by foreign governments. He didn't know them then but he joined them in thinking to get rid of the military government that had wiped out an entire generation by terror and murder. He had no idea that the patriarch had taken power by getting rid of his predecessor as that had never happened before in the history of the Abyssinian church. Normally, a patriarch is replaced only when the previous one has died. It has to be done through prayers and the decision of the elders but this time, it was rather a political process than a religious process. Gech only knows this patriarch was rewarded as a representative for world peace, but he died just a day after the Chairman of the TPLF had died. They both died naturally and people accepted the phenomenon as a divine message. '*Spiritual life never needed promotion, because it's already promoted by God. A patriarch doesn't need medals and rewards; he's already rewarded by God. Even I have never needed a reward as a soldier to serve my own people because to serve was my reward.*' He realises what this life has rewarded him with now – a refugee life. He had lived a life that honoured his name until now, now that he's become a refugee.

It's not the end of the world. There really is another world beyond this chaotic third world, he said to himself, to find courage to face the future. They started to talk, a heated talk in which the issue was centred on which ethnicity was to be blamed for the fall of the East African states.

"The royal system was cool, but the last Emperor Haile Selassie I let it end because he was old and wasn't ready to hand the crown down to his successor voluntarily."

"And it was too late; the socialist militants were organised and their revolution was nearly exploding. Even the elite people used to feel backward about the fact that they were still led by a three thousand year venerable crown. And there was Russia..."

"It was also too late; Eritreans and the entire region needed a change."

"Nay, Jah was a real soul."

"But he was bad."

"Well, Mengistu was worse."

"Woyanie was even worse than him."

"I think it's how it's supposed to be."

"The days of Ethiopia are finished."

"What do you mean?"

"It's a failed state."

"It's nothing new. The state has existed for thousands of years, longer than any other world state has; uniting all the Horne of Africa and beyond. It might have been weakened by foreign intervention and by the strategy of divide and rule, but it has never failed. It only gets grey, petty and fragmented; but it'll rise and regain its power again. Trust me," Alem says, wishfully.

"It's only politics that are the problem."

"But, politics, I mean it can cure or ruin everything you have."

"Avoiding the shit is our problem. We are supposed to deal with it."

"We grew up hating politics, because when we talk about it only bad things follow."

"We have to avoid ethnic-centred political systems."

"Federalism is essential. But, a federal system must support unity. The problem is that there is no system of equal and proportional power distribution that encourages solidarity among ethnic groups," said Alem.

"There are more than eighty ethnic groups in Ethiopia, and therefore there would be more than eighty different countries in East Africa."

"Then they'll fight over borders as usual. Without knowing it, so many people will die for nothing other than for the benefit of political opportunists."

"That's what was planned by TPLF."

"God save our brothers and sisters."

Alem felt fed up again thinking that this is the reason he is a refugee now. He dreams of the rebirth of that great nation to return to the state before things went wrong. He wants to communicate with the spirits of his ancestors to know how it looked when Africa was more united and with richer states. He wants to meet Mansa Musa - the richest person in the history of mankind who made himself rich without being a gambler or coming from a privileged class. Alem remembered the story of how Mansa Musa had stretched his camels across the great desert of the Sahara with gold bound for the rich and holy land of Mecca, sharing his wealth on his way to the Arab nations; how he created a fortune for centuries to come. Alem imagines how his forefathers managed to accept their Middle Eastern guests as religious refugees and European diplomats, missionaries with more than normal respect and privilege. His forefathers identified the false messengers of European monarchs from the true brothers of European scholars. They dealt with them wisely and hospitably. This enabled Abyssinia to be recognised as a fierce nation no one dared to colonise; that was until Mussolini came back to seek revenge with a forbidden weapon blessed by the Pope. His forefathers endured those weapons and fought the Fascists for five years alongside the whole peace loving world and secured their territory from the scramble of Africa. They had been a role model of freedom, peace and love. They had been a symbol of togetherness for more than half the world that had been under the darkness of slavery and colonial oppression. They had altered the history of the world just with a single battle called "Adwa". He wants to meet their spirits and ask them how they had managed all that. He wonders how it came about this way. He can't bear all the nonsense going on now and this makes him hope that things will change at some point. He shakes his head unconsciously.

"Are you angry, Alem?" Paulos asks.

"We are all here because of this" he answers firmly.

"See we are all refugees here. In a way all humans are refugees in some respect anyway." Gech gives him courage as he raises his right hand and shouts, *"We are not just refugees, we are citizens of the world."* They all repeated it after him.

"See we don't care how we differ from one another." Mohammed added.

"We are on our own."

"And we have each other."

"We shouldn't focus only on politics, folks. Let's talk about the real life out there, let's talk about families. Let's talk about breathing fresh air, let's focus on the great things that our forefathers handed down to us." Gech grabbed everybody's attention with his golden voice. He had a deep sadness in his heart, and burning eyes. He talked like an angry lion in a cage. Nobody knew he was a General who had worked for the EPRDF[11] until only a few days ago. He was hungry for simple, everyday talk. He was thirsty for alcohol, for a time of relaxation drinking wine in the family yard. His story started when he lost all of his family during the Dergue Military junta twenty seven years before, when he was just ten years old. That's how he'd joined the liberation front. He was selected as a musician first. He inherited his musical skill from his parents. As a kid, he had grown up with music, laughter and parties every day, until one day his story changed completely.

---

11 The Ethiopian People's Revolutionary Democratic Front

He remembered that very day. In the evening an official came to the house and accused his family of sheltering and supporting protesters calling their deeds as *nech shibr* 'white terror' which was a response to *key shibr* 'Red terror' that's literally an official declaration of genocide – killing people who disagreed with the soviet socialist ideology or who refused to serve this evil revolution. Generations had lost their lives for nothing. There had never been such an open outrage in the history of East Africa. The protesters were a group of youths from Eritrean, Ethiopian sub-regions and university students from different parts of both countries. When somebody was accused of something it was inevitable that the next day they would be hanged in the market place to terrorise the people. In the middle of the night Gech's family were all rounded up by the military; the families fought back but were all killed while only he escaped. Then he joined the protest movement. Even if he was very young at the time, he was an adept soldier and talented singer. That's how he joined the world of gunners. He fought for about ten years until the death of the socialist military regime in 1987. Without thinking, he kept serving the system that was gambling with the lives of the people and the state he was serving until he was finally forced to give up.

Though it took him his entire life to be a General, partly because of ethnic discrimination, he was a devoted soldier to his mission. He'd had lots of adventures that were kept secret from the monotonic, dominating officials and so he was not promoted as he deserved. He accepted it as his lot in life. *After all, I am only a soldier,* is what he told himself. Completing whatever mission came from officials was the only role he had been trained for until one day he received a most wicked mission. After he had received the mission from the ministry of defence of EPRDF, he was thinking about it while drinking tequila at a traditional pub located near the Arat Killo Palace, Addis Ababa. It wasn't an easy task to take in. It was brutal, inhuman and more destructive than any liquor he could take. Pretending to forget about it, at least for the moment, he drank more tequila than he ever had before. He was also listening to the poetic lyrics of a minstrel.

Chapter Thirteen

Muachiw balie gedayw wondmie,
Endet bye lalks hazen teshekmie.

He felt the minstrel was singing about him. He gave him the words. This is how it went:

I married a prostitute, from whom I cannot get a divorce,
All her friends invite me to fight; now I haven't got a choice.
I don't know what to do with my life,
Every night different men keep taking my wife.

Everybody felt this was the only place they could say whatever they wanted to say. The minstrel took the poetry and sang it back to them. The minstrel reminded him of his childhood. General Gech accused himself of going back to his birth place not for his family but for worse. He ran away from home when he was young and dumb following music, following freedom; now he's going to go back much older and with the mission to perform a political massacre, with forces armed with heavy American weapons. He thought of his family members who have survived the 'red terror' by God's providence. It was New Year's Eve, a season he had missed being with family and all the exciting holidays of *Demera* (Founding of the Cross), *worha tsgie* (Season of flowers), Christmas to follow with the spirits of family past, present and future. He missed the scent of fresh summer flowers. He remembered how the fresh air of September springing from the yellow red and green New Year's flower 'Adey Abeba' covered all the land with an aromatic smell; the piles of red, yellow and green harvested plants. He thought of the romantic, royal and spiritual hymns, the dark winter's farewell folk songs that he grew up with. He missed the time when he could sit with his brothers and talk about anything without fear of anyone spying on him. However, as he became a colonel and then a general, he learned how to cover his fears; his consciousness grew in the opposite direction, but not for long. The minstrel had succeeded in taking his attention away from the next day's nightmare, at least for the moment. He adores him, the way he can take words from his customers quickly and clearly, and give it back to them with lively melodies. He can say whatever he wants, not because it's his democratic right which this government can

127

give and take; but it's his cultural right which his people have had since the formation of the state dating back more than six thousand years.

"*Take this!*" said an old man, pointing at a western poster on the wall of the pub that depicts a group of monkeys, dressed smartly, playing snooker and covered in the clouds of their cigars.

'*Chimpanzee chairman, a monkey deputy, a donkey General;*

The minstrel repeated it with his *Fano Baty* scale melody; watching left and right in fear of spies around. The old man kept giving him his last line stressing each and every word he was saying.

I have never seen such a miracle,
I've never seen such a failure.'

Amongst the cynical drunken laughter of the crowd and the noise of guns, the compound suddenly turned into hell. Federal soldiers shot at the body guards and took three of the elders. The General went out and talked to one of the soldiers after showing his ID.

"*Yes General, they are terrorists.*"

"*How do you think those old men could be terrorists?*"

"*Wa! Because they are supporting the Amhara and Oromo protests.*"

"*Agreed!*" he knew he couldn't argue more. Of course, he'd noticed they were commenting on the political situation but they were honest and ready for the consequences as usual; he felt they should have the right to say what they believed because that was what he had been fighting for his entire life. He knew that in past years even kings used to go such places disguised as ordinary men, not to spy for their own benefit but just to hear what their common subjects were suggesting about how the administration could be improved. He remembered an old saying '*leaders and people are like the back and front of a coin.*' Now he understood how even if they are intertwined, even if their lives depend on each other, they can never see each other's faces directly. He is a state soldier but forcefully and systematically submitted to the political will. He suddenly grasped that wise, spiritual and poor people were set against gangsters who have succeeded in dividing the nation. He was going to do the same the next day anyway. He was the donkey general according to the elders.

The next day

He'd flown from Addis Ababa to Gondar, and two spies were employed to follow him; he was given forces from an ethnic group of TPLF to make sure he executed the order. He knew why. Different ethnicities could be harsh and strict with their mission. They sent these two people with him because of the previous week's incident when two protesting colonels had flown to Eritrea, the worst place, just to escape sudden execution or atrocious prison conditions. They'd gone in a jet, armed with expensive weapons to help them shout out to the world in case anyone could hear.

Gech was confused as to why he was no longer trusted, but at the same time he was just awakening to the reality of what he was doing, what he had been too blind to see before. He arrived at the camp near his birth place. The mission was to watch over the demonstration, control the peace and security around there – that he knew of, that was what he wished for, what it should have been; but the mission went far beyond just wrecking the demonstration, to become an irresponsible and terrible act of genocide. Before anyone came out for the demonstration it was his job to scare them not to go and if they did, he had to *'take a democratic action'* which according to TPLF's political definition is translated as *'kill them all, and level them as terrorists.'* He knew the state had never had any terrorist happenings throughout its history, it had never agreed with the culture, lifestyle and history of Ethiopia. *So, where does this alien evil come from?* He couldn't understand. He questioned himself while reading an alien document he couldn't understand, a copy of the top secret document sent to him to execute his political duty.

North Gondar, Jan Amora/Royal Eagle/ district

He had his armed forces nearby and ready. They are waiting on his orders. He'd visited the town moments before the demonstration time. He begun to grasp and take in the situation. The people are living in a desperate way just as they used to when he was a kid. He started to open his mind and could see no changes at all. Even more, he had begun to witness the damage, even worse than ever. Everything is still yellow and grey and unhealthy.

North Gonder - Dabat/My father's home/ District

It's very quiet. People had changed a lot. The giant trees he knew had been cut down, all the elders he knew have died. It seems as though only the palace of Dejach Ayaliew Bru stands tall, defying time. It's not easy to find smiling faces among the youths and people he grew up with and he's been sent here to make it even worse. Flying up in the helicopter, he looks down on a tiny line of demonstrators, streams of angry young people all over the abandoned town of the district that used to be a glamorous city during the reign of the last Emperor of Judah – Jah Ras Tafari Haile-Selassie I.

Now it looks like an abandoned town after a devastating bombardment.

The City of Gonder

Half the people gestured showing the oppression with hands crossed over their heads shouting out slogans:

'*Stop dividing us; pushing us to hate each other.*'

'*Stop plotting false stories that makes us fight one another, for your own political and economic gain.*'

'*Stop leading us into unending war and division, please.*'

'*Give fair distribution and equal attention to all ethnicities.*'

'*Free our brothers and sisters. They are our voices not prisoners.*'

'*It's my brother who is dying here.*'

'*Down with TPLF*'

'*We are people, not terrorists.*'

'*TPLF is not our government but terrorists.*'

'Enough of American gangsters.'

This city has always been a bridge to freedom. There is always a voice in a silent, ruined old capital city like this: a dignified voice that calls out for freedom for the entire nation. A sign of a rainbow that warns and promises that the storm needs to come to an end and things will settle down after. He saw his young brothers boiling in anger and ready to die fighting for their and their family's freedom. They had been quiet for a while, with a hope that one day the TPLF will learn and change. That has never happened throughout the past couple of decades. This was enough. Green, red, bold, young eyes pointed directly to the front; eyes fiercer than bullet shots. He felt his young self among them, remembering when he used to think like them, that he could change things and everything was possible. But then, he realised that it hadn't come to be. He felt his coldness and weakness for the first time. He felt he was older but very tiny and insignificant in this yellow city. He realised how the system had made him older than he looks, weaker than he is. He wanted to be young again and fight for only what he should fight for, at least for this day. But it's not as easy as it was when he was young.

Now he has a wife and couple of children to take care of; he has a mission to keep. If he doesn't keep to his mission, his heroic action could ruin the life of his little family forever, with a cost to his nation, his family and everything about him. What a bloody official mission, a violent reply to a democratic question asked by the entire population, just because TPLF officials don't have answers for their evil deeds. *How could they?* He totally excluded himself, as he realised the difference between him and the TPLF soldiers. Growing up here, he himself knew that when a united people say *"enough"* together, he knows it only means one thing: ENOUGH!

Here many brave youths had been sacrificed for the liberty and dignity of the whole nation. This place had been one of the centres of protests under different rulers: Dejach Ayalew Biru and later Ehapa (Ethiopian people's revolutionary party) over the three regimes from Haile Selassie's feudal system, Dergue militants, and now the patriotic youths over those corrupt officials. This was the birthplace of many heroes and heroines even until now. Maybe for the first time in the history of Ethiopia a peaceful, unauthorised protest demonstration had happened. It had been led by no particular person but by all the youth banding together. It was a peaceful direct attack on the governing party and the Prime Minister who had been ruling the country for twenty-five years. Governing officials were embarrassed by the dangerous demonstrations even though the protestors were quiet and peaceful. Even so, the officials were angry at the protest but it was difficult for them to aim at a particular person. The people were holding the national flag of the country which was against the current constitution. They should've been holding the flag of their particular regional and political party with the pentagon star on it, but they were holding the flag that symbolised only the green flood, yellow flowers and red blood – their symbol of unity – a rainbow. This flag links them with nature instead of some sort of symbolic subjugation to western misinterpreted divinity.

This flag represents the colours of more than seven thousand years of history. It's the flag for every nation to enjoy as it waves across the sky. It's the pride of these people; hence the ruling party hates it as it may bring the people together and be seen as a danger to the opportunistic systems of government. Anyone could see their relationship with the land, their pride, love and heroic actions shown by their peaceful uprising. The demonstration was calm, loud and energetic. *What's wrong with it?* he asked himself attentively observing the demonstration. Meanwhile, the brutal federal police force was tensing up, waiting for an order, but it was only the general who could give it. This was in his 'job description', his responsibility.

"*We are waiting for your order,*" said Colonel Goytom, who had been secretly assigned by TPLF to spy on him.

"*Nothing to worry about, there is no sign of violence, Colonel.*" He was wary of the man – a cowardly soldier whom they had secretly named '*death himself*'. No one knows how he got the title of Colonel. With his arrogant comments and his background everyone came to realise that he's spying on General Gech. They all know that brave soldiers had lost their brave leaders because of Goytom. Gech smiled at him.

"*Why are you smiling?*" Goytom reprimanded him arrogantly.

"*Address him with his title, Colonel,*" one of his colleagues said disapproving of the Colonel's approach to General Gech.

"*It's okay.*"

"*Sorry sir, I mean General,*" Colonel Goytom added, as they were all making fun of him.

"*It's okay, relax,*" confirmed General Gech.

"*It's not okay; we need to take the democratic action we came for.*" He tried to use his privilege to impose a decision to take a hard, political action over the wiser action that could benefit both sides.

"*Here you start your evangelical rant,*" whispered his colleagues, realising he hadn't got any sense of a disciplined soldier.

"*We have command over the lives of our families who gave us everything. But, unfortunately we are sent here to terrorise our own people with no grounds for a disciplined army to take such a brutal action over these poor people. If we wanted to do that, we should've become gangsters, politicians or killers. Comrades, never forget that we are soldiers. Our job is NOT to kill, but to save lives.*" His speech had begun to turn radical and unpredictable for most of them. A debate started between the forces as they divided into groups based on ethnicity. But everyone kept silent as he commanded. He's being tested and he knows why. He'd rather fail the test, free his soul and accept the consequence than do as the system expects him to in order to get promoted and become a demon like the rest of the officials. '*What's all this sacrifice for? Call me selfish if I do this. Let my parents' bones pierce me to death if I put my hand on anyone ever again.*" He thought that neither he nor this people needed to be a victim in order to increase the power of the TPLF gangs.

"*These people are protesting against the constitution.*" Goytom tried to initiate violence and lead half of the force to attack the demonstrators.

"*They are people; they were around before our constitution. Do you even have any idea what you are saying Colonel?*" The General directed his penetrating eyes straight at the Colonel. The Colonel had no idea, but he was planning how he could use this situation for his own promotion and his ethnic- based party's sake. The demonstration was still going on peacefully; people were shouting simple slogans. Some of the slogans were clear and democratically asking the government to free detained journalists and peaceful protesters, to stop one ethnic group dominating the rest, to stop creating plots to worsen ethnic hostility, to help the refugee crisis, to stop using international terrorist law to terrorise its own people, to give power to a different party.

The General couldn't find a single reason to attack these people; these questions were the reason he'd become a soldier. He nearly cried out that these basic, democratic questions were still not answered. *After all that sacrifice!* He felt these people were far superior to their governor. *No more sacrifice*, he decided for himself. Brave soldiers never attack peaceful people. War is between two opposite forces, and his mission should be as peaceful as theirs. He knew he was stepping to a different rhythm from any of his fellows. Another of his men commented,

"You are thinking well."

"Eh? Colonel Bekele? I am a General but imprisoned by my title. What can I do, brother?"

"We all are, but you have the heart of a lion – a true general...Shh... just once in your lifetime do what your heart tells you to do, General."

"You are a true soldier, Colonel Bekele."

Pushing aside the soldier, Goytom who was a government spy came closer to ask him what he was doing.

"I am trying to find a reason to stop them".

"I suppose they will go home after they are tired of shouting, bastard minstrels!"

"That's correct, but no comment is needed, Colonel!"

"Yes General."

He felt how he usually felt after a battle is won. He had taken a lesson from these brave and wise people. Even if he knew no one was going to hear their questions, he knew that was how to start the real change, winning through peace and doing nothing violent. International news feeds were attending the demonstration so that at least the world would know and possibly help. He stayed until it was finished, praying that the day could end in peace. He had control over the situation at least for that time; he had schooled his army as to how to treat a decent people like this. He told them of the legacy of people exerting control over political gangsters. He reminded them of the Italian people who had helped Ethiopian patriots; of the uprising over the Fascist Mussolini who was poisoning Ethiopian fighting patriots with chemical weapons even though their use had been forbidden by the League of Nations. He remembered Hiroshima and Nagasaki. He reminded them of Hitler versus confused Christian and Jewish people. Then he made them realise that at the end of the day people will stand united. He learned for himself the power of forgiveness; he understood; he awakened. He cried at last feeling much lighter. He knew the consequences of his actions that day, so he secretly left everything behind and joined the life of many – the life of a refugee.

Now he was with his real-life comrades. He would protect his friends as he used to protect his country from foreign enemies and inside scum, and so he was thinking about how they should plan to cross the dessert. He had been there for a couple of months, so he knew some of the places. He had been here for training during the time of Gadhafi, when the country used to have its own rightful king. General Gech has learned a lot since then.

Shared problems form them into a brotherhood.

The problems that they all faced had made them as a family, as brothers. They had taken an oath to help each other as they wandered through the greatest desert in the world. There, people either turn into absolute monsters or saints. Nobody knows what's going to happen. There, the sun is the king and the moon is the queen. The wind is a soldier. There, nature's harshness governs; there are vicious insects, especially scorpions. In the country around, there is always confusion and violence. Any group could suddenly come and attack the other. People first have to be organised to survive. If they stay together, then the bigger the band, the more they can organise and help each other.

Day and after day, meeting people after people, they managed to build their small squad of refugees and together they could entrust their lives in order to survive. From here, at the barren border of Sudan, Egypt and Libya called Mount/Jebel – Uweinat – Musselles, where you can dig for gold - they plan to march through Kufra and Sabha, avoiding the deadly militia and detention centres of Gharyan. Then route to protect themselves from the ruthless and inhuman smugglers that have turned the desert of the dead Ruler into a slave market. Thanks to the 2011 NATO-backed ousting of Muammar Gaddafi, thanks to the Turkish and Qatari oil company's extensive support for giving explosive weapons to extreme war gangs and traffickers, thanks to the American government for the irresponsible act of contributing to the evolution of ISIS, this place has become like hell. It's a land of abundant wealth, but a hell-hole for many. Here you can dig for gold and be rich or die at any time. This is the only place on earth where oil is free. It was the place of Mansa Mussa – the richest person in the history of mankind – so what do you expect? Everything is cheap, but also a place of great danger for everyone, including the lives of thousands of refugees.

For Rahel and Emu-Hiba, it's going to be even worse just because they are women. They have double the trouble awaiting them ahead. They need to pass through a higher risk of gratuitous and sexual violence too. At every border crossing and checkpoint in particular, they have to take precautions, contraceptive injections and emergency protection. They are going to be sexually enslaved by the uniformed Libyan officials and militia and they will have no one to report their sufferings to. They have to suffer emotionally to save their own men's lives, to save them from being assassinated, sold into slavery and beaten to death by jealous human traffickers, smugglers, ruthless rapists and terrorists. They all are aware of this, but they keep going because they need to.

The more they thought, the more they prepared themselves for a better and safer journey. At last, by the cold fresh beautiful moonlight they collected water, food and sticks for making their shelter. They need it when the scorching heat and freezing cold can be fatal. They learned from the first chapter of their journey that it was all for all, helping each other in all circumstances, through any eventuality.

"Every moment is always the beginning of the future, boys." The General kept up his motivational speech as always.

They noticed that they were still in the middle of chaos so they left the inhabited areas to go into the desert seeking a life beyond this barren, sandy land.

"Every moment is always the beginning of the future, boys," echoed Alem as the rest followed him. He found solitude for a second and opened a book as it was time for prayer. Moussa followed wanting to check on him.

Alem read a psalm every morning, his rapid reading sounding like a chorus of bees. Tizzz… tizzzz… honouring their queen in the silent stage of the wide open desert. After he finished, a Somali boy, who had been his audience for a while, glanced at his laminated leather book.

"It's different."

"It's sacred."

"I know how to read Amharic, but it didn't sound the same. I think you read fast."

"Yes, you are right. It's not Amharic, it's called Geez' meaning 'the first language. It's believed to be the first language between man and God."

"Aw! So you can speak the first language."

"I guess so."

"Cool. Please teach me."

"Why not, if you want."

"*Who wouldn't want to know the first language of man, brother?*"

"*I will teach you every morning after prayer. But you must teach me more Arabic in return.*"

"*Sure. Thank you. So, there really was a time when there was only one language?*"

"*There was only one language before the incident of Babylon, I learned.*"

"*I wish there was still only one language throughout the world so that people could communicate more easily.*"

"*It's not bad to have different languages. In every language there is always unique knowledge and wisdom.*"

"*How many languages do you have in your country?*"

"*More than eighty, can you believe?*"

"*Possibly to your surprise Nigeria has 516 languages and Papua has 820 languages.*"

"*Common sense is the best language we have.*"

"*That's so true.*" Silence. Moussa is lost in thought as if something is troubling him badly.

"*Have you got any money yet, to pay for the smugglers?*"

"*I don't really know what or how I'll pay when we get to the coast.*"

"*Don't worry, I'll pay for you.*"

"*No, you have Emu-Hiba.*"

Alem insists and gives him a couple of notes.

"*Thank you.*"

He's always shared everything with his friends. As everyone is blessing him, so he blessed Arron who helped him in need. Within the blessings, he remembered Arron. It's normal for somebody to help others to get them out of a brutal situation. Alem had told Arron that he was going to try to make it to Europe and Arron had sent him enough money to pay the smugglers, not because he had confidence in them but because Alem had to travel with a group of refugees for his future wife's sake, to guarantee her protection. They also believed it would be much safer than getting lost or harmed on their own.

Alem started to compose a letter to thank him:

'I received the money you sent me, and I am sending you only a paper in return. I know that you will understand its worth. I hope you will profit from it. I care for you as you do for me. People say we are all human beings even before our parents give us individual names, before we speak their languages, study their cultures and hold on to their teachings. But with all those different identities there comes a cost when just being human is not enough to fall in love and care for each other. Among countless differences only our common humanity is valuable and a reason to survive. Throughout the universe the spirit and soul of a man has worth. Above all the beauty of nature, human life is the most precious. So keep yourself from dangerous and destructive activities. When you are about to commit something wrong think about the shame you will bring to the essence of humanity. Respect life. Live as if one day you are going to miss all of those things around you. The best battle ever worth fighting for is against your negative desires; the best victory ever is overcoming your bad thoughts. Our happiness lies with this, within ourselves!

I am writing this without a desk in a chaotic town somewhere in Libya. So, 'see you' in another letter until we meet again somewhere in Europe.'

In England Arron was reading another of Alem's letters. It was highly decorated in the traditional illustrative style of Abyssinian drawing called *Hareg.* He smiled. Arron's smile was like a sunrise. At least Charlotte told him so. His bedroom was full of papers filled with lots of memories. He enjoyed rereading Alem's letters. He thought they had power over him. They encouraged him, kept him happy and inspired. He passed the traditional greeting paragraph and continued reading the rest aloud. *It helps me get closer to his mind*, he thought.

> '*Don't be hard on yourself. Get tired when you have to, be a child when you have to, sleep when you have to if it doesn't cost you, and it definitely will profit you. We are renewed and reborn every day, that's why we sleep. That's why we learn, that's why we fall in love every day. That's why we hope, that's why we live. We think that when we get tired or older we are going forward to our death but the way we get older makes our destiny – the next eternal life that nobody has ever seen but hopes for. Don't worry as we are in the process of strengthening our future. Being born, growing up, dying, with all those steps you grow more powerful if you value and believe in yourself. Don't be afraid of being watched – we are all being watched by everyone. You might have heard people saying we don't live longer than our possessions, but our name is eternal. Don't be afraid of changes, some changes are like being reborn. Every time you are reborn there is a new world waiting for you. Whenever you die, hope there's a new eternal life waiting for you. Think as if you have fulfilled the requirement of your graduation to the next level – to be an eternal being...*'

He read it again and again, summoning Alem as if he hears him singing these words with his golden voice. It's been a long time since Arron heard Alem's voice on the phone. He didn't even know where he could be. He is aware that he's a refugee, but where? Everywhere should be a home for refugees, yet nowhere is home for refugees. From one fire to the other, they keep going until they can rest somewhere in peace. That's what everyone does anyway. It's what it is but, *what might happen to him?* He knows it's not going to be easy. He has been there, he has been sold from smuggler to smuggler, and he has been hungry and thirsty almost to the point of dying. Yet, what matters was that at the end he survived. *Would it be the same for everyone? No. Would it be the same for*

Alem? Would it be better for his friend or would it be worse? God knows. He prayed for his friend's safety.

Chapter
FOURTEEN

At the Libyan border...

They were still in the middle of chaos; it's been their routine all along so it's just a normal day, but windy. Sand was flying all over their faces. The refugees are exhausted. Their legs are aching, their stomachs are empty and their mouths half dried. They slowly follow each other's footsteps. There is no clear way they are aware of, yet every direction can be a way, a way to nowhere. They've lost their planned route already.

"Oh..."

"Who says ohh?"

"No one says ohh..."

"Just say it."

"Oh..."

"I love my life."

"Are you kidding me?"

"Seriously"

"Yeah"

"You have an adventurous spirit, you can walk to the end of the world."

"Then you can call me Christopher Columbus."

They have to live in the desert in order to seek a life beyond this barren land. Gech was telling them his battlefield story. Slowly and precisely he talks, with silences between every word.

"I'll say people never liked war, but they still fight."

"I'm not a soldier but I still don't understand why people think human beings can never avoid war."

"If leaders were fine, we could."

"You cannot blame gravity for falling in love."

"We made ourselves sin by saying we are sinners. How can we be saints, then?"

"Can we conclude that the propensity for war is part of the human character? No! That's only our conclusion based on recent experiences that we've had. The truth is we were created as angels. We can be saints too for our own sake!"

As he was weakening, he kept his silences longer until Alem took over from him. Alem was giving his motivational speech.

"At least, it's not always dark. The full moon is with us; the full sun in the daytime. At the end of the day, we have love, freedom and unity."

They kept on walking quietly...

Moussa was providing the latest weather news, teaching them facts.

"Today is going to be windy all day; it's not going to be a good crossing over the Mediterranean Sea. I heard that sixty two people drowned yesterday."

"Stop being a nightmare, Moussa," they all shouted at him.

"It's not me, it's the news."

All bent down in silence while another screaming wind took control in the other direction, pushing them forward, more like casting them deep into the hell of the desert.

They kept on walking...

All the girls were trying to cheer them on by proposing clever strategies for their journey. Here they were a family in a foreign land, all seeking to claim their freedom.

The squad now seemed set to cross the largest desert in the world, the Sahara Desert. Everybody appeared to be silently praying, contemplating what they might face in this massive barren expanse.

There was a brooding silence until Moussa broke it for a moment.

"Which country is your dream land?"

"I don't have any," Paulos Amon replied.

"Well, I have. Everybody has somewhere he dreams of living."

"Not in a dream land. I hate dreams."

"Why?"

"Maybe it's because I have never had a good dream in my life."

"I have."

"Where?"

"Nowhere land." They laughed at his accent.

"Nowhere land, aha"

"Whatever. You laugh but some people say it's a cool place."

"My dream is Holland, it ... don't ask me why, but it's Holy and land."

"Germany – welcomes people."

"France – a country of love."

"Italy – Pizza."

"If I end up in Portugal – I will be a brilliant footballer too." Moussa adds.

"England, I don't know why but I like the union flag, mate. Nice crosses."

"And the Queen and the royal staff. It just reminds me of the good old golden days of Africa before Mr Coloniser came." They all pass on a laugh as if to say, 'You've never been there, bro'.

Nobody knows that Alem is a prince from the house of Solomon the Wise and Queen Saba. Who knows that he cares nothing for it, even that he's cursed for it? Who knows what is awaiting him? Who cares about him anyway? Nobody knew that he had failed in his fight against the corrupt government that keeps killing his family, friends and all. He learned that protesting wouldn't change a bit of it. He abhorred their way of iron fighting. He wished that he was a soldier, so he could have fought and died like a man at least, but he was a priest and a writer. He changed nothing. It made him believe that he had wasted his time hiding, studying, fighting with a pen, playing with words and ideas: for nothing but for this life. With no destination he could think of. He's jealous of the others who at least they seem to know their destiny.

"*I will not stop till I get to Las Vegas!*" claimed Moussa, trying to break the silence again.

"*Why?*" he got a reply after waiting a while.

"*I promised my ex-girlfriend I'd send her a picture of me with MJ, 2pac, Nipsey Hussle.*"

"*How about King, Malcolm and Jesus, hahaha?*"

"*I was joking.*" They all laughed.

"*They're dead, bro.*"

"*No.*"

"*Dead.*"

"*No.*"

"*They all died.*"

"*But I've seen them on the telly, and heard that their death was just a conspiracy thing.*"

"*Dead!*"

" *No, alive.*"

"*Dead.*"

"*No.*"

"*You saw the recordings, brov*"

"I saw it on the news, people saw them alive."

"Ghosts."

"Dead."

"No they aren't."

"Yes, they are."

"No."

"Yes."

As usual, a silly argument began. Alem thought for a moment that he was going to miss all this, once everything's passed. That's how they killed their miserable time, arguing foolishly; acting silly was so much more fun for them than holding guns like some of their friends were doing back home. At least it was clean fun. They were the same souls with the same principles.

"How about you, Alem?"

"What?"

"Which is your dream land? If you have one."

"My country is, at least was... I have no dream land other than seeing my own country returned to its previous glory and dignity. I'd love to see a United States of Africa."

"That's impossible to see."

"It's a dream anyway."

"It's not realistic, though."

"It was real for Africa back when the rest of the world wasn't even populated with a civilised society yet."

"Now it's just a memory that we can see buried under the giant lion symbol of African greatness, mistaken by western imagination as the thing called – sphinx? What is a sphinx?"

"That is all nonsense."

"Yeah, dreams are not real, mate."

"Dreams are not always unreal either."

"Just a memory that's already past."

"Memories are not always the past, bro. They form our internal reality. It's all within our heart. It is all stored in our DNA. We can still build pyramids, we can still calculate the age of the universe using only our mind. We can give life or the human species to the other planets without being hostile to our universe. We have an enduring heart, a heart that links our minds and our hands together. It's one of the thousands of invisible senses we have." Pointing at his heart, *"It may be more real than what we see and feel with our corrupted five senses, those we know and usually depend on."*

"If you say so," Emu replied with a long sigh.

"How about you Emu?"

She always preferred to keep silent to giving a wrong answer. She knew that she had no idea where she was going. She was just following her heart, Alem. Maybe it's there, where the earth and the sky embrace each other. There, two lovers could kiss freely in a peaceful park and look at each other without worrying about barriers, like the earth and the sky – two lovers, forever. They seem far away from us, of course, *why are they so far from us? Maybe they are shy* she thinks, or *they fear people.* The closer she was to them, the further their kisses were from her. Her dream was be there, where the earth and the sky fall in love and marry forever, each day and night giving birth to the sun, to the stars and the moon.

She stared at Alem the way his mother stared at him when he said her farewell. Again a grave-like silence fell over the band until the girls started chatting about relationships. It was mainly about Emu and Alem. They all agreed that it was better to be a couple in this hard time, helping each other, weeping on each other's shoulders, shouting at and teasing each other. They also exchanged cultures, and new words in different languages.

Then she said, "*England.*" She knew Alem liked England. He had told her "*England is green.*" He worried that it was going to be a long way off. If they couldn't settle somewhere before, there will be a long troubled path waiting for them ahead.

Moussa is always at his side.

"*Don't worry, we will make it to a safer place, okay. We will find somewhere safe to settle, eventually.*" He comforted him by starting to sing a popular song. East African young people have lots of things in common, especially songs. They all know Teddy Afro and Aster Awoke's music. They can sing them, even if they don't understand the language.

> '*Abro menorun legna kalalelin,*
> *Eski enfetnew degmo teleyayten...*
> *Sdetnetie, yshalegnal, sdetnetie*'

They knew each other's special interests and if they had a question, they knew the answer would come from one of them.

"*I don't want to lose you guys!*" Moussa bent down his head.

"*Don't worry if you feel that we are like one cell in our universe, but remember there are lots of different directions within it. The direction you choose leads you in to a different destination in a unique world. It doesn't mean we are parted from each other. We are always next to each other.*"

"*But our reality is so bitter.*"

"*It's not only ours. Suffering is the story of mankind, we are not alone. There is also someone out there who cares for us, who tries to help us. The fight is not only ours; it's the fight of mankind even if we are in front of the battle. The universe that displays the divine truth of love and togetherness is on our side.*" When he started to make such an encouraging speech, everybody focused on his words.

"*Tell us more about this unique universe.*"

"*There is a universe where only a star and a moon live in the emptiness of an infinitely wide cosmos; only the moon and the star are pink. The sky is green. You don't have to breathe, drink and eat there to survive because love provides everything. Once you stop loving, you die. There is no earthly law as such because the word love guides everything. I hope that will be my place after I die. The problem is I will be with the star and Emu with the moon – so that we will never meet. But we will look at each other forever until the moon and stars meet across a bridge that will be built by ourselves and our children after the trials and tribulations of billions of years. That's love as strong as the colour of green light, red and pink, as beautiful as nature!"*

"This one is a sad story." Moussa bends his head down again.

"You are like an astrologist... oh... you know everything, mate."

"Where did you study all that?"

"There is only one source of ultimate knowledge that we all have in our nature and it's called 'just being human.' The difference is that we perceive it in different ways, we sense it differently. Most of us rely on our limited experience, by ignoring the divine findings of our forefathers. We deny millions of sensors in our consciousness and say 'I won't believe unless I can see on my own eyes. That which I cannot hear, is not real at all...' If you have an open heart, knowledge keeps knocking at your door at any time. Some sense it through Art, others through Science, some through dreams and so on."

"I don't understand."

"If you are ready for it, just one deep breath can change your perception."

"What do you mean?"

"Think that you are not alone; think about your connections in this cosmos that you already know, and beyond. You will feel the energy of everything that is in you; you have all the energy that the cosmos has: its power, energy, wisdom, health, wealth, healing, knowledge and so on."

"How could I have it?"

"Pray for it. Believe in it. We are as one, as you can observe. We breathe the same air, we enjoy the same sun and moonlight, and we walk the same road all the time. We are joined by the same wires, the same chemical

molecules and biological cells. We share the divine thoughts of our cosmos together with others throughout infinity!"

"I've no idea what you mean."

"Think about it; use your brain to discover the limitlessness of being human. The human brain is bigger than the size of a skull. It consists of a unique cosmic system that no one has ever seen. Every cell of our body has a unique cosmic system of operation to function. We are infinite!"

"I am surprised!"

"There is no magic in it, it's all natural! There is only one magic – the creation of the first energy. Everything is a multiplication and manifestation of that source. Everybody can do amazing things if he or she understands and is able to make the connection to that energy that governs the whole being. Do you know in our Abushaker[12] calendar, one day in God's universe is one thousand years in the human calendar? When I was a kid, my grandfather told me God promised Adam to save him after five and half days, but Adam had to wait five thousand five hundred years to witness the saviour – Jesus! Well, I'm just saying."

"God always comes to earth disguising himself in human flesh."

"I don't believe there is god!"

"Maybe a force that I don't mind calling 'God'."

"Fair enough."

They all tend to agree. Sometimes they think he is manifested as Buddha, full of wisdom, or the incarnation of Jesus Christ, a human god, who died for love of humanity.

"And that force includes all of us, as a network within the infinite cosmos. The universe is both complete and under creation, and we know that it's still growing."

"I think God's plan is to continue developing it, and stop every motion when it's perfect, like 'heaven'."

---

12 An ancient Abyssinian calendar based on orthodox religion.

They look reflective, like serious scholars debating abstract discourses to help themselves to pass this time of uncertainty.

The flowers in the desert...

They walked a long way through the beautiful moonlight, joking and discussing with each other to ease their fatigue.

"*Oh!...*" they shouted in unison again while they kept on walking.

"*Who is saying 'oh..'?*"

"*No one said 'oh...'*"

"*Oh....*"

The desert was still a desert, with no end. They'd travelled miles through the mountains of sand until they resemble the colour of the sand themselves. It's getting hotter. Their expression of tiredness only makes them more tired but also relieved from their sore joints. But, to hasten their journey, they made it a rule not to repeat that expression.

"*Who said 'oh!' earlier?*" asked Moussa.

"*No one said 'oh...*"

"*Someone said 'oh...;*" they all shared in their tiredness and decided to take a rest. They sat between the sandy mountain chains which was the coolest place.

"*Come here.*" Emu-Hiba hid herself in Alem's shadow.

He covered her from the beating sand blowing in all directions.

She was thinking that she was really lucky that after her long and tedious life of suffering, she had a new reality – Alem. She thought it must be very rare in one's lifetime to come across one's own soul mate and Alem also felt lucky in return. At last he had begun to feel the same way as someone else, to share a common vision of what life could be.

He stared into her pupils not only to make sure of her feelings but to find his infinite happiness. Then he looked intently to explore inside her deepest thoughts. He wanted to find himself there, looking for a space in her heart and wondering where her soul could be. She didn't ask him anything, but just let him catch her soul as if she were casting a spell on him.

They explored each other's internal as well as external territories. She couldn't resist. First he tickled her until her laugh started to go deep into her throat and as he hid his fingers in her armpit she began to moan, and her lips went red, thirsty and hungry for his kisses.

"I know your weakness."

"Yeh, you … always discover… my weakness." The words went from her mouth directly to his; a perfect unison, a single heartbeat. It was a romantic symphony that no one had ever composed before. He felt no one had ever tasted lips as they did; experienced such perfect first kisses.

"Tell me what my weakness is … tell me …" she whispered and struggled with tears and caresses. It was either the beginning or the end of her world; she wasn't sure.

He tasted her tears, the fruits of joy or … he felt love more than anybody had felt before. They discovered the magic of a first kiss. They taught each other what it means to be together in unison of breath and in their souls. It felt life could be so good despite their desperate situation, or maybe it was this strange wandering life which heightened their emotions in this uncertain time.

"Kissing your lips, any man could die."

"Have you died?"

"Not yet."

"Don't kiss me again then, I want you to live longer with me."

"But I want…"

"Then don't stop kissing me."

Chapter
FIFTEEN

Libya – the screaming wind

Almost dying of the stifling heat, they kept walking through the deadly desert.

The howling wind kept screaming and changing direction; pulling them backwards this time, as if to say *'please stay away of danger ahead.'*

"Ouch!"

"Alright?"

"Yeah, I'm fine."

"We should wait until it dies down."

"Keep moving."

"Ouch!"

The wild wind wins and they can't move farther. The desert is the queen; it has power over them all. Nothingness reigned. The wind wore the crown and silent chaos sat on the throne. The scorching sun is staring down; making sure that it's hot enough to be a deadly desert. It seems as though the whole world is empty and all the troubles are here. There's nothing but sand and wind. Nothing is happening in this arid desert, but suddenly something could happen. Someone might die, be born or killed or ... dry up to nothingness.

When the wind comes from the opposite direction, they think it will take them back 'home' and drop them in some battlefield littered with corpses. But it only stops their progress for the moment, covering them with dust.

"It's a fight between the wind and the earth, the sands standing guard, trying to protect their mother earth from the anger of the wind."

"At least nobody loses."

"I think it's only a fight between two opposing winds. This kind of wind is supernatural. Some call it the harmattan." She gives him a scientific explanation.

"Devils. See, how much sand is displaced from their beloved ones."

"Who cares about sand? It remains sand wherever it is displaced."

"Place matters for life."

They waited, enduring all this. Time was the only hope they had. Time is king. They realised that in the evening when the sun sets all this chaos of nature will return to calm, the sand will settle, so they can move faster. The weather switched from the hotter to the colder temperature of the desert. It's better as at least they could breathe fresh air without sand stuck in their mouths and noses. When the wind calms the beauty of the desert is exotic, unlike its daytime character. Regardless of its hostility, anyone would say: *'There's no such beautiful place anywhere on the planet.'* To Alem, the smoothness of the dunes resembles the bodies of beautiful women lying side by side. Who knows what those curves are? Who knows what this means? Earth looks like young women eager for love softly rising and falling. Who knows what's in them? Who knows what was happening when the wind was screaming and roaring? Those hot muscular bodies hugging each other make it seem as if the whole desert is in love with nature now. There is no more peaceful place than this, at least for the moment. He imagines a silent death, quietly, without action. He can see the high-bridged nose of Cleopatra, the curved neck of the Queen of Sheba, the curved shapes of their bodies, hair blowing in the wind. All the while Alem and Emu cling together at night, embracing each other against the backdrop of this sensual landscape.

Their band is proud of surviving the night and of being part of this natural beauty. Even if they don't have time to stand and appreciate nature, they feel part of it, blended into the landscape whether they like it or not.

They are still in a barren land that leads only to more endless sandy desert.

"It's only you and I," she says as she forgets everybody around her.

"Can't you see the others?"

"I can see only you." She jokes like one who is drunk with love. She feels she's part of an epic story, her love is as intense as the surrounding heat, and she thinks only of him.

"You are crazy," he says, placing his head on her neck, her long, brown hair covering his head. That's what covers him from the troubles of the world; that's what makes him forget every problem that may be facing them. Here, with no habitation and harsh temperatures, the world seems empty and hostile.

Keeping walking

With such unpredictable hot and cold weather of the desert, they travel more miles than in their previous travel, until they get exhausted again. The desert is now flat and you can see very far ahead, nothing but a flat and endless desert. They don't know of places nearby to rest.

"How long can we walk?"

They've finished all their food. They have nearly finished their water. They must keep walking until they can get more. Without food they managed to keep travelling. At least no one is pointing guns at them for now. It's like a no man's land. Safer? No one's tied them up laughing and staring at them. No one is pinching their manhood with a needle or a heavy bottle hanging on it just for fun. They've escaped all of that. But this is not a place of living things at all and silence is their story. Keeping walking is what they do. All their stories are with their silence and all their futures are determined by their footsteps.

Then sometimes they met other small groups of people in a tent they had made in the middle of nowhere. They felt happy that they could find at least some water with them although it was mixed with petroleum. They would need it when they'd finish all their water anyway. They shared everything. They shared their stories about getting robbed by war gangs; beaten by their own friends employed by detainee Libyan militias; raped by war gangs. They were auctioned, leased and sold as slaves in the squares, car parks, slave markets and farmlands in Sabha and Gharyan (60 miles south of Tripoli) where a lot of refugees were held hostage. Somehow they'd managed to escape and tried again just to trust their luck to the trap of the deadly desert again.

"Our smuggler ditched us here again. Because we were too many, the tyres of his car sank in the sand so he ordered us to push his car. Then we knew we were dead again."

"When we three were ordered to get down and push, it helped move the tyres but then it drove off without us."

"Like ninety miles per hour, mate."

"Leaving all three of us here."

"We ran and ran but it was gone."

"Far from us."

"We tried to hang on first of course…"

"But, the other ones beat our faces."

"Beat our hands."

"And left us here to die."

"Here we are waiting for nothing but a miracle."

"Here you are our relief." Alem and all his crew showed compassion and gave them a little fresh water.

"You can join us," proposed Moussa to help them.

"*We have no more money, so we are going to the Tunisian border, to find the UN to help us.*"

"*We are in the same situation, so we can help each other.*"

"*You can join us if you trust us.*"

"*Not really, but what choice do we have? Let's get somewhere before we die.*" General Gech approves. South Libya is too hostile for them to keep up walking as fast as before. Everyone is tired and sleepy, so they decide to have a rest for a while. They lie all over the place, praying they will get a bit of sleeping time and wake up safe and refreshed to continue walking more miles until they can get help from a UN refugee camp.

Chapter
SIXTEEN

Enderbury, the rhythm of the club...

Charlotte is not too shy to follow him without him noticing. For his safety, she follows him into the club to spy on him and to check that he will be ok. She wishes he would get drunk so that she can take care of him as she used to. She remembers the first and last time she has been to clubs with him. It was the same club that they are in now, she remembers. He too thinks of her while he is dancing with his friends. He wishes she were here now. He has missed dancing with her, but not today. He needs more time away from her, even if he misses her.

She had been the first girl to introduce him to lots of clubs and it had been her first time as well he remembers. She had been waiting for her eighteenth birthday to join the group of regular clubbers and she took Arron along. Now, it's months ago since they had been to the club.

Friends' tales

They were sitting drinking and smoking in the smoking area of the club. Next to them they could see a group of mature men and women celebrating. They were all dressed up and seemed to control the atmosphere with their drunken laughter.

"Aaa... Mothers' Day."

"My mother's day is made anytime she sees me around her" his friend Lucas said. *"I don't have any real family feeling. I've a father and an older brother but they have been so hard on me. Sixty percent of the men I have met have been bad to me; that's how I understand and feel what 'father' means."*

"I haven't had a mother, since I was born." Their silence seemed louder than the rhythm of the music and the drunken noises of the smoking room.

"But, ninety percent of the women I have met have been so nice to me. That's how I feel what 'mothers' are" added Lucas squeezing his finished cigarette and trying not to remember what his step father did to him.

George, another friend joined in. *"Mother's day reminds me of only my grand mom."*

"My granny is especially important to me too. In fact, she is everything to me."

"Grandmothers are twice a mother," adds Arron.

"Welcome to my story." John mourns, remembering his granny.

"Anything can happen in life, but mothers are miracles." They puff their cigarettes in unison.

"If all the girls could be like a mother and a father to their boys, the world could be like heaven."

"If all men could be like a father and a brother to their girls, this world could be like heaven."

"Why can't fathers be like mothers?" Lucas complains.

"Hey get a life mate. Not everyone's the same."

"All the same, I feel helpless and lonely here."

"We look out for each other."

"That's the point," John confirms.

"And you have a family."

"Yeah a foster family." John sighs as he reveals dozens of secrets he has never told anybody before; he had introduced Arron to his foster mother as if she was his biological mother.

"So, she isn't your mother."

"It's nothing new, almost all of our friends in the college live with foster parents."

"To be honest it is not bad, it's like having more than two parents, if you can see its positive side, if you know what I mean," adds John. They all laugh except Arron. To be fair John's foster mother is more motherly than many mothers in the UK. The first time Arron met her she asked him if he smoked, drank or gambled. He replied 'no' to all her inquisitive questions. Although he was lying, he appreciated her care for him and his friend. Since then she's believed in him and given her permission any time John wanted to hang out with Arron. She knows Arron is John's only close friend who helps him to mix in with the others at college.

"Hey you've got lots of Asian friends."

"Yeah sure. They are great, mate." Thinking what to say about his Japanese friend Miyuki, he added, *"they are so friendly to get on with, I mean they never pretend. Their hearts seem pure and warm"* That's all he could say about them.

"Well it seems to me that it's hard to know and understand them."

"You think so?"

"How about me?" asked John, a little jealous.

"You know you are the only true friend I have in the college and vice-versa." They smiled at each other.

Realising they are all boys dancing in a circle, the girls in the club see them as a threat. But then a club- crawling girl pops up in the centre of their circle. His friend John loves dancing and sex more than anybody, but only with his fiancée Diane. Arron joked, *"John's death will be between Diane's legs."*

*"I am already dead, mother f*r."* It was funny the way he swore. 'Posh swearing,' Arron called it. But, Diane has been in and out his life since the beginning of their relationship.

"Enough talking, let's dance with the club ladies." John pushes Arron and they get onto the crowded dance floor. Accidentally, Charlotte sees him

just as he saw her, but they pretend that they haven't seen each other. Grabbing a stranger and starting to dance, she pretends that she is dancing with another guy she knows. Arron is confused but pretends as if he hasn't noticed. He leaves the club without saying goodbye to everyone. Outside the club, her father is waiting inside his car. Arron sees him, but he hides and walks away to the bus stop.

Downtown at the bus stop, there's a man speaking nonstop nonsense, loudly. He's smoking cannabis in public. Arron can't believe this, but he hears swear words flooding from his mouth with the familiar odour as he takes in the drug. 'Why in public, why doesn't he keep to his own space' Arron thinks. The man is mad, and allowed to be wild. No one cares for him. Everyone shies away from him. Everyone looks down on him. He could be a father, a husband... No one pays any attention to what he's asking for or what he's doing or what he's saying. Arron tries to listen to him, but his English is hard for him to understand. Had this been back home, Arron would have tried to listen and help him. Something about the man reminded him of home, of a crazed man who lived in his town, who spoke whatever came into his mind.

"Smon" He remembers his crazed old friend's name.

Arron recalls Smon talking loudly as he looks at this demented person in front of him.

"Four plus four is forty five... who knows... the possibility and probability of... this and... that... Who cooks BBQ at a burning winter... freezing wind... in the mid of the night. I smell snow man's nose... marshmallow... it's me burning... It's I. Leave me alone. You never understand what I'm saying; maybe it means nothing to you. But... three...seven... twelve... It means something to everyone. It's all about humanity, having one language...beautiful! If life is not being human, believe me or get drunk, there is no purpose for living. If you waste your day with toils just only to get high and forget every night. Life and time are infinite... another night will come and go... Humanity is a shit of love. Being human is... is... loving all this shit! It's our identity. Our identity is...shit without shits. If love dies, we die with our shit... No names... no interesting stories. If we do not have stories... we don't exist at all. Hate is a shit of failure in

loving... living in your families tomb like me until you wake up when the time past... thirty... three years old... but... relax... the eight thousand years monster will get baptised soon anyway... get me outa'here!" Arron remembered what Smon had said without forgetting a single word.

Smon was a decent man, but turned mental after he lost his only son who had been shot by the government in a mob uprising. He couldn't believe the fact that his son was dead. He disappeared after the burial without anyone noticing. Nobody saw him go, or again until a couple of weeks after his son was buried he instinctively shouted out from inside the family tomb. He had been with his son's body crying silently, without any food and water. Since then, he's lived permanently at the cemetery next to his son. *He has lost himself to the devil* people used to say. He is fierce to everyone, except Arron. He hated wearing clothes until Arron forced him to wear trousers at least. He used to see Arron as his son. Arron used to bring him food every time he went to the church, which was next to the cemetery. Now, Arron misses Smon, his buddy in his lonely childhood. He used to call him 'My friend Doctor Arron'.

Chapter
SEVENTEEN

In the morning

"Bang Bang Bang-bang…"

The gunfire up to the sky freaks them out like in a nightmare.

"I'm a lion!" Gech unconsciously shouts as usual.

"Where are we?" Moussa shouts out.

They find none of the strangers.

"They are gone."

"Where?"

They try to find them, looking around, thinking they could be shot already. They look for their bodies until they see them coming back towards them, caught by a well-armed military gang.

"Fools!!!" shouted Gech.

The three of them had taken all the water for themselves.

"They are coming for us."

"They said it's safe to stay here while they go to the Tunisian border to look for a UN refugee camp."

"And they bring back an army trying to trade us for what?"

"Don't panic."

"They are just fools."

There are about four hundred heavily armed gangsters coming face to face with a band of forty refugees weakened by hunger, thirst, a long journey and post traumatic issues.

"Let's run away!"

"Don't even twitch!" They all aim their guns at the refugees.

It is too late. They are encircling them at every corner and Alem's group have realised that the desert is not for runners but for fighters; not for legs but for wings. They wish they could fly away or be swallowed up by the ground or blown along with the sand, rather than confront such intimidating machine guns. They make a tiny circle, calming each other until the gunners separate them into two groups.

"Keep it down. We just want you to join our dream!" One of the soldiers looks down and laughs at them. They separate the boys and girls first. They take the boys into a container on the back of a lorry, so they can't see where they are taking them to. Inside, the boys are together in darkness.

The girls are inside another truck. Rahel is crying and Emu is shouting out for help, but she only receives mocking laughter back.

After a long time sobbing, Rahel faints. The gunners take her out of the container and leave her in the middle of nowhere; there was no excuse. Emu is going mad inside that infernal truck unable to help Rahel or herself. It is not going to be easy for her.

"Rahel! Alem! Moussa!... please, let me go! Where is everyone?"

"Would you calm down?" a gang member standing on the corner of the truck shouts back at her.

"I cannot. Why is this happening?"

Someone hit her in the teeth with his gun, forcing her to fall back.

Usually smugglers sell them to groups, just ordinary gangs who use people's lives to get money from their families. This group is different, they are well armed, more like an army and they have a name and a black and white flag. It says EDASH/ISIS written in Arabic.

As she becomes conscious again, she shouts again.

"You'd better keep quiet, that's what's best for you right now," a girl next to her whispers.

"Who are they? What do they want? If they want money, I can give them whatever they want. Just leave him alone, they can take and use me if that's what they want."

"They don't want you the way they want them."

"Why him? Why not me?"

"Think of escaping, nothing else," she keeps whispering again, more like praying this time.

Life is precious, yet very cheap. They have been used to the suffering while together but they will miss even this from now on. Now, they have to face things by themselves. It's personal now; the curse of their unavoidable national heritage it seems.

In Libya the local cruel militants and bandits have more control than ever before. Especially the cities and town shelters are getting extremely dangerous. The countryside shows you the good side of a country's people; cities show you the negative side these days; the chaos. Those fighting for freedom wanted to put an end to the years of anarchy which began it all. People are fleeing outside the occupied cities of Libya, escaping from the bombing of this war torn country. People rescued from militant terrorist groups and refugees have no idea what is going on here; they are simply the victims of the chaos.

After a long ride to the north of the desert, the truck carrying all the girls and children arrived at a temporary terrorist camp. Not so long ago, gun shots again broke up the silence of the desert but when the evening came air strikes targeted the war zone and this particular ISIS group lost the battle; the helicopters went back to the North East. A group of foot soldiers broke into the prison and freed the prisoners. In a small cell, there are over a hundred people; only women, children and disabled prisoners are left. Emu is there; she notices they speak East African and Arabic languages and they are all wearing different uniforms. They are a group of Egyptian, South Sudanese and Ethiopian humanitarian volunteers.

"Take all the women and children first, before they come back again."

"Move! Move! …"

"Where is my Dad?" A young boy hugs and holds the child.

"Daddy will come for you later." Colonel Bekele comforts the child, holding him in his free arm.

One of them strides towards Emu.

"You too mam."

"I am not moving anywhere until I see my husband come back!"

"You must save yourself for now." He forcibly grabs her, but she is stronger than him. They struggle and fight until she finally loses her resistance and is taken by them just before another ISIS attack. There's fighting and shooting; the firing continues until they are stopped by another air strike. The helicopter displays an Egyptian flag and is an immediate response to the beheadings of twenty one Egyptian Coptic Christians by this ISIS camp. The resistance in Libya were expecting this as soon as the video of the beheadings was released. So, they had planned to use this chance to save as many surviving prisoners as possible, at least the women and children. Emu sees volunteer soldiers dying and risking their lives to save prisoners they don't even know. She returns to her senses. She remembers that she was a soldier once. She stares at a gun lying on the floor between two dead ISIS bodies. She must pick it up. She is witnessing the horror of real war for the first time. She has never been in a real battlefield like this before. Although she was once a soldier she gave it up because she hated it, she hated killing instead of saving life; but now she has no choice. She holds the gun; it seems heavier than any gun she's carried and trained with before.

The air strikes stopped the terrorists from entering the prison and so all the prisoners escape, arming themselves and voluntarily joining the resistance fighters on the other side. Emu shields herself with the bodies and starts using the skills she's been trained in. She shoots a man and is not afraid this time. She can see and identify anyone from afar. She never misses. She kills two, three, four... and more enemies. She feels nothing at this moment; Alem is the only one on her mind. It's not going to be enough for her. She keeps firing at the last ISIS man's body. The leader of the resistance group, Colonel Bekele is waiting for her to stop. His eyes are filled with tears for her, stopping her from firing at the dead body. He hugs her as she cries uncontrollably on his chest, the way she used to with her father and Alem.

A long silent sleepless night has passed. She has buried her head under her knees throughout the night. She reminds him of his sister, mother and wife who've lost their lives for no reason. Not only is she a woman, but also a brave woman just like his mother and wife. He thanks her for helping him to save more lives in the fighting. Eighty one refugees have been saved. Today, he felt fortunate to have saved more prisoners than on the other days. He comes close to her.

"May I?" He sits next to her without waiting for her to respond. "What's your name?"

"Does it matter?"

"Not really; but in case I need to call you, how can I?"

"Emu."

"Okay Emu."

"You were a soldier, am I right?"

"Does it matter?"

"Not at all. Well, I was an Ethiopian soldier who came to help Rwanda. I came knowing I would have no reward - since I am not from the group that governs the country- but then I left the army. When I returned, I found out all my family had lost their homes even in my own country. So I thought if I had protected my family first I might have done something to help."

"Well, are you telling me you are proud of deserting your country?" There's a silence.

"Ehm, I guess you're right. But, I am here in search of my relatives too."

"Whatever., Thank you for saving me."

He realises that she is in pain thinking of someone, just as he has been feeling since he lost the most important people in his life, his family. Now the only meaning to his life is in saving others; by doing so at least he can save someone else's family at least.

"Everything will be alright, Emu. Everything will be okay. I'll leave you alone." He put his hands on her shoulder and smiles. She smiles back miserably.

It's his birthday, but Alem's in jail where innocent people are waiting for the justice of unjust gangs. He's begun to be scared of their version of sharia law too. He wonders where Emu and Rahel might be. He doesn't even know where he is anyway. He's praying for her. He knows she's praying too.

"Moussa, I do not care about myself."

"I know what you mean."

"Emu, I had promised Aba Tso…" he tries to cry, yet he cannot.

"We tried to make our fellow travellers safe. We'll be okay. I hope we'll join them again." Moussa prays. He is sure that the soldiers who captured them are not Libyan. The Libyan uniform is being used by some other terrorist group. He didn't suspect ISIS but he fears that too as he can identify their black and white flags.

"Do you think they will let us go?"

"I think so. Or maybe I just hope they will."

"Do you really think so, or is it just wishful thinking?"

"They want a ransom, they want money from us, but if they knew we are worthless, they wouldn't have any reason to keep us here." He just said it to comfort himself. They know nobody cares, nobody will pay their

ransom. They are not American, they are not European, they are not even Egyptian; they are lost boys from East Africa. Which government is going to pay for their lives? It's a joke that any government would pay to save them, but for them it's a matter of life and death. He's wondering what has happened to Emu; he's searching for a sign from her, but there's nothing. There are almost a hundred prisoners in one small room. He sees a family with a child. He stares at the child with his sleepy and exhausted eyes. He sees his own childhood reflected in the boy. He wishes he could escape like him, close his eyes and vanish into oblivion. Trying to adjust to his situation, he begins to rationalise his feelings by composing the boy's story.

'I am only four.

I've got a story to tell. My story.

Who said a child has no story?

Here it is.

I left my home, like everybody else.

Don't ask me why.

I don't know where I am. Who knows where he or she is anyway?

It's full of danger this barren land, full of doubts.

You have no idea at what time you're going to die, who knows when he or she going to die anyway?

That's life.

I thank God, because I am still with my family at least; my dad, my mom and my little sister.

My father's face is stranger than ever, not as he was before. It's so red and dried up but still with the flame and sweat over his face. By this I know some terrible things are happening.

My mother looks more worried than ever, nearly ....'

He saw her crying like a child.

"*Are you crying mama?*" said the kid staring at her tearful eyes.

"*No, have you seen me crying?*" She's trying to hide her pain, but it's too late.

He knows a mother must never show tears to her child.

Alem continues his story.

'*I saw her tears, although she tried to deny it, as if nothing was happening. No! It's because you can never accept that your mother is crying.*

You always see her fighting to manage.

You can't stay to watch your mother's tears.

But you have to do something – anything to make her happy again.

You plan to turn the world into somewhere with no tears.

You want to build a snowman and make your mother smile just a little in this desert, something magical to escape from the bloody reality of this awful place.

You dream of a safe and joyful home for your family at this moment,

You want to build a playground for your little sister

You want to hold a party in this prison for your friends and community

You want to turn this desert into a jungle.

But you can't perform even a single miracle, because the power is all on the side of the devils. Slave traders and colonisers are still alive hiding in this vast desert. Goliad is still laughing looking down at poor young David. David doesn't have any power left to pick up even a single stone.

The place is still a desert.

The prison cell is still a prison.

The masked men pointing giant guns around you are still there.

Your family is still crying,

But you and your father are not meant to cry.

Because you are a boy and he's a man, you are meant to burn inside.

But when your dad starts to cry,

That is the end of the world.

He was the only hope,

And you were the only hope

But now there is no hope...'

When the gunman took the kid from his family, Alem's eyes filled with tears knowing he will have more misery ahead. He cried in unison with the kid's farewell tears, accompanied by soft crying.

Darkness reigned. The prisoners cannot see the faces of their torturers but they can still hear them as they set a price on them.

"They are bony."

"They don't even have a kidney."

"Okay. Deal."

"Isolate every man and boy from their families!"

Next they select all the boys and transfer them into another truck. They're in complete darkness.

They are taken to nowhere. Alem suddenly misses Aba. He dreams about him, the father coming with life-giving water. Believers think him to be a saint, nonbelievers thinks he is at least a good magician. However, Aba won't turn up this time. Alem misses Aba Tso's golden, spiritual voice.

'Be courageous!' He remembers.

"I am jealous of your courage and love." Paulos breaks the silence in the darkness again.

"You have your own. Leave me alone and be jealous for yourself," Alem replies in defeat.

"It's not like that, she shouldn't love me anymore. I mean if she is still alive, obviously."

"*She does,*" Alem says encouragingly. "*Head up, never let anyone force your head down.*"

"*It's not that easy, she is special to me. You know why… last time she said 'oh…, if you were not here I should despair.' What does it mean? I don't think she could exist without me, bro. She is not used to it.*" He can't imagine himself without her next to him either. He felt that she must be dead now. He feels dead himself; he's not used to this.

"*She loves you well.*"

Emu wonders what is happening back on the other side of the desert where the boys have been taken. Her companions are wondering how to get out alive. A messenger arrives. He whispers to the leader.

"*They are near the other coast with prisoners.*"

"*Number?*"

"*About thirty five boys strangled by a whole brigade.*"

"*Ah… huh?*"

"*Yeah, a whole brigade.*"

"*We are outnumbered. We will stay until the sea is calmer.*"

"*We'd better hurry up in case they find us here.*"

"*Do you have any idea about the prisoners?*"

They talk silently making sure nobody can hear them.

"*Why don't you talk aloud!? They are our brothers, fathers and husbands,*" Emu shouts.

"*Calm down, nothing is happening to them, yet. We can't reach them, that's all.*"

She cries, silently.

"*I know what's happening, of course.*"

"They've just left with the prisoners," says a fourteen-year-old armed messenger.

"Quick, they will soon be back at their camp."

"Emu, you have to leave now."

"I am not leaving unless..."

"Listen to me just this once. I promise I'll make sure that nothing bad happens to your husband."

"How do you expect me to go without him?"

"Inshallah. Believe me, I will try to find him and send him after you. But now, you have to go and be safe for him. Okay? Please!" She doesn't know him but he's an angel; she doesn't even know his name. She doesn't ask his name but she will never forget him. He took all of them to a small Isuzu truck; a hundred or more people climbed up into the truck till it screamed fighting with the sand to let it move.

They are all stacked over one another, but they have comforted themselves by being sandwiched between each other. For Emu it's different. It's going to be a lonely journey. She's looking back already, looking back to her friends feeling neither here nor there. She feels numb, dead already. She wants to join the Colonel but he said no as her father had. He taught her love, peace, togetherness and forgiveness. She's learned that not all men are evil because of these two, but they are not here by her side now. They are like candles. *How many candles burning would be enough to lighten the darkness of man?* she thinks. A man killed her father, her freedom and peace. Although she had met the boys who could have been the hope of the bright future she was dreaming about, the hope of African dreams who could set the whole world free of ignorance, she didn't know how to get them back. How could she get her strength back? Nothing would cure her pain more than being a soldier now and finding Alem, taking revenge for the loss of innocent life. But again, Alem once told her *'Revenge is weakness and cowardly. Revenge is for thoughtless people. To seek revenge is to lose before the battle. Revenge is an instrument of the devil to further his job. You have to forgive. Winning is leaving everything aside only to give it time to cool.'* He resembles her father who raised her hating war and avoiding fighting. She loathed it again. She thanked the man who saved and sent her away from the chaos. Whatever his motive is, she'll remember his bravery forever and repay him one day.

Chapter
EIGHTEEN

Arron saves John again...

This time it was from attempting suicide. This is how it happened. The day before his birthday, he'd texted his ex-girlfriend Dian begging her to stay with him as he'd planned to spend his special day with her. Since they'd broken up nine months previously, she'd had three different boyfriends. John still loved her and she liked the way he was not giving up on her. Every time she broke up with him she felt lonely and since the previous month she'd kept coming to his house. He was hoping to bring her back into his life.

'Hey baby'

'Hey baldy!', she texts back.

'Hey, stop it.'

'Why have you called?'

'To let you know that tomoz is my birthday. Xx'

'HBD, lol.' That's it.

The next day - morning

He'd slept all the morning but phone calls finally woke him up. He'd got eighty birthday wishes from his Facebook friends. While he was reading them, he felt as if life was playing a sadistic trick on him.

'I hope you have a nice one.' Hopeless.

'Wish you a happy bd.' Which is only a wish.

'Mate, Happy birthday.' Which it is not.

175

He was planning a birthday party, but now he was going to spend his special day sleeping. Imagine. It's your birthday and the one and only person, the one you love most in the whole world didn't want to spend a second with you. That's how he felt when he woke up from his bed.

Messenger

'*Happy birthday John. Hope you have a good one.*'

'*Thx, at least I'll be able to sleep all day long.*'

'*Have a good day.*'

'*You've ruined it already, thx.*'

'*Why so sarcastic? You can make it better.*'

'*Sorry, you don't understand.*'

'*What's the point of saying 'you ruined it' then? Um, I'll stop myself from complaining cos it's your birthday today. Sorry for ruining your special day anyway. Have a great day. Bye.*'

He felt that being born was the worst gift that his mother had given him. He wanted to end it all – his life. He wanted to remember the old Dian. When she was at high school she was innocent. Now, she's grown up and she's seeing other boys, but John can't change. He's still a poor boy and he can't get her go out of his mind. He wanted to draw her with his smoke, but it kept forming clouds – making a dark thick figure like a dragon or some other kind of monster. *She's no different*, he thought. She was calling a deathly spirit down on him. He couldn't stop himself thinking of her. He had got engaged to her once hoping she would be with him for the rest of their lives. She was happy even if she was too young, but now she's not here anymore. She's left him broken again. He hadn't realised how much space she had been occupying in his brain. Every time she left him alone like this, he was as empty as a vacuum. All he could think about was memories of her. When he tried to forget his past he saw her with another man, a man who could be one hundred per cent better than him. Then he tended to let it fester and burn away throughout the day. Trying to forget her, he slept all day until the evening. Imagining the next day, he dreamt of her having multiple weddings with different boys even to one of the boys who had bullied him since elementary school. Even if he's his friend now, dreaming of him with his ex-girlfriend burned him with jealousy. Trying to get her out of this nightmare he stopped dreaming. He stopped sleeping. She controlled his past, present and future. Forgetting her would be equal to forgetting himself. He felt that without her he would have no history, life or hope. He stopped writing; he was trying not to write about her, he hated writing. He was angry at himself.

"Damn me!!!"

He was on the second bottle of Jack Daniels with his Winston cigarettes, but he could not get drunk enough to forget his troubles. The more he drank and smoked, the more he burned away inside. At least he had the courage to end it all. He thought that death would be much simpler than living. Living is harder than dying.

Message from Arron

'xoxoxo. Yo, brov. I wanna see you in my house, hurry up!'

'Why? I am sleepy.'

'I want to drink. I am so fucked up. So stressed.'

'Welcome to my life.'

John could not say no to Arron. He could not forget what he had done for him the previous time. He had brought purpose into his life again. That's the meaning of friendship he thought. So, he obeyed Arron and went to his house. When he entered all of their friends where there with a surprise birthday party singing *Happy Birthday,*

He blew out all the candles on his birthday cake in one go even before they'd finished singing.

"Make a wish," Miyuki, Maho, Lucas, George, Maria, Arron … said in unison.

"I wish to be dead by tomorrow." He was laughing by this time.

"Seriously?" shouted everybody at him.

"I wish there were no more break-ups." He nearly cried this time.

The usual banter and party events began - cards, gifts and real wishes.

"How was your birthday so far? " Arron started a random conversation.

"Well bad."

"Have you been drinking?" asked Maho.

"All day long."

"You are drunk."

"Not yet."

"Your eyes are half shut."

"And yours too." They laugh at each other.

"Your face is red."

"It's my birthday."

"Fair enough."

More drinking, shouting, music, dancing...

She held him like a nurse; at least he felt that she was nursing him. He thought that she was far better than his ex-girlfriend who had led him down to such despair.

Moving her lips softly around his face, she whispered,

"Do you have a girlfriend?"

"Not yet."

"What do you mean?"

"I was single till I met you just now."

"And now?"

"Too soon to say. Now I am with you."

"I would like to be with you as a friend."

"That's alright.".

"How old are you?"

"Exactly 22 years and 15 hours."

"Very precise! We are almost the same age!"

"Ehm... a hundred more years more to live."

"Absolutely."

More drinking, shouting, music, dancing.

"Thank you, Arron. You saved me again!"

A toast!

Chapter
NINETEEN

The revelation of Alem ...

"Are you a Christian infidel?" Silence.

"Why don't you answer my question?" he kicks him repeatedly in his face until it's full of white mucus. Moussa can't speak, but he hasn't lost consciousness totally as the other brothers have. He signals *'yes'*, making a symbol of a cross with his face. Only Alem and Gech know he's lying.

"He is lying, because he wants to die with his friends. Haha... what a martyr!"

"And you?" Silence.

"Why don't you answer?" Alem can't speak because his mouth is covered with a thick, cloth gag. He shows him his pendant – a cross.

"And you?" he asked everyone the same bloody question and nobody lied except Moussa, who thought life without those brothers couldn't be better than this, knowing that if he has to die one day it couldn't be more honourable than this.

He used to say,

What's death compared to love?

What's time and age, or long life compared to love?

What's even a million women's affection compared to one true love?

What's even living a hundred years compared with this everlasting bond of true friendship?

Of course, Alem didn't like his idea; he wanted him to live longer with his gift of a smiling, open face. With that face he would tell this tragic story with some sort of false sense of humour hiding the real pain. He would tell their stories, so it won't happen again.

"And you?" he asked Alem again.

This time one of the bandits untied the gag in his mouth. He felt this was his last chance of freedom to speak and so wanted to use it properly.

"This is a time when your questions have no value. A time when none of us care what you ask us or whether we are Muslim or Christian. As you can see none of us care about culture, language, gender, race or whatever differences you want to use as a cause for promoting difference. The time is coming when the world will be watching a single screen, a screen as vast as the sky, as fast as light. There'll be no such person as a refugee – no 'refugee question' because we can all be anywhere at any time; there will be no need for a place to hide from bastards and cowardly criminals like all of you because everything will be seen by everybody. Nothing will be hidden, nothing will be far away, nothing will be impossible.

"Western prophet!"

"Infidel!!!"

" 'I am from East Africa and a Christian'... will not be my answer any more as there will be no divisions between us and any region of the world. I am Eastern, and I'm going to be a citizen of the world, unlike you narrow-minded villagers. You know that the fire you lit in your village is burning us now. You have destroyed all your own people and civilisation, all your historic buildings. You will end up with nothing, no sense of your own culture and history. Now you are turning on us and our women and children. You are blinded by blood to the civilization which is spreading enlightenment throughout the world right now. You are going to pay for all this, your history will judge what you have done to us and you will live with shame and loneliness until you beg for your death."

Three of the guards blabbered in one of the languages he knew back home. He was filled with hope. He hoped that they could help him as a fellow countryman would, but soon he realised that would never happen as one of them approached and scolded him.

"*Change your religion and join us, then you may live and serve Allah with us.*"

"*Or else?*"

"*You'll be dead by tomorrow.*"

"*Why should I?*"

He explains that it's to expand the state and scare away western influences.

"*This is just blasphemy. This is just a lie. Allah is everywhere; he doesn't need your state or territorial expansion at the expense of his creation. Mohamed cursed anyone who killed,*" shouts out Moussa.

"*We are giving you a choice. Believe or die.*"

"*That I'll never do, have you not read the scriptures?*" Alem and Moussa replied.

"*This is it … Come, be brave... let's see how long you can hold on to your bravery.*" He kicked them trying to please his Arab comrades.

"*I understand. If you cannot help us, get your hands off us. I'll stand for my principles and yet I'm not looking forward to dying.*"

"*Yes you are! You have no idea how it feels like to die. It's new to everyone, you know? You will see if heaven and hell are real. Isn't that what you are looking forward to?*"

"*Yes! Of course, you may be right and I'll see if it's right.*"

"*You'll go to Jehanem with your friends.*" He tightens with ropes, in a line.

A masked monster comes to them and injects each one of them. The needle is as thick as a nail. Alem gets high and for the first and last time he wants to write his story on the paper of his mind before he loses consciousness, but he doesn't know where to start.

'*I am not a soldier, I would hate to be a soldier but if I were one, I could build a beautiful world. I am not a poet, but I eat and breathe verses with new words of dreams and forgiveness. I can touch and feel the smell of love. I am not a musician but I still touch the rhythms, eat the notes. I can kill incredible dance steps, discover more planets bursting with life, I could create my own universe out of sheer happiness. I am not a sportsman but I could jump from galaxy to galaxy, until I see the smile of God filling the universe. I could run from the very beginning of the universe to its end, if it had one. I am not really a painter but I see colours and draw the hands of God up in the sky. But now, I hear liars talking and roaring to tell a monstrous tale. They say 'there was a dragon called ISIS made up of several heads of monsters. Here in front of me, now.'*

Alem fights against the chemical that has been injected into him and is running through his spinal cord until he feels as if he has a tail. He makes sure that he's able to realise what's going on around him. Some monstrous ISIS soldiers were playing with a kid's bottom. "*Sodomite!*" said Alem powerlessly.

"*Take him. I can't do this to an infidel,*" says the other monster.

The wind is tired, the sand is sleeping and the world seems still. Pause. Life is just a photograph. He sees his picture inside the eye of a camera; a miniature of his soul. His eyes are half shut. He sees chained legs in front of him. Moussa's long legs tied to Gech's legs, all tied to his legs and his legs tied to others behind.

The way to Golgotha...

"*Go! Quick!*" shouts one of the heavily armed guards holding their necks. Chains tied their hands, legs and heads together. A camera man is recording everything, the injections and the bruises from beatings as they walk to their cross.

"*Go quick.*"

"*They cannot hear you.*" One of the guards smacks one of the prisoners behind until they are all next to each other.

Most of them are as dead, numbed by the drugs they've been injected with.

"I don't know why those fools carry barely living people to slaughter. Cowards!" says Moussa, trying to resist the drug they've injected him with.

The lambs are tied. The martyrs are ready for ISIS's devilish display soon to be enacted. He wants to ask them a question, in case they are unaware of what they are doing.

"Do you know Prophet Mohamed was raised by an Abyssinian woman?"

"Do you know, Bilal, he who first taught you how to pray to Allah?"

"Do you know, the first family of Mohamed were refugees and protected by the Christian kingdom of Abyssinia?"

"Do you know you are acting against the essence of Muslim belief and ethics?" Moussa murmurs as if no one is listening to him.

"But, this is an international shame. This is Nazism, TPLF-ism, colonialism. This is not the work of human beings at all. This is evil. This is how we came to know that the devil exists. It's following us everywhere and through time, where there could be a much better life than this", Gech adds in front.

"I left my mother for this!" Alem recalls his mother. *"Here we forever seem to stay, but the sun and the moon die every day,"* he remembers from a classic British text.

The guards neither hear nor understand them. If you have ever seen men who wear the cloak of the angels of death, then these are them. Now, they are near to the beach. He can see it afar. That's one of the edges of Africa; the end of his world. He wonders what they are going to do with them. He remembers that he can't swim anyway, but he would try to flee by swimming.

Now he's happy – beyond limits, because it's the end of his trouble. Most importantly, he has a great reason to die. He's not ill, he has never become tired of life, he hasn't tried committing suicide; he loves his life. He's totally healthy. He's ready to write a story – maybe it will remain unpublished, like one of the stories of brave men he has admired throughout his life, freedom fighters, prophets, scientists, lovers, martyrs...

He laughs at his executioners who wear heavy black clothes, strange and forbidding in this burning hot place. And their flags resemble the skull and crossbones of other bandits. He doesn't know what it means, but it's something to do with Islamic State. He knows these are his opposites. They represent death while he feels really alive for the first time. He feels brave even if he's tied and beaten up and still kept prisoner by heavily armed forces. Still life goes on until death, until its last drop.

They finally arrive at the coast. They set up a camera in front of them, the confused, tired, hopeless and beaten faces... Alem, exhausted stares as he struggles to say something to the camera. *'My untold life story ends here in the desert.'*

"Kneel down!!!" They push them all down on their knees in a row, facing the shore of the Mediterranean Sea. Alem couldn't see anything fully. The camera man is still recording the show. He has amazing stories to tell, but the camera knows only his dying face, sucking his power and leading him from the light of the desert to the eternal darkness. One of the gang makes a nonsensical speech to the camera. A middle aged Arab stands behind them; masking his evil face with a black cloth like a robber, one hand pointing a pistol and his other hand against the camera. Half proud yet full of cowardly gibberish in an alien accent, he warns the Western Christian states with this East African prey. Alem heard him saying, *"You will not have safety, even in your dreams, until you embrace... us...."* All the boys were confused by the speech. *What's really going on? What the hell has that to do with these poor boys? This is only the work of ignorance and cowardice. This is just mental,* Alem thinks. They all hate the voice of that ignorant man. They don't deserve such a childish speech on their final day on earth. They want the truth on the camera that is recording their last day for their families and the whole world to see what has happened to them. So they are determined to show how they managed to try and fight all this. They opened their eyes straight to the camera and began to tell everything while smiling. Without words they tell that ISIS is an inhuman institution

that will never bring safety to whoever connects with it. The fire they have brought on themselves will prey on them even in their dreams, until they die. On the boy' faces, it is not *an eye for an eye* but silent forgiveness. Not revenge but a speechless message to the world; a love that breaks and melts heartlessness. The message of the tired boys says *'Enough'* to political manoeuvring that's costing their lives. They smile at the barbaric angles of death. With their smiles, they invite the world to witness their bravery; what it means to stand on one's principles, belief, understanding, friendship. Their entire story is within their smiles.

Alem hasn't seen green for ages, he misses staring at grass and green plants. He wishes the sand could be green. The black guns, the flashing knife, the camera... he sees blue water across the desert, the Mediterranean Sea; small green algae. He hasn't seen a drop of water or anything green for a couple of days. Now, he wishes to dive into the sea – dead or alive – he doesn't mind. As he day dreams, he witnesses his friends' blood mixing with the waters of the Mediterranean with the rest of the martyrs before their souls leave their bodies.

He finally remembers his last dream, when they were back in the desert.

In his dream, he was flying near to the surface of the earth. He felt exhausted from flying too long. He wanted to land, but the ocean was full of beasts and the land was on fire too. He searched for somewhere to live but he couldn't find anywhere. As he was flying he hoped nothing more than to find something green, something that would give him courage to make him keep flying. Not burning, not drowning, but flying. As he could not defy gravity anymore, his wings grew powerless. He started falling. Then he'd woken up from his nightmare and he remembers Emu-Hiba was next to him. He remembers that he went back to sleep in her lap immediately. He was dreaming of green until the gangs came and changed their destiny.

Now he knows that once his eyes shut, there will be no more green in this life; but he's looking forward to how green heaven could be, if there is one. He knows after he stops breathing that he won't be able to smell flowers, but he's wondering how the scent of heavens' flowers would be. He knows, after his brain shuts down, he's going to forget all of this. He hears the voices of his friends being slaughtered. He hears them fighting and surrendering, losing and winning, screaming and fighting at the same time. 1st, 2nd, 3rd... Alem realises it is Moussa next... Alem cries out for the first time.

Moussa..

Looking at his friend's execution and the blood flowing from him, he's not afraid of death. *'If nine deaths knock at your door, let the one in,'* he used to say. He is a man, a proper man. He's thinking of himself as a hero now. *'The best way of dying is to go deep into a new kind of universe, knowing the reason and purpose of giving your life, proud of doing it, believing in it, doing it, not just trying it.'* That's what he's thinking about. That's what he has learned through this experience: to stick with his beloved friends, loving his friends until death. He was even feeling lucky that he had met those incredible friends. *'That's what Allah wants – to love everybody as yourself.'* He'll never leave his sweet friends, no matter what. Together, they used to hear the dialogue of the flowers in the wind. They used to speak with the moon. Now, they have almost no feelings; instead they have blurred memories and broken dreams that they can hardly remember anymore. Now that they are nearer to the other life, they are closer than ever to each other, almost like one. He doesn't feel any pain even when a savage hand with a knife is cutting his throat until his arteries break, until he feels dizzy with his blood spurting all over him and on the ground around. Death is flowing through his veins. His own blood is choking him, making him feel he's still alive, until he sees all his blood running over the ocean. Then he faints and can't breathe properly anymore. Still that cannot stop him smiling.

No matter how tough he is, the door to the other life seems tightly closed and Moussa has to push hard, knock hard. Knock! Knock! Knock! And knock! It seems it won't open at all. But he can't go back either as he has nothing left. All his blood vessels are emptying; all his breathing tubes have stopped functioning. His flesh is mixing with water and sand. He has lost all his breath to survive. His body is not his anymore. Helpless: he has legs that can't walk. He has eyes that are shut, ears that can't hear.

He feels lifeless. Lighter. His soul sees his lifeless body and wonders. '*Is it really me?*' and '*Am I dead?*' Now he'll know that the door that was hard to open is already opened and finally he feels the endless breath of freedom: the other world, omniscient; the uncontrolled, free spirit. And he said to his soul, '*At last, I am free, now.*' Freedom bought with a sword, people say. But, he finally says '*My freedom bought not with a sword but a sacrifice for a loving friendship and being human.*' 4th...

General Gech

For him, life has been harder than death. The same thing is happening now. He prays for the rest of them, as he can't save them this time. He can't even save himself, but his suffering has a meaning now. His friends are the meaning now. He's not alone at all as he used to be. Living was too high a price for his life. He doesn't know how much it costs, because every minute he's lived he's been paying too much. He has paid a lot and this time has to be the final. He has seen lots of death traps and he knows there is no better death than this one.

"*But, I don't want to die.*' He groans inside. '*Death why are you always fighting me? When will the battle end? Heaven, how far away are you?*" Life felt like a dream at this moment. Frozen. Stopped. He misses his family, the breath of a child, the warmth of a mother, the smell of his wife, the scent of his homeland. He found nothing here. It's a burning beach, nothing else to lay his eyes upon. He closes his eyes; looking into the shadows within himself, the shadows of ghosts he knew from previous battle fields. His memories flood in until he cannot remember anything anymore. Finally, he simply gives up. 5th...

Paulos Amon..

He used to be the fastest, he had the fastest mind, the quickest thinking of anyone, and the speed of the mind is the greatest of all speeds. The speed of a bullet can't beat it; the speed of a dirty hand wielding a knife couldn't darken it. His mind wanders to things he's been reading about Indian culture as his consciousness fails. He flies back in time to the seventh cycle of the seventh universe just after God Siva destroyed the previous universe and created the new one. He finds himself right there. Then he goes forward in his mind to beyond the next cycle of the cosmos, rearranged and recreated. There he sees that having died once, there can be no more death; the dark has lost its power, the sun has got brighter, all the galaxies and planets of the universe are populated with life. Deserts are no longer hostile places. People know with their brains before they see with their eyes, think with their souls rather than their brain. Then he found himself there, and he smiles with his heart first. He explores all the cosmic ages, infinitive and endless. He sees Rahel crying alone and laughs at her; she replies with a smile a hundred times more radiant than flowers can smile. Black out! 6th...

Alem..

Alem feels sorry for his mother and his unfortunate wife. He wants to conceal his real fate from them. His mother became a nun after he had left her to follow the river and the moon. Now, she was going to lose him forever but he doesn't want her to know the details. He wishes to soften the blow by writing a letter or sending a message to her, his wife and friends.

In his mind he composes the letter:

'Dear Mother, and Wife, Aba and Arron.

It's I, Alem.

I have been in trouble for a couple of days and I was thinking I was going to die, but a king's daughter with her guard saved me and in return I had to marry her quickly. I was more than happy to do so. Can you imagine, for a man who was seeking his fortune, I got it just like that! I am indeed lucky and need no more than this. You might think I've completely forgotten about you and you are right. I must admit the nature of the palace where I now live doesn't give me time to think about my earlier life. Besides my princess is already pregnant; life is quick and

miraculous as you can see. I hope you can forget me and I hope
that I will see you again. All the best.

This way nobody would suffer or grieve for him.

As his life ebbs away, he's finally able to see the green across from his own red blood, now mixed with yellow sand and the blue ocean, across the ocean to a new world, 'the garden of Eden' he might call it if he could: a new world with a new sun, a new moon and new refreshing air. When you are dying you go far away, long and fast. In no time, he's witnessing a foreign land with nothing in it but quiet spirits led by the light of the moon – the way to heaven- looking exactly how he had dreamt it, the moon tattooed with the image of Emu. At last he wanted to say *'Moon, do you even know me as I know you?'* But, he is mute; he can only follow the leading moon.

The lonely moon is still leading.

The dusty moon is still ahead.

The half moon.

The moon.

Moon

All the friends are dying in the Ocean, mixing with other African spirits deep down in the heart of the ocean. At last, they are all singing together, united and knowing even more about each other. There, at last, Moussa is not just a Muslim, Alem is not just a Christian, Paulos is still the fastest and the biggest, Gech is still a lion; they are all united in one divine human spirit. Silence. Silence is their story. All their stories are within their silence.

The silence was broken with the release of the video recording of the massacres. It's been posted on a militant website called 'al-Furqan media arm' and shared on other media such as Youtube. This remained the worst news of the week throughout the world, showing half dead and blood-splattered bodies under the guard of the vile, black clothed ISIS soldiers. Most of their mothers, sisters and relatives don't have internet access so they wouldn't know about it easily. The Ethiopian government tried to hide the news from the people for political reasons too. They were not interested in saving people's lives because they were only interested in protecting their own positions. However, the people knew all about it. Facebook is now the most accurate communication system. So, after some days almost everybody had heard about it and were pained by this horrible incident. Alem's mother was one of thousands of mothers sharing the same fate as her. Even though everybody was coming to her house to comfort her on her loss, she chose not to believe what had happened and remained seated just outside her door, watching for his footsteps, wishing he'd come back soon. Here she was just another unfortunate mother like all the millions of mothers who had lost their beloved ones fighting for their own natural freedom and the right to live in the land of their birth -fighting the angry desert that has no mercy on living things, fighting the stormy ocean that has no sympathy even for a helpless child, fighting with savage humans who have become like beasts and with no sense of humanity at all. In a foreign land – fighting for life! That's what everybody does anyway. Mothers know all these things will happen to their child; they have a special telepathic connection. She knew he might die, but how could she believe that her prayer of 'let me die before I hear bad news about my child...' had been reversed? She refused to believe that he was dead; she said yes to believing in his incarnation.

"I will wait for him until I die! I am not the only one; everybody is waiting for our beautiful ones to come back into their mothers' lives again! Have faith mothers; don't let negative forces take over your souls! Remember your mothers, who fought and won over evils even worse than Mussolini! Let that spirit be with you so that you can defeat the curse that comes upon us! Have faith and pray; you will see miracles, you will see your sons again!"

Eventually people stopped asking her to cease grieving, and let her be herself. Shouting and praying at the church, in the square and at the cross-roads... everywhere, she was more like a prophetic nun than a mad woman. Everybody loved her not only because she was mad and spoke the truth but also because she helped everybody equally. She was sympathetic by nature. She always cried, prayed hard and even laughed with people sometimes. She often sacrificed her own safety to protect young political victims, thinking she was doing this only for the sake of her son. Nothing would stop her from communicating with him, doing good for him, pleasing him, praying for him, waiting for him – for ever.

Chapter
TWENTY

Away from Charlotte...

The fact that Charlotte had seen him with a Japanese girl annoyed her, and even more, the fact that he seemed be ignoring her which was painful. It made her start playing a game to make him jealous, but she failed because he seemed not care about it.

"*I have a lot troubles going on in my mind.*" That's what he said to her. So she decided to leave him alone.

Gregg was his friend; they'd the played guitar together several times. He plays the bass guitar better than anybody else he knows. Now, he sees not the guitar in his arms but Charlotte. He is no longer his friend.

John was locked up in himself all day. He knew why.

"*I hate break ups,*" said Arron to break the silence.

"*Do you?*"

"*Yes I hate break ups.*" He said it again as he had said it a hundred times every day since he had seen Charlotte with Gregg last Friday night. He knew what happened every Friday night. Lots of loves die, and new loves replace them. He needed to get over it, but he couldn't help himself. Once he loved somebody, he fell for them completely. Now, it was different. He had to move on.

"*What's wrong with me? It's all my fault, not hers.*" he checked himself from top to bottom. She'd left him with her pictures and texts. The conversations he'd had with her, lots of 'love and kiss' emoji, lots of promises, lots of jokes. Now, there was only one feeling left, nostalgia but with the remnant of love – eternal, jealous, vengeful.

Unintentional experience of drugs ...

"*What's up, how do you feel?*" Lala asked. He was his best mate from Albania who liked being high enough to keep himself afloat.

"*It's not special really, just like a cigar with different taste,*" he said. He didn't feel anything at first. He was expecting a much more extreme transformation to happen.

"*Shit is gonna happen, wait and see,*" said Lala with his 'One Love' melody. Slowly he noticed he was in a transformation process, a transition to a different kind of hell; a hell better than earth. He felt the roar of various monsters coming out to break his inertia. He felt fire burning through his throat, his tail growing through his arse, his horns through his head. Lala was higher though. He started to lose control. Arron realised that something disturbing might happen if he stayed with him in this mood. He knew he was a boxer back home and had suffered brain damage, so sometimes he loses control. He was well trained and knew how to attack special parts of body that could kill quickly. So, Arron went outside.

"*Why? Enjoy; it hasn't started yet.*"

"*I need to get fresh air.*"

"*I will come with you, man.*" But he couldn't manage to take a step.

"*I will be back, brother.*"

Outside was not 'outside' that day. It was not really cold, not really dark. There were no swimming fishes, just wind and water chasing each other from the middle of the Atlantic Ocean towards the little shore of Enderbury.

He started a dialogue with unidentifiable creatures.

"*What a fucking liberty.*"

A crater as deep as a volcano rocketed through his stomach, through the mouth, touching the sky and turning the colour of the blue sky into bloody pinkish mushroom clouds and creamy rain – burning like citric acid.

He found himself eating and smoking a lot to get rid of his headache. Suddenly a call awakened him from his mental state. It was Miyuki. She called him as she usually did by this time.

"Where are you?"

"Near a beach by my house"

"What are you doing there in the middle of the night?"

"It's in front of my house."

"I know that."

"And, I can see the sea; it seems like a fantastic dream with its smooth waves in the night."

She realised he had taken something.

"Take care. Don't forget us – your friends, while you are having fun by yourself. It could be dangerous."

He was expecting more insults than this but, she was positive. Had she been Charlotte, she would have said a lot of bad things. 'When you find out the fact you are a dickhead, it's like a nightmare that you will never wake up from.' That's what she'd said to him the last time, when somebody told her he saw him smoking weed.

He loved her, but he didn't like the way she wanted to control his feelings. He's not that kind of boy, one who could make her happy only by surrendering all of himself. He didn't want to even see or talk to Charlotte now. Even if he missed her, he didn't want her in his mess right now.

"Go away!" he shouted at her, more like a roar, when she'd last tried to advise him. He had never scared anybody with his strong reactions until that day. She ran away from him quick as lightning. You could tell she was embarrassed.

His social worker took him to a different school, an English language school where international students learned English. It was a break from his college friends and he met lots of international students with whom he could share feelings and experiences. They talked and listened to each other's stories, interesting or not. They were different people from different parts of the world but all about the same age, with the same understanding and common principles. He made friends from Africa, America, France, Japan and China.

Miyuki was his first friend from among them. She was the cutest girl in the class. She was different, silent mostly but occasionally the silence was broken by a low voice which he found attractive. She was a brilliant speaker.

"I live with my mother and grandmother," she said.

"Name?" shouted the teacher to encourage her.

"Sorry!!!" She felt embarrassed instead, for the moment. She stared at him as he fixed his eyes on her. He thought she was like an angel when she spoke in front of the others.

"My name is Miyuki. I am from Japan – Kansai, from Kansai University." She was a very shy girl and the cutest thing is that she tried her best not to seem so. She didn't seem to like talking too much. She made him change his mind about loneliness and not meeting people, especially girls after he'd been so messed around by them. The one he couldn't forget was a girl called Stella, her dim face imprinted on his mind. She didn't look normal. He didn't like the idea that most boys get damaged by sluts, and most girls get destroyed by bad guys. He hated the way relationships could be so destructive and until then he'd been one of the victims. He had been in the worst mood he'd ever been in. Who was there to help him take the shit out of his life and teach him how to handle it? She could be the one.

He reflected on the usual conversations from class-mates. It usually went,

"Where you from?"

"East Africa." He didn't like such *nerdy* questions. Immediately he started to hate them and felt they didn't like him anyway. Why labels, why does he have to provide a context?

"Is there polygamy in your country?"

Here we go. Now he had to fight the battle again. *"Actually we have a more conservative culture than you have in Italy."* Sayk!

"Are you anglophone or francophone?" as if all Africans fall into just two groups.

"We use languages even older than you have in your country."

"Are you Muslim or Christian?"

"My father is Christian, my mother is Muslim and I am neither." He managed not to show his anger, because he knew that there were a lot more inane questions still to come.

"We used to govern East Africa." This was what Arron really did not want to talk about, but he must not give up.

"Finally you have come to the point." She was a history student, but he knew a lot about history too.

"We were the ones who shamed those fascist ideologists, who think all the world belongs only to them." She kept quiet for a moment, but not for so long.… She has to battle more. So, she took it far too personally.

"Hey you know I really don't like you! Why don't you understand? I tried to tell you lots of times. You are too much! Niga…" she finished saying more in her language so that he wouldn't care or understand. He heard the last unfamiliar word, but he didn't have anything to say about it. He lit up a cigarette and took a drink while everybody tried to make her shut her mouth. He realised that there really are people with a mind-set stuck in the Middle Ages. Some people's thinking is as ancient as the world itself. If there were such a thing as a time- travel machine, he would help to transport such individuals to the time where they belonged. Then he thought that the world would still not be free from Hitlers or Mussolinis and you just needed to take all this shit or put it to the back of your mind.

Loneliness was the obvious cure. He started to think this way. *Indeed, loneliness is my faithful friend. It has been with me from the day I was born. It will not desert me even to death and after. Its soothing gifts are priceless: concentration, contemplation, and self-love. It gives me time to see the whole world in a different way from how other people see it. I can rise above my present state and see the universe, as God sees it from above.*

But that day Miyuki had changed him, making him feel better again.

"Are you shy?"

"A little bit, but not like you." She added, *"you seem more shy than I am."*

"Me?" she'd made him smile.

"You never talk to anyone here."

"Well, I didn't used to be so shy but bad experiences have changed me back to being a shy boy again."

"Bad experiences? What do you mean, what happened?"

"Forget about it." He suddenly fell silent; for a long time. This silence was powerful. He wanted to restart the conversation. *"Of course, I was shy in my country because I didn't have any choice."*

"What do you mean? Is it a choice to be or not to be shy?"

"I mean being reserved, it's part of our culture."

"The same as in Japan."

"But now, here, we are not in Eritrea or Japan, so we have no need to be shy really." She laughed. It was the first time he saw her laughing; it was like magic. Dimples appeared on her cheeks reminding him of his mother. He always liked girls who bore some resemblance to his mother. He started to compare the two. She'd got dimples and a smile just like his mother. She was of average size and height just like his mother. She was quite shy. She told him that she liked sweets, just like his mother did.

When she said, *"you are my first friend,"* he felt positive as if she'd said that he was the first boy she had ever met.

"How come?"

"I am scared of meeting new people."

"Why?"

198

"Maybe it's because I don't have any self-confidence."

"You can have confidence from now on, and make lots of friends."

"I wish I could, but how?"

"Just feel everybody else is just like me."

"Not everybody can be like you. It's difficult for me to make the first step in friendships."

Arron felt a sense of renewal and began working with an unknown excitement. *Where does this happiness come from?* he asked himself. *What has changed him?* Well, there are times like this. She gives him a positive vibe. She becomes his motor.

He started meeting Miyuki after work. He enjoyed her company, because she made him forget about Charlotte and Gregg, at least for the time being. They talk about how they'd spent their time. He tells her what conversations he'd had at work.

At the hospital where he was working, he said 'good morning' to every patient he met. Some said 'good morning' back, some stayed quiet, some ignored him, and some didn't hear what he said. One day a man in a side room took the time to talk to him about his journey to Eritrea and Ethiopia long time ago.

"I've visited so many countries that I cannot finish counting them all, son."

"You made an adventurous journey, mate."

"I like travelling around the world."

"Me too."

"How old are you?" he moved his pillows down to his neck; trying to look at his face. *"I am eighty-four,"* he added.

"Twenty-four"

"Oh, you still have a long way to go."

'*I've come a long way already,*' he was going to say, but the man kept talking of himself, of the things he'd achieved when he was twenty four; with pride, as if he'd reached his destination.

"*Life is just so.*"

Chapter
TWENTY ONE

Waiting for the boat ...

Unsure of what has happened behind her, Emu-Hiba must go forward by herself. Everyone is new to her now as she sits waiting for the boat to take her on her journey. She doesn't know anybody here and she is completely alone. She's lost all her travel companions, lost everything except her memories. She remembers all of them, Moussa teasing Rahel; Rahel braiding, untying and braiding her hair again and again; General Getnet telling them about the adventures he'd had when he was in the war in Somalia; Mohamed reading his scruffy half paper, half dust book; Paulos Amon sharing his knowledge, future plans and dreaming of NASA. Above all she remembers Alem fondling her, with Getnet as their watchdog, and Mohamed who took responsibility for their emotional state when they were without hope. He read them a poem; he couldn't survive without writing.

> *"I saw that what can't be done is done,*
> *I saw a rat giving birth to an elegant elephant,*
> *I saw the dark come out of light and light fade into the dark,*
> *I witnessed an angel become a devil, a million times over,*
> *I saw this and this...all"*

She remembers the last Christmas Day spent with him. She remembers especially the Christmas carol he was reading to practise his English reading skills, but he understood it in his own way:

> *Summer's wait*
>
> *Life grows short and the walking dead fall,*
> *Soldiers are mocking, with their guns in hand,*
> *Around the wall of chaos,*

Consuming human blood as petrol floods over, the fire is lit.
The prisoners sit and watch the end of their life,
Sit and wait for death. It'll come fast.
Hands grow numb in the burning cold,
The dragon is locked in its flammable hold.
Man and beast are mostly in a deathly sleep,
Across the floor the angel of death creeps
They all wait for revelations,
The sand grows deep, a death angel sings,
"Where is peace, where is the king?"
No bright star shines light in a dark sky,
But oh! So far, so high!
All wait for the dream.
Sleep is over, let the war pass,
The peace has shown the world at last,
That death is defeated, Christ is come,
Man's wait is done,
All praise to God's son,[13]

Everybody was laughing and comparing the original song to his own hashed up version.

"*Bravo! A freezing poem in the barren desert,*" exclaimed Alem, declaring his love of literature.

"*Like an ice-cream!*" Emu laughed.

Smiling, she's woken from here memories by a new voice.

A small rubber boat big enough to carry about sixty people is waiting for them off the coast.

"*Get in the boat, take care. If something happens you are on your own. Nobody is going to help you out. I know you are grieving but you should also know that you are in danger. You must get over it.*"

The smugglers are not in charge any more. Everybody wants to save their own life and escape from death or ISIS. All of them, whether rich,

---

13 Words adapted from Robert Tear (1939-2011)

strong or weak… experience the same tension, more than they have ever known. The only outcome of this next stage is either life or death. They are all subdued by the storm in which an angered nature unleashes its monsters following the carnage and blood of yesterday. It's life or death, nothing in between. In fact she has no idea what's happened to her husband, but deep in her gut she doesn't feel good. The boat goes with the waves and her heart trembles. In her gut she feels she's going to die. Everybody is going to die. None of this frightens her, but uncertainty about what is happening to Alem does. She is dreaming about him all the time, even when wide awake.

'There is no escape from the hands of ISIS', says her gut. But she hopes, and declares…

'Christians never give up hope. Nor Muslims either.' She starts talking to herself. She knows Alem will never give up his life so easily. She will meet him at some point, she thinks, to give herself strength.

Only life and death can release us and this boat means life; it seems the safest place for now, the only place. Until it says, *'I am death'.* She remembers Moussa quoting from his favourite verse,

The boat is floating on a sea of death.

That's what life is about, anyway – staying afloat, staying afloat, until it's your time to sink'.

She is lost in thought, just daydreaming; it's the best way of escaping realty. She realises that she is afraid of death. She's dried up and frozen like a rock, silent as the grave. She understands neither sadness, humiliation nor defiance.

"They are religious people."

"Are they?" She hears random conversations around her about ISIS. She doubts whether she is a Muslim when she considers that she has lost her father to a faithless militant and her fiancé to a radical gang. *How come no one understood that this is not a religious act at all?* She felt very lonely.

"So why do they kill?"

"Because they have rules."

She thinks *Hell is their rule. I hate being both religious and political, especially when 'religious' people exploit 'politics' and wreak such disaster. It's neither political nor ethical, it's rather ignorance.* She brushes her tears away, and she says aloud,

"Tell me a religious rule that tells us to kill, create terror for children, mothers and men. What's wrong with these believers?'

She wonders if *atheists* have rules. *They have principles rather than rules ... like 'live your life for yourself and leave the Goddamn God alone.'*

She thinks he might be dead, but he must defeat death. *I must bring him back to life, as he gave me life. I will make him keep living inside me forever.* She promises him she won't let him down. She dedicates her life to him to make him live again. He told her *"everything is for the good."* She believed him and prays for him now. *Let it be.*

"Forty degrees centigrade?!!!" the man in the boat shouts and brings her back to reality. It feels as if the world is about to catch fire and the Mediterranean is boiling. The rubber boat is melting and burning the skin of its passengers, delivering them to the dancing sea creatures now wrapping around them as if to drag them down, now staring at their banquet, the spirits of death.

The man's face is masked by his beard and hair, but his skin shines through and looks tanned and greasy. He has been staring at her for a long time, knowing she's lost and alone, feeding on her beauty with his eyes as if it's his last hour of life.

Fool, she thinks to herself and means it. He stands at the edge, standing guard over her in case she falls. Here you can't talk about safeguarding, because danger is normal, expected at any time – they are in the mouth of death itself - yawning death. There are no rules about behaviour and how to act but she realises that he has kept her from not only the waves of the sea but also his giant shadow is protecting her from the burning sun. Still she doesn't feel anything. She's like a dead woman with no fear or feeling. Her ability to feel seems to have been left behind with the corps of her beloved.

"I am Sicilian. My dad is famous out there." She doesn't have any energy for meaningless conversation. *"But I grew up in Asmara - which gives us something in common."*

She hates it when somebody keeps talking without the consent of their listener, especially, if he starts talking without even introducing himself.

"I am going to be reunited with my forefathers, if I survive the boat, I mean." He explodes with laughter but is soon ashamed of himself when no one responds to what he says.

"I am from Asmara."

"I am from Assab."

"Amche."

"Ah..., here we go."

She is done now. Ethnic problems followed them across the desert and now the sea; what a shame, she thinks. Which is more to be proud of, being human or being an African? Why be more proud of being East African than any ethnicity? We are all just people with common circumstances and sharing a common fate.

"My name's Davi Romario."

"That's an unusual name."

"Romario was my grandad."

"So, you keep to your culture by using your grandad's surname."

"Not really, but I loved my grandad, he was a terrific gambler, my mom told me."

How he could be so proud of having a gambler as his grandad? Even facing death he is proud of the sin of his grandfather. She's lost everything and left her homeland because of people who gamble at a national level. She wishes Alem were here. If Gech or Moussa could hear this man they'd wonder why on earth intellectual people struggle so much in life while ignorant people thrive.. She wishes she had the guts to bear the situation. She wishes she didn't regret anything that had happened to her. She notices he's dressed in long boots and tight clothing like a gangster.

"Fine."

"It's Italian style."

She tries to imagine how Italians look. Are they all like him, greasy hair and tight-cut clothes? She keeps listening to his mumbo jumbo; she's no idea what he's talking about.

Even if she isn't enjoying his company, she has no choice but to be near him and in fact feels a little bit safer with him there.

She dreams of Alem in a different form. She sees him at her thighs, disguising himself as a leopard. What surprises her isn't his incarnation as a leopard, but that she isn't afraid of it. Somehow she knows it's him, feels it's him. Then he changes to his original form.

"Marry me."

"We are already married. We are united in one body of love." She replies hugging herself and feeling underneath her breast.

She's aware that she is only dreaming. Now, she's in a new world. She can't see the same mornings she used to see before. She can't see a full moon or naked sun. She already misses waking up in the desert in Alem's arms, filled with the smell of his masculine odour. She misses his rough touch as he woke her every morning. She feels the pain ten times sweeter than before.

She travelled without noticing the beauty and the wildness that the sea has to offer. It's sharing her journey as she thinks of Alem all the way to the Italian coast. Then she realises that a rescue team has come to take care of them. Things seem different here; it's calmer. People have orders; no one has guns in his hands, people smile when they see each other. Women are like men, men are like women here. She sees togetherness. This was the world she was dreaming of; the world Alem, Moussa, Gech had promised her. They have kept their promises partly. She has made it to Italy. Staring cautiously at everything she looks like an idiot. She wonders how she got here. The day after they'd been rescued, she tried to figure out what happened on the boat before the rescue ship arrived, but she can only remember the crowd shouting and then the sea coming in over the boat. They could have died if the Italian border police had not rescued them and brought them back to life. She is now aware that she is in detention. She was hoping to be in a refugee centre, but they took her to a detention centre instead, for more interrogation because she's not only a refugee now, she's an illegal immigrant.

Thoughts from jail...

Davi was following her as she headed to the women's detention centre.

"*Chaw, Davi,*" she is staring at him with a lifeless stare. Davi thought she liked him, but now, noticing her blank face, he became aware that she's interested in nothing at all. Besides, sometimes he's seen her eyes suddenly go crazy too. *She's hot, but she's no fun,* he thinks. Silence is all her story. All the stories are within her silence.

She couldn't even beat the police officers questions within questions. She's tired of men questioning her.

"*Come ti Chiama, signorina?*"

"*Eh...*"

"*Chiama!*"

"*What?*"

"*No name!?*"

"*Emu-..*"

"*Huh? Quick, in there Seguimi.*" They took her to a cell without wasting time to interview her and having no clue about her.

She learns that people living here are always busy, as if they are running out of time, always doing something. Is this a normal life? She is feeling rather queer; all the city scenes she saw recently are mixed up with her dreams. Still, she hopes things are getting better. She still thinks that the promises her friends made are going to be fulfilled. Even the prison cell seems alright, better than those she had experienced before, she thinks.

She's never been free; the only difference now is that she is physically bound within four walls. She still is free in her mind to fly and think beyond the four walls, this roof and floor. She already has long experience of how to live in such kind of places. She knows it better than she knows herself. She has never tried to be a heroine; she hates heroes who try to bring peace through violence, death and destruction. Even religious leaders and establishment figures were accountable for the death of numberless WW2 victims, accountable for the loss of many other lives as well. Whichever hero you mention, they have destroyed humanity in some way. If mankind really wanted to live in peace, then only through love could we be cured.

Chapter
TWENTY TWO

Arron met Miyuki at their usual café.

"How is it working in a hospital?"

"Good."

To be honest, he thought, it's the right place to learn about life, to know the boundary between life and death. It's the right place to witness real love but also feel the sadness of life, sometimes happiness, sometimes silence. There, all feelings are real.

"How are the people working there?"

"Nice people. Well, nurses are like mothers". To be fair they are more than that, he thought. The difference is that we call mothers at any time, but we only call nurses when we are facing death. They all give us love and care. We all give love back to our mothers, but to nurses? It depends.

"And, patients are like children or real humans. I mean they are natural." In fact they are good teachers of real humanity and love. They don't care about race, gender, religion, or other forms of discrimination.

The next day ...

After their usual meeting at a café, Arron took her to his favourite pub, Wetherspoons. She told him that it was her first time in a pub.

"How come it's your first time?"

"It's not usual for Japanese girls to go to pubs and clubs."

Her face had already turned pink from drinking, making her more attractive. She laughed without stopping. She was trying her best to make him laugh too.

"You said you have never fallen in love."

"No, not me Arron."

"Love is shit! Love is embarrassing." Arron felt he had not been lucky in his love life. Now, at least he had got friends to share things with.

"Loving is like being reborn."

"With the same shit." His speech was more bitter than his drink. He likes whisky more than anything in life. Of course, he's funny and entertaining which draws most girls close to him, but he thought that no one had ever been a true friend to him. When he started to love someone it never lasted long.

"Do you know what I am feeling right now?"

"Happy?!"

"It's a feeling, but it'll fade away by the morning."

"Fortunately or unfortunately, life is feeling! A wave, a vibration." They seemed to find life from the waves of a vast ocean, bubbles rising from their drinks, smoke curling and turning them into their real selves, clouds, wind, and the blond hair of dancing girls flying to the rhythm of the music.

"Let's dance!" The dance floor seemed to be full of dancing angels. The lighting and the rhythm of the spotlights created a kind of illusion in the darkness that made you feel as free as if you were on the wings of your guardian angel. It seemed like a series of bright pictures of love spirits dancing against a clear sky, legendary pictures that could tell stories of thousands of years of friendship. He saw Alem among those spirits.

Morning...

In his room with his friends, Arron was writing while everybody else was asleep except Miyuki. She made green tea and a coffee. She brought him a cup of coffee.

"I wasn't expecting green tea at your place."

"I love green tea, not more than my coffee though. Thank you."

"Liar, you told me you don't like tea at all. Since when did you start?"

"Since I met you." Silence.

"You like it?"

"It's lovely."

"Just like you... I mean lovely."

"I know."

She kisses him on his chin. They smile at each other. By that, he knows that they are just close friends.

The next day ...

She read the story that he was writing about his friend Alem and said nothing.

"Do you have a girlfriend?"

"No."

"Nor have I got a boyfriend, I told you. How come? It seems you have already fallen in love with one of your characters."

"Deep down I have."

"But you could find one in the real world."

"Sadly no, God hasn't created anyone like her. Oh, they are just words, they don't complain, they could die if I wanted them to..."

She left without saying anything. He still thinks that they are just friends.

The next day she came back.

"Sorry for yesterday's tiff."

"It's not serious – don't worry. Why did you leave?"

"I felt embarrassed, but life is like experimenting with right and wrong, success and failure; like sweet wine and sour, it makes you relaxed and drunk, laugh and cry at the same time – a blood-like drink. And all these things are love."

"What do you mean?"

"Arron, we do not have any other choice but to forgive and love."

She always enlightened things. However, whenever she wanted to tell him something personal, she never told him directly, but talked in riddles, hoping he would understand what she found so difficult to say.

"The secret of nature is this, it's beauty with ugliness, wisdom with ignorance. Can you imagine why we don't think that all creatures have languages to speak, legs to walk, civilisations to be seen as in human eyes, but what if they really have more than we have?

Even water, who knows the secret union of two particles of hydrogen to only one of oxygen to produce water? Who knows why all plants stay still? Is it because their enlightenment depends on contemplation? How about the ancient trees that have stood and observed humanity for hundreds of years? Even fire and water, how have they learned to live together?"

She's soulful, she doesn't speak a lot. But when she does, she speaks with feeling, deep down her thoughts are sweet and sincere. Deep down she is natural, she's a poet.

Drinking her tears, he became drunk with love, and she did the same. Her round face looked almost divine; it was as if he was hugging a soft, pink moon, crying out of happiness. He said to himself, *there is no beauty like her in the universe.* Even though they considered themselves to be good friends, they couldn't find the power to fight back their feelings. They wanted to be near to one another and that day their friendship went to the next level. With the courage and company of alcohol, they quickly began to drink in each other's souls with a soft and gentle kisses.

In the morning, he finds himself in his bed and she is curled up on the sofa. She feels cold. He was feeling happy but now unhappy when he sees her happiness gone. He feels sad and confused at the same time, trying to remember the night. He can't figure out what had happened.

"Anything wrong, Miyuki?"

"You were drunk, and you were talking about Charlotte."

"Really?"

"Yes, you love her so much but I still want to remain your best friend for ever."

"Fair enough."

"I love you so much but only she can make you happy and so I want you to be with her."

"I guess you are right, I can't deny it." He hugged her and she tightened her arms around him.

The last time - at Miyuki's and Maho's farewell party...

Charlotte came with a boy again. He wasn't jealous because the boy was a friend of John's who is her cousin anyway. He couldn't really talk to her as Miyuki was there. For now, everything seemed to have settled down, and they didn't find any strong reason to be together. They decided to just wait and see.

Miyuki was jealous, knowing that they were still in love.

"You still love her, don't you?"

"I don't really know."

"Think about it."

"I'd better not." He hugged her knowing he could divert his feelings as well as avoiding the topic she'd raised.

"You are more than anybody to me now" she said. *"That is what I want you to know now."* He nodded.

Charlotte acted as though she was not jealous as she saw a girl with *her* boyfriend. She befriended Miyuki by inviting her to dance while Arron went out for some fresh air. John followed him. The rhythm was overtaken by the voice of a billboard hit song, *'Can't Feel My Face'* by Abel Tesfaye – *'The Weeknd'*. With each beat of the rhythm Arron misses the old Charlotte.

He couldn't cope with all the misfortune he'd faced after he'd broken up with her. He had stopped living before Miyuki came into his life; a different engine - made in Japan. She'd switched him on to make him fall in love with all things Japanese. He would miss Japan as he missed his own country Eritrea. But now he wanted to be back with Charlotte again. As he saw Miyuki dancing with John's new friend, he felt a little bit of jealousy towards Charlotte who easily recognised it and felt happy that he still had feelings for her. She remembers him saying that *'A little bit of jealousy is required'*. So it works, she smiled.

The next day, she decides to text him to see what he's up to.

'Din din din.'

"Morning" He'd got Charlotte's text that very morning.

"Morning" he immediately replied.

"I want to talk to you."

'Ring ring...' he picked up her call quickly. They talked for nearly an hour and he said, *"but don't ask me why I haven't been to class."*

"Where do I stand with you?" she asked directly.

"What do you mean?"

"Do you love me?" He wasn't expecting that she would make it this easy.

"Oh... yes, a thousand percent more than before." They both agreed that he'd dated Miyuki only because he thought it would free him of Charlotte, and her of him. Miyuki wasn't really his type anyway.

It was a sunny morning. He felt hot now. He was tired of the intermittent mist and drizzle every day. Now winter was dying and giving birth to summer. The rays of the sun smiled down on the city, spreading from the south east to cover everywhere in warm light. The people of Enderbury were tanning themselves in the beauty of summer's warm, young sun. Their tense brains were being massaged by the beauty of the city, the fresh new flowers and pervading odour of spring. There, he found a reason to get inspired; there he found the right season to begin making his friend immortal. *Nobody is going to destroy me,* he promised himself. *I want her to be my inspiration.*

This season I must tell a great story! A story of friendship.

He decided to share his plan with his mentor and with Charlotte. Every day she taught him new words. One day she taught him a new word: manipulative. It described her well. He promised her that he would let her do as she wished. She felt refreshed after not seeing him for a long time. She told him she had been bored since they had broken up, explaining to him that was why she had put on weight.

"It's all your fault."

"How should I make up for it?"

"Come and drink with me," she replied.

It was a Friday night. They met at his house after work. A pen and something were rolled between his fingers. His mouth was filled with smoke, his mind breathing incredible words onto a piece of paper. He is not a writer. It's just his life; paper and coffee in a smoke-filled atmosphere. They drank and got high before she took him to a night club. It'd been a long time since he had seen drunken people and semi-naked girls like this.

Then, Charlotte said, *"Dance with me."* He had never been high in a club like this. He said okay but in fact he couldn't stand it. He preferred sitting in a corner alone. She couldn't resist the beat so she left him to go back to the dance floor, that's what she'd come for anyway. A man started dancing with her. He watched as their bodies moved to the rhythm together and that was the time he knew that he really loved her. She's fair, she is innocent, she is … her smile was bolder than any girls in the club. She attracted everybody with her moves. He realised that almost half the boys in the club were dancing around her dancing to one of *Weeknd*'s songs remixed. When he saw a man trying to put his hands in between her legs, Arron got into a state that was impossible to describe. He leaped across the dance floor and she clung to him so fast that her whole body fell under his. He wrapped himself around her. She moved all over him to the rhythm of the song. She wanted to get inside him and dance in his heart, and so she did. He hugged her from top to bottom until they were completely at one together.

The more the DJ warmed up, the more the atmosphere built, the lights of the dance floor made it even more magical and the excitement spread even more through the dancers. It was like a series of pictures, between the blackouts.

He wouldn't forget this night for ages. He spent such a good time with her.

Then she said, *"Take me home."* He thanked her while they made their way back home.

Then Charlotte said, *"Touch me here"*

"Kiss me here."

"Do me here."

She had not changed; she did the same things as when they'd gone out for the first time. That was how he had lost his virginity that year. That's how they started their relationship. Together, they did everything to give pleasure to each other without saying a word. The waiting had ended.

Chapter
TWENTY THREE

France ....

Calais, a hell in Europe, she thinks.

In Calais too, men are busy doing so many things. The more they do, the busier they become in their limited time on Earth. The more they explore the universe, the more there is to find. They're busy at school, busy with schedules, busy with conferences, busy with festivals, busy with war and peace, busy with love and hate, busy doing nothing – come on take a break she thinks.

Alan found her when he was busy giving a lift to some of the unfortunate travellers. She was in the middle of nowhere, alone and unwell, faint from walking across the villages of Normandy for twenty days. Now she has neither the strength nor will to go on any longer. She is certain that she is going to lie here forever. Now he is taking her to the hospital but as soon as he gives her water to drink, she wakes up and says '*no*,' so he returns with her to the refugee camp.

In the camp she doesn't like the way boys fight for food and second hand clothes, the way charity workers make them stretch their hands up high for a piece of bread. She's grown up where dying with honour is better than begging.

Emu feels something inside her; contentment. It comes from something living; not because she is in a better place, at least compared to places she has been before. She was not sure at first, but suddenly she'd realised that she was pregnant. She is going to give birth to her husband's child. It may be a boy, if she's lucky. She'll name him after his father's great grandfather *Theodros* or some other name that reminds of her of the short but intense time she had spent with his father. Alan had tried to convince her she should live in France, but she was determined to fulfil her dream and Alem's to join the group of people who were heading to the UK.

"I'm still in the jungle." One of the refugees shouts over the phone that she has no battery left and thrusts her phone back in her wet pocket as it switches off by itself. Emu realises that this place is called the Jungle; a European jungle where she can see hardly any trees.

The Jungle is not a real jungle; it is a hellish place. She witnesses lots of horrors she has never seen before, it's a different kind of death, a different battle, with different villains, people with hidden weapons, constant surveillance and suffocation. She once saw twenty-eight people suffocated in a fish truck and the pitiful driver. She looked at the police and was surprised the first time she saw them; they seemed friendly but hard to define. She still remembers those angels of death who took her husband's life in the far off desert.

Here in the Jungle she remembers Dingl or *Virgin* as they called him. *"What happened to him?"*

"He died in the chassis of a truck!" He'd stayed in the jungle for about a year and half trying every day to make it to the UK but he wasn't lucky enough. Everybody in Calais knows him. Finally that is how his life came to an end.

She heard another story about a famous refugee named Bridge.

"And Bridge. He was great too! What happened to him?"

"He jumped from a bridge; not to commit suicide but he was trying to jump on to a lorry to make it to UK. He was unlucky and fell into the double tyres of the lorry before the quadruple tyres ended his life and turned him into a mash of flesh".

"Why he do that?"

"Because he couldn't afford to pay the smugglers, so he needed to try by himself".

How about swimming? Why are you so near that I can see you from right here? England, you are near to my eyes, you are akin to my dreams, you are the home of my plans; yet you are still so far from my reach!

She once heard that a group of refugees ended up in the wilderness of Russia, where almost no one lives. They were not thinking of a trip or a holiday, they were dreaming of the UK but arrived in a massive icy and empty desert instead. They called back to the jungle and informed them that they had decided to live wherever luck took them to safety. There are several refugee stories she heard that are really hard to believe. She learned of the sacrifices people made, looking for a better place. *But this is suicide*, she thinks.

She also reflects that some of the smugglers do more to help the refugees than the charity workers. They sacrifice themselves to help victims out of here. It's not even related to the amount of money they get from their customers. They hold your entire bodyweight to carefully raise you up to the highest points of the loaded lorry. They appear like fathers caring for their children, a shepherd caring for his flock. They like Emu as she is beautiful and strong and the wisest of all the women in the camp. She helps them a lot in managing the refugees including the handing out of food and clothing.

At her first attempt in the middle of the night, border security police caught her with ten others like her and took them to a detention centre. She's used to detention by now, but she is tired of it. In detention, her friend's cry reverberated so deeply it touched into her soul.

"Hey, what are you doing to her?" nobody replied.

"Be quiet and wait your turn, then you will know why she is crying."

"Why are you crying like this? What have they done to you my dear?"

"They took my finger print! I'm finished, I heard it's a bad luck," she cries. Emu breathes long and laughs at her for misunderstanding the situation. *"Don't worry, we haven't done anything criminal. Obviously, we are in*

a foreign land and we should obey their rules, if you know what I am saying? They will help us and understand our situation. Be comforted, at least we are not alone here. We have each other."

They give them a piece of paper to enable them to travel by train only within France, forcing them to agree that they will pay back when they start earning money.

"Tu es libre de partir."

"What?"

"Get in, into the car."

The police shout at them, pushing them into their car. They are all used to this humiliation by now. Emu is feeling accompanied at least, finding another refugee group that can at least remind her of her friends, brothers and sisters back in the great desert of Africa. It used to be the wealthiest, healthiest and safest place in the whole world once, but has swallowed all her beloved ones now. She can still feel it like yesterday. The difference is that the desert is warm and it's freezing here. She still wants to escape this place and all her memories. This is not the life Alem had promised her. *Life is not what we think it is,* she reflects.

She's again caught by the border security police while with her friends trying to cross another sea: a frozen one this time. An angry police officer is not aware that she is pregnant, so he treated her as usual. After they collected them inside the border security check at the port, they drive them back into the forest, ordering them to run away to the jungle, the refugee camp made by smugglers and Christian volunteers. They all get frustrated, thinking how to escape a beating. A police officer opens the car door wide and takes his position.

"Courir les gens," he shouts.

As everyone has heard that the police will release their dogs, the crowd push each other to get out of the stuffed car and escape before the dogs are released.

"Out! Out! Go, hurry up!" leaving them in the middle of nowhere.

"*Go! Go!*" They insist.

One of them pushes Emu as she hesitated. The others try to harass her by pushing. "*You should be comfortable with that in your belly, ay?*" he whispers in her ears. She nearly falls hearing and thinking of all this. She would have been injured unless a refugee called Abas had not protected her.

"*She is a woman. Can't you see she is alone and needs help?*' All of them were pushing and shoving him while he was trying to help her; in the foray he fell to the ground and saved her from falling on the stony ground that could have put her in danger.

"*You rescued me.*"

"*What?*"

"*Thank you, you saved me.*"

"*Aaa... not me. Allah saved you.*" She is shocked when she hears him mention the name of Allah. In his name, ISIS had put her life in danger and her husband had been executed in the middle of a vast desert.

"*Are you afraid of me because I am...*"

"*Never mind, I was a Muslim. It doesn't make me fear you. You helped me.*" He'd also faced the same problem back in his homeland because he was of a different Muslim sect from the majority. They are the same birds sharing the same fate and feathers flying alongside each other, searching for freedom.

"*You look like Alem, apart from the fact you are a bit reddish in colour.*"

"*I wonder if he's your good friend.*"

"*Good friend indeed.*"

"*Eh?*" they seem to be having a problem communicating, but they understand each another. The train is flying. Abas and Emu sit beside each other looking as if they are friends. It's better in silence. She wants to tell him all about Alem. But how? Ironically, she starts to speak in her language so as to narrow the gap between them.

"Can you hear a tale beginning? Once upon a time there was love, genuine love. But, that time was a bad time. A sorcerer by the name of religion was eating humanity and destroying it. He buried love in her sons and daughters. He ate uncountable numbers of young people. One of those young victims was the father of my future child: ambitious, intelligent and lovable. When people kill others it's not only people that die but all the love, hope, wishes, aspirations, wisdom- all die with them." Even if he doesn't understand the language she speaks, he seems to understand what she is saying. He has the ability to understand people just by looking at their faces. Living here for a year and five months has taught him a lot, and he seems to be made of grit. In the Jungle, he'd started to explain how hard it was to enter the UK.

"The gate to heaven, I call it, because it's so heavily guarded. To reach there you need to have ID stating you are 'Legal'. Otherwise you need to risk different forms of death because the way is as narrow as a piece of string. Death is on each side, if you fall."

"Can you believe it? I have been here longer than the other people you see in Calais."

"How do you spend your time here?"

"I read books." His hobby of reading books was part of his normal work back home, when he used to be a teacher. Abas taught Biochemistry in The University of Kurdistan Hewler (UKH) for five years, while he was studying for his Masters. There, he found himself in prison for a reason he still doesn't know. After a while the prison he was in was bombed and became empty. Only he managed to flee to safely. He had never thought he would escape and find himself here in this cold wilderness. He never thought that he would be so lonely. *"My book is the only friend I have now, in my book I can meet all my family right here,"*

"What do you mean?" She just wanted him to tell her about his family.

"I lost all my family in the war. Now I am alone."

"Me too. In fact I am pregnant. I'm going to have a baby." Silence

"You may have my company from now on, if you like."

"It's a blessing to have a friend at such a bad time."

"You're welcome."

"I had only one friend in my life time, he was everything to me."

"What happened to him?"

"He's gone."

"I'm sorry."

Her eyes fill with hot tears until she is ashamed of herself. He unexpectedly hugs her. His hug could make her forget everything, but she couldn't stop crying. He hugs her tighter, and she keeps on crying.

He lifts her up to climb into the refrigeration lorry that's awaiting them and then he gets in as well. He hugs her again to give her his warmth and encouragement.

Dover...

They're in the truck passing through the port security check point. After a couple of hours and the train ride through the Tunnel, they are in Dover, UK; Alem's dreamland. The truck left the train and travelled a couple of miles away from the port of Dover. The driver called the police after hearing something knocking inside his truck. The refugees were still in that truck dying of cold, coughing and spluttering between life and death. They could have fainted and slept forever, if the abrupt arrival of a police crew hadn't woken them and rescued them in time. She saw them as angels at that moment.

"Out! Hurry up! Out!"

"Who are you? Where are you from? Name? Age?" They stare at her and at Abas. *"Are you partners?"*

"What?"

"Are you her husband?"

"No…"

"Don't lie. Don't lie."

"I'm not."

"No lying, okay?"

"We are just friends," she replies.

She is still listening to herself whispering *'Angel-Land'*. Who knows her name? Who knows that she's feeling like a loser just hoping to get back her identity and purpose in life. Who knows that she might be pregnant with a child from the great line of Judah? Who even cares about all this? Nobody, honestly. Thinking all this makes her optimistic and strong as a pure diamond, or gold that has been tested with fire over time. She still hears a familiar voice calling from somewhere in her stomach: 'Engel-Land' – like choral chanting.

But the weather … The sunlight doesn't reach the soul and in the summer, it burns more than it warms. It comes and attacks the skin like boiling water and then goes suddenly without letting her feel it. They say it doesn't come directly from the sun, but across lots of mountains. It looks no stronger than the light from a florescent bulb, radiation but not heat. She wants to pull the sun out of the sky. She wants it to swing and dive into her. Its light is like cold shadows. She wears a large hood that not only keeps her warm but also makes her feel covered and protected now she's on her own.

She contemplates the different worlds that she has witnessed. There, the sun always shone but there was no one who dared to stare at it. The moon was nearly always full. When the sun sets it sends a hidden bride to the bridal chamber and when it rises it brings hope for ambitious youth. That's the time when the moon and the sun are hidden from our eyes and are doing something together, even making love. That's the only moment dark and light meet. The moon appears as bright as day time. There, clouds form and fade quickly. The wind brings sudden relief as it passes softly and gently. There shadows are more vivid than their objects. All the time you see your shadow growing slowly and boldly.

It's your companion throughout the day, all the way from birth to death. You know every bit of it. It makes you forget the fact that you are alone. There, life is hot and dry, rain is a miracle, water is blood, and blood is nothing but thick red water.

At the Police Station ...

Drunk with cold and wet with tears, Abas explains to his interviewer the situation he has escaped from.

"For them humans are just like onions, they just chop them up."

She saw him with his sad face and wished to hug him to comfort him. She saw him being interrogated while she was ahead of him in the next interview room.

Her interview questions begin. Blinding pictures and the intimidating looks scare her. She imagines she's shrinking. She realises how hard it feels, being interrogated while semiconscious and cold. It's like a nightmare; all she wants is to sleep until it's gone, but she's lost her power to ask, think and speak.

'Do you speak English? How old are you? Where's your family? How did you come here?

Why did you come here? Where are you from? Tell us what happened.'

It's a long story! She feels overwhelmed.

But, where should she begin? She's lost it all. She wishes just to forget about it all. Yet she can't say a thing. She isn't ready for this. She sobs.

"You okay?" A social worker interrupts.

"Yes, thank you."

"You want a little rest before your screening interview." She feels protected. She trusts that they absolutely know what they are doing. But, she knows she doesn't, so she keeps silent. Silence is her history; her history is within her silence.

Chapter
TWENTY FOUR

Emu in Enderbury...

They placed her with a local family and she feels at home. She is reminded of the hospitable culture she came from. She used to hear it said *"Habesha are the most hospitable people."* Well, she feels most British people are similar.

Mr. Book she calls him. No one could really be called *Mr. Book* but his love of books is beyond her comprehension. He has read hundreds of the books he's come across throughout his rich and full life. Most of them are on philosophy, history, British culture and local knowledge.

He told her he was the mayor of the city during his fifties, but his experience goes far beyond this as he reminisces about the past. *"When I worked at such and such a place..."*, *"When we were living here and there ...."*, *"When I was this and that...."* He is just sweet.

After some time, realising more of her story and her separation from her husband, social services provided her with somewhere to stay and the local community looked out for her. She had worried that her baby might be taken from her if she had no means of support. She'd heard of such cases and dreaded losing her only link with her past, with Alem. Her fear continued for the months of her pregnancy, finding it hard to come to terms with the hospitality around her, the fear that she'd wake up and be back in the days of her migration. As weeks went by, she learned to trust people, to relax while still not knowing Alem's fate.

In the hospital she feels lost until she hears a baby crying. That makes her smile for the first time since her loss and she falls into a deep sleep.

"Is she okay?"

"She's okay; she's just lost a lot of blood because she was circumcised probably when she was a child."

Waking up, Emu finds Abas playing with the new baby.

"He looks like my son."

"Suggest a name for him."

"Rasselas."

"Thank you. But what does it mean? Hang on - I heard the name from Alem."

"The Prince of Abyssinia. I read it in a novel written by Samuel Johnson."

"Ras Alem, the crown of my love Alem."

"The prince."

"Tell me the story."

Now recovered and back to her normal energy level, she is happy just like any other new mother. She's no longer worried about her pain or the result of her asylum application. Giving birth to a boy that will be the centre of her life forever has changed her dramatically. She's not a wife now but she is a mother and Alem lives on through the child. His presence is still with her in his son. She loves the hospital, as it has given her back the life she lost in the Libyan Desert. Now, she feels alive again. At last she begins to feel like a human being again; she can sleep and feel hunger and pain. Now she can feel so many emotions, not only tears but also joy and fresh hope. Finally, she can sing the songs of life; she can tell her stories and listen to others.

'Thousands of years ago, there was an Abyssinian prince, and he had never been outside the palace. He was happy all his life long, as was the only son of the Emperor, but he wanted to experience a happiness that the palace could not give him. His dream was the happiness that only the outside world could give him. It's a gift more precious than being a prince – to be an ordinary man. He wants to feel what it is to be human. He wants to experience true love, life. One day he begged his father to give him permission to explore the world. His father, who had never denied

him anything he asked, let his son go anywhere he liked without any security or royal formalities. And then'

Emu and the Prince slept as Abas was telling them the story.

As she wakes up, she kisses the baby for the first time in her life. It reminds of her of a year ago when she had kissed the boy she loved for the first time – it was Alem's birthday. They were exchanging their breath long before they'd started to kiss – fresh, hot air. *I can still smell it,* she utters. *It's like a sunshine rose breath... even more than that, its life....* She kisses her baby over and over again. She remembers Aba Tso and his prophesy and how he had mysteriously rescued her from the Real Devil and transported her to being Alem's partner on their perilous journey.

At the time Arron first met Emu and her son Prince Rasselas they were not sure of Alem's fate. Stories went round, rumours of capture, imprisonment and sometimes miraculous escapes. No one was sure though in her heart Emu's hopes were fading as the weeks and months passed. Arron had insisted that she tell him all about the journey. He made notes as she spoke. Her story was full of hope mixed with doubt, love mixed with hatred, joy with sadness, life with death. She showed him the pictures she had of Alem and his mother.

Arron immediately wrote a letter to Alem's mother, pretending that he was Alem; to give her the impression that her son was still alive.

Hello dear mother.

It's me, Alem, your son. I couldn't contact you for a long time. Don't blame me please, mother. I've been very busy. Don't worry; I am actually very happy. I have got a beautiful wife and an adorable son. A boy! My wife thinks he looks like just me. You know what I mean. My friends named him Rasselas. Don't ask what his name means. It's an Abyssinian-British name, I guess. So you have a grandson. I'm sending you pictures of my

*new family. They keep me very busy. I hope you can understand
me, right? Better than anybody, you know how it feels to have
an adorable son, don't you? I hope one day I will be able to see
you with my children.*

See you soon mother.

Your beloved son

Alem

He attached a copy of pictures of Alem's parents, Emu-Hiba, Alem and
Emu-Hiba and their child Rasselas, edited to make it look as though
they are all together. He sent some money in it too, so Alem's mother
could celebrate that her prayers have been answered.

*"It's like I'm seeing my Alem. I am thankful to have you and his baby
beside me. It makes me feel closer to my real love, as if my love is forever
with me."*

"You are a true friend, Arron."

She gave him all the papers that she'd kept from Alem's writing.

Then one day, after Arron had recovered from the shock of seeing his
friend's death, he suddenly realised that Emu might have seen the
pictures too. He hadn't kept in close contact with her after the baby was
born because he'd heard that Abas had come back into her life; faithful
Abas who had lost his entire family and felt it his mission to stand by
this brave woman and her son. But Arron awoke one morning feeling
that all might not be well. Was his friend still trying to communicate
with him even after death? He had an intense feeling that he must go
and check on Emu.

The pavement is covered with fresh dried leaves; the winter is advancing.
The flowers have long died, the branches have fallen, tree trunks are
becoming pale and naked. The sacrifices have been made to preserve
life, to keep the cycle of nature. Arron is not only used to all this but
he has made it part of his adventurous life and blessings. He wanted to
make sure things are going right with Emu-Hiba too. He hadn't seen her
since he saw her leaving the hospital with her child.

He tracks down the place where she's living, the far away sun reflecting back to him from the stained glass of the front door. He screws up his eyes against the bright light that seems to be blinding him like a powerful and divine spotlight from a faraway land. It reminds him how far away he is from their ancient homeland, from where the sun sets after the moon rises. To protect his face from the cold wind, he bends his head down and breathes on his hands. He reaches the door, dismayed by the cold of the doorbell as he presses it.

'Ringgg… ggg.

Ringiggg…gggrrr

Ringiiirrrrrgrrrgdrrr…'

Standing on dead leaves, he keeps on ringing but no one comes to open the door. It seems as though no one is inside.

He sees a 'knock loud' sign and bangs hard on the door.

'Knock, Knock, knock …Knock, knock, knock…'

He still can't bring himself to leave and walks round to the back of the house. Where would she be with a baby on a freezing day like this?

The door is still firmly closed. If someone is there they could be dead, but he couldn't stand there any longer as he has no power left to bear the cold anymore.

He murmured to himself, "*Have a happy New Year. Rhus Hadush Amet.*"

He begins walking away, and as he walks along the frozen pavements, a shaft of winter sunlight strikes him in the face, again blinding him for a moment. He stands still and then involuntarily finds himself walking back, retracing his footsteps, almost running as he approaches the silent house.

'Knock, knock, knock'

The door is still firm. The house is still quiet as if no one is inside but still he persists and walks round to the back again, his hands and ears numb with cold.

'Knock .. knock'

He murmured… *'Have a Merry Christmas.'* He tries calling her social worker, but can't get through.

'It's not been possible to connect your call.'

'The number you dialled is not responding;' he calls a different number.

'The number you are calling is on another line, please wait.'

'Your call's been forwarded to an automated machine, please speak…'

He tries calling Abas, though he's almost certain that he's gone away for a few days on urgent business trying to help a friend who may be about to be deported.

He bangs on the door but still there is no response. He sits on the cold step, unable to move from the spot when he hears a muffled cry, almost like the first sounds of a new born lamb, a tiny thin sound of something or someone in distress. This time his body fills with an unfamiliar strength and he breaks down the door instinctively. He doesn't even realise that he's hurt his leg badly until he cannot move forward. Then he sees Emu-Hiba peacefully resting on the sofa, the baby lying in a cot on the floor beside her.

In her hand is her mobile phone, battery now dead. She still has the headphones around her neck. Arron wonders how long she's been like this. At first he thinks she's dead but when he checks he finds that she has a faint pulse. He picks up the baby, cradling him to his body to keep him warm, then dials 999. Waiting for the ambulance to arrive, he goes to the fridge to find the baby's bottle and begins to warm some milk.

"Just in time", the ambulance man says. *"Another hour and she'd have gone"*.

As they gently carry her away, Arron sees a note addressed to Abas on the arm of the sofa:

Abas,

I've never stopped searching for news of Alem; every day I've searched the internet until finally I found a film on YouTube. I've been watching it over and over again. I cannot move; I cannot live. I want to lift our child but I have no strength. My final effort is to write these lines which Alem said to me before we were parted:

"Suddenly, I got up in the middle of a deep sleep, and you were beside me – my star with the stars above. When I see stars I see you differently, I see myself differently. Without you I am half a person; you are the queen of the stars, and the full moon is our witness. We are twin souls like the two faces of the moon. Time is our road, endless but divine. As we travel, our hopes die each passing day but are reborn every night; for our love springs each new day from the sheer happiness of our own creation."

'Damn *YouTube!*' He hates the fact that she had almost forgotten about Rasselas and her friends. She even forgot about herself and everything is still about her love. He says goodbye to the ambulance men, checking on where she and the baby are being taken. *"I'll follow on when I've sorted things out here,"* he says and sits quietly in the now silent room. He gathers her belongings, her phone and her bag and some things that she will need for her and Rasselas in hospital. Then he looks for her charger and plugs in her phone. He can see the last thing she looked at, her lover's face and his blood flowing into the Mediterranean Sea. As he sits holding it, the same bright shaft of winter sunlight enters through the window and falls across his face.

Then he sees another note on the table in front of him.

Arron,

You have been kind to me and all of us. I thank you for the help, but I'm blind to see a life without Alem. Yesterday my neighbour asked me when will I go back home and I told her that I'm sad, alone and countryless. I told her my country has gone with the heart I fell in love with and that I needed to look for him. I've missed him and I can't forget him. I wanted to follow him. Now I know his bloody end and I can't go on. Do me one last favour. Let, Rasselas know about his parents; how they used to live for each other, how they used to dream about their future... him ..."

"*You fool!!!*" Arron cries.

It was then he decided on his plan of action:

"I will write his story and yours, no more, no less; just as it is, to please his soul, and so that he will not be forgotten."

He starts in this way,

I saw that what can't be done is done,

I saw a rat giving birth to an elegant elephant,

I saw the dark come out of light and light die with the dark,

I witnessed the angel became a million times the devil,

I saw this and this...all....'

Because of this, hundreds of people like Alem died on the way, the desert dried them alive, a knife took their breath away, the beasts of the sea swallowed and feasted on them. Moussa, Gech, Mohamed... Alem, they all were visionaries, good-humoured and generous boys.

Back in class...

Unlike in previous days, Arron loves his class dearly. It's the place where he has met the nicest friends he's ever had. Here everybody passes through lots of ups and downs and everybody is open and shares their problems. Somebody's pain is for all the class to share. Somebody's success is for all of them to celebrate. Here teachers are like close friends while back home teachers are feared as fathers. Together they were listening to a speech on television.

With their sacrifice they opened our eyes, so that we can see; they opened our ears, so that we can hear,

Their death enlightened our minds so that we can think; they paid our debt that we owed out of our ignorance.

Some people are killed because they are criminals, but those youth died because of our crimes, because of the world we created. We still have debts to be paid as we lose our diamond stars. Why are so many innocent people all over the world, every day, still paying for our mistakes? Let's end it. Let's take responsibility. We human beings are responsible for either the destruction or the renewal of our world. We are not moving forward, just repeating the same mistakes over and over again. Does it have to be like this? Is there a terrible inevitability about this cycle of violence and destruction? Let's go forward to a better future... let's live in peace and love.

John is in a hurry to sit beside his best friend as he has a more important piece of news that he can't wait to tell him.

"Finally she's said yes!"

"Shh..." Charlotte shuts him up so as not to disturb her beloved Arron. He's listening to the speech with the rest of the world. He realises that the storm has passed; John is happy because now he's engaged at last to Maho, even if there is a lot of pain yet to come for him – the pain of a distance relationship. She's gone to the other side of the world filling his friend John with a fresh happiness, and Arron said to himself, *those Japanese people might have come from the garden of heaven, bless them.*

Arron felt that he was not only listening to one man's speech, but hearing every human being throughout the world throughout time - people who build their homes high above the storm, people loving each other, people devoted to changing the world into a better place. There are still optimistic people who hope the world can be as in heaven. He thinks and wishes that *the brainwashing would stop, that the old game would be over; the devil is in retreat and then mankind will eventually come to its senses.*

Thinking about baby Rasselas he felt refreshed, renewed. He has never before felt so settled, hopeful and motivated in his entire life.

Epilogue

Arron continued with his studies and adapted to his new environment. He watched the flimsy relationships of his college friends, their constant break ups and contrasted them with his friend Alem's brief but intense love.

Emu did recover and with the help of Abas, concentrated on raising Prince Rasselas. She couldn't see the future but kept Aba Tso's prophecy in her heart knowing her son was special.

Meanwhile, far away:

"*Congratulations*"

"*To all of us!*"

Alem's mother received the letter with some pictures and money. That was enough to make her share the good news she had been waiting for with her community. She called every mother of the city to tell of the miracle that her son was still alive! She framed the letter and pictures. Then she hung them in front of her door, so that whoever came by would see and believe her story.

Aba Tso's presence gives the festivities more colour and blessing. He's kept an eye on her over the months knowing more than she knows but confident that the prophecy is still alive.

"*Thank you for tolerating my madness for a long time, but now he has written me a letter to say he is still alive. He said 'see you soon mother'. That means he will come soon. You'll see, he will be here soon. You have to believe me, Aba.*"

"I always believe in you, my child. I BELIEVE YOU!" There they cried together for the last time. *"Don't ever cry again; that will bring a curse to your son and grandson. Be thankful and grateful for this. Thank God! Now, we have a family to be happy about, to love and pray for."*

So be it.